LOVE LOGAN

Tilly Keyes

A NineStar Press Publication

www.ninestarpress.com

Love Logan

Printed in the USA

ISBN: 978-1-64890-178-2

First Edition, December, 2020

Also available in eBook, ISBN: 978-1-64890-177-5

WARNING:

This book contains sexually explicit content, which may only be suitable for mature readers.

Zero's teleportation machine is the talk of the town, but opening night, it fails, leaving him a laughingstock. However, unknowingly, the machine pulls someone from the twentieth century and spits them out in Zero's time.

Logan has strange, dull clothing and bland hair, and when he opens his mouth, it gets worse. He's afraid of everything, but worst of all, his talk of love grates on Zero's nerves.

He vows to fix the machine and send Logan home no matter what. Zero's best friend, Honey, has other ideas. Despite Logan being terrified of her and labeling her a cat-person, she finds his talk of love enlightening.

With Logan about to go home, Zero needs to realize there's more to life than going down in history before it's too late.

Chapter One

Each shuffle of clothing and stomp of impatient feet increased Zero's thumping heart. The curtain muffled the words of the audience, but they increased in volume until a unified grumble shook Zero's bones. Being ten minutes late was part of his plan to build anticipation, but he hadn't envisioned the wait would have him close to fainting from nerves.

Zero pursed his lips and exhaled slowly. He brushed his sweat-soaked palms on his suit, then removed his top hat and wiped his brow on his sleeve. He wanted to wear something more flamboyant with tassels and twinkling lights, but he softened his look and chose a stripped black-and-silver suit, and his trusty black top hat. The night was all about his invention, and he dressed down to put all emphasis on it.

"This is such a bad idea."

Honey's words pulled him from his thoughts, and he turned to her, widening his eyes.

"You're here for support, not to further my anxiety."

Zero could see her normal ellipse shaped pupils had narrowed to a line of black, splitting her lime irises in two. She was afraid for him, and he couldn't deny that fear when his heart tried to escape his chest.

"If—If only you'd tested the machine."

Zero pushed his hat firmly on his head. "I have tested it."

"But never like this. You haven't done this with a living thing—"

"It will work," Zero said.

Honey gripped his arm. "But what if it doesn't?"

He frowned and glanced at her paw that gripped his arm. She blinked then retracted her claws with a softly spoken apology.

"This is my moment. I can feel it in my bones. My life is about to change."

"Dying is life changing, life ending," she replied.

Zero shook his head. "I won't die—hopefully I won't die, and if I do, I hope it will be quick."

"What if you walk through and only half of you appears on the other side?"

Zero lifted his hand and tilted it one way and then the other. "Well, if that happens, I'll die quickly, so it's not so bad."

Honey hissed and flattened her ears. "Don't make jokes."

"I wasn't joking," he said, turning to face her. "If it goes wrong and I die, then you know I died doing what meant the most to me. Besides, I couldn't live with the shame of a failure, so let's hope it is either roaring success and I appear in the opposite arch or it's unable to put my atoms back together and I die instantly."

Honey shut her eyes and bowed forward. Zero rubbed at her arms, but she didn't straighten to look at him. She sagged further.

"I can't go out there until I see your smile," he whispered.

She sniffled and shook her head. "I don't feel like smiling."

"Please Honey, for me. I need to see it. You're my lucky charm."

"Fine," she said with a huff. "But you better not die."

Zero thought better than making that promise. It was a strong possibility, not that he admitted it to her.

Honey lifted her head and twitched her cheeks. Her nose rose, and two daggered teeth showed through her narrow lips.

"Thank you," Zero said.

The second the words left him, her smile dropped, and she breathed heavily through her nose.

"Right," he said and clutched his lapels. "Here I go."

"Wait!"

Honey moved her arm fast and Zero flinched at the elbow near his face. He straightened when he realised she was using the fur of her forearm to mop his brow. He sighed and closed his eyes. Honey smelled sweet, and her amber fur was soft and warm.

"Thank you," he said.

"My fur's super absorbent."

Zero chuckled lightly. "I meant being here. Being...being by my side."

She dropped her arm and stared at him. "Don't say stuff like that. Don't di—"

"Yes, don't die," he said, then pinched his suit lapels. "I mean, come on, I can't die wearing this bland thing."

"I think it looks good on you. The silver's the same shade as your hair, and the mauve lining is the same colour as your eyes."

Zero pulled at his suit and sneered at the shiny material inside. "My eyes are a nicer mauve than this."

Honey rocked back on her heels and flicked her chin out. "Stop stalling. If you're gonna do it, do it now or else I'm gonna cling to you and drag you from the stage."

"Please don't do that...again."

Zero turned from her and walked up to the quivering curtain. He glanced back to check Honey had left the stage, delved his hand into his trouser pocket and clicked the button for the force field.

The curtain vanished, and the mumbles of irritation went with it.

He had everyone's attention in the theatre, and he paced the stage linking eyes with as many as he could.

They were the first thousand that would marvel at his teleportation machine, shower him with praise, and cement his importance in history for centuries to come. He wanted to remember individual faces, wanted to see their eyes widen and their jaws drop in shock. There were some hot life-forms, some that he would enjoy getting acquainted with after the show.

His nerves dispersed, and he chuckled, then winked at the human in the front row with the emerald hair. The man smiled in reply and winked back.

"Zero!" Honey hissed from the edge of the stage.

He shook his head to be clear of any rising lust and stood in the centre.

"Ladies and Gentlemen. I have gathered you here today to show you an invention that will change our world forever."

Zero paused at the edge of the stage and lifted his hat from his head. He rolled it down his arm then gripped the edge and flipped it back on his head.

"Prepare to be amazed."

He walked to the other side of the stage removing the hat once again. He twirled it hypnotically fast in his hands before slotting it over his hair.

"This will blow your mind."

He walked to the centre of the stage and gazed out at the dimly lit theatre. His attention lingered on one member of the audience and he swallowed hard. Not the emerald-haired man but someone else.

Apollo, his ex-boyfriend, sat a few rows back. His blond hair hung long and luscious against his face, and he pouted his rose lips. His suit was gold, and even in the low lighting of the theatre he managed to shine with his importance. He noticed Zero watching him and smirked into the back of his hand.

"Focus," Honey said out of sight, and Zero snapped out of his momentary paralysis.

"This is an invention so amazing, so miraculous, that it will make the flying car obsolete and old."

Apollo dropped his smug grin and narrowed his eyes. Zero inwardly grinned at his reaction and rubbed at his chin.

"I promise you, what you're about to see will be the single most incredible event you'll witness."

Zero turned and wagged his finger at the arch closest to him. A rainbow of wires wrapped around the frame and vanished beneath the floorboards of the stage.

"I will walk through this arch...and reappear through that one."

The audience mumbled and whipped their heads back and forth to take in the stage. Only one arch shared the space with Zero, and he waited until the agitated mutterings got louder. He pressed his forefinger to his lips, and like obedient children the voices faded to silence, and the life-forms stilled in their seats.

Zero pointed up, and the eyes of the audience followed his cue until they caught sight of the other arch. It stood on a clear force field, fifty metres off the ground. The rainbow wires hung down from the ceiling and wrapped around the metal frame. The arches appeared identical, but it was the one by Zero's side that had taken him years to perfect. He had tinkered and experimented for almost a decade to get the machine in working order, and he was finally ready to reveal what it could do.

Zero waited in silence to build more anticipation. The audience murmured and shook their heads, and he pressed his hand to his chest.

"Hold your scepticism and wait and see."

His words were a cue for Honey to switch on the machine. The lights and force fields of the theatre flickered, and the metal components of the arches sparked. A static noise increased, and bright white light appeared in the centre of the arch. The light twirled and danced and Zero dropped his gaze to spare his eyesight.

He blinked at the floor while his sight adjusted then glanced up again able to stare at the hypnotic white.

Apollo bit at his knuckles and shook his head, and Zero wondered whether it was for fear of him being killed or worry at the invention outdoing the flying car.

He lifted the hat off his head and bowed. "See you from the other side."

The audience gasped and got to their feet.

The light from the arch pulsed towards him, and he stepped forward with as much confidence as he could muster. His skin tingled to the point of pain, and his mind muffled to nothing as the white light consumed him.

A deafening bang drowned out the gasps of the audience.

The ground beneath Zero vibrated, and he struggled to open his eyes. A repetitive pressure shoved at his shoulder, and through his clouded hearing he heard the desperate shout of Honey.

"Zero!"

He wasn't dead, which meant his invention must have worked. He tilted his lips into a smile and braced himself to hear the unified cheer and applause of his audience.

Zero forced his eyes open and linked eyes with Honey hovering over him. He blinked at her with a frown, wondering how she got up to the high arch. He saw the theatres ceiling beyond her head. Not close as it should have been, but far above. He breathed in the scent of burning and gawped at the remains of the second arch smoking above them.

Zero rolled towards the audience and propped his body up. They were out of their seats and leaving the theatre. The stage shook with the many feet that passed by, and Zero focused on each mocking expressions and stifled laughter.

Honey crouched beside him. She puffed her amber fur out and flattened her ears. Zero's hearing sharpened at her hiss, and the sound of his failure attacked him in full force.

The arch that hovered on the platform had broken in two, and the one beside him had a flume of smoke escaping it. They both spluttered sparks of defeat, and Zero's eyes watered at the contamination in the air.

The theatre that had taken an hour to fill emptied in mere minutes, and the last audience member to leave was the one man Zero hated.

Apollo climbed to his feet and dusted his hands together. He didn't move to join the queue of people exiting but walked towards the stage.

"That was it? You believe that would make me obsolete and old?"

Zero swallowed and bowed his head.

Apollo smirked and unbuttoned his gold blazer. He stroked his hand down his neck to his chest and grasped the medallion that rested there.

"You will never get one of these, never be remembered for millenniums to come. You are nothing, Zero, just like your name."

Apollo lifted the medallion to his lips and kissed the circle of gold.

Zero climbed to his unsteady feet and walked away from the mocking man. Honey hissed furiously, and Apollo released a bark of a laugh. His footsteps plodded from the theatre, and Zero collapsed to the floor. There was no need to switch the curtain back on when the theatre was empty.

Honey rushed towards him and crouched down. "What happened?"

Zero laughed bitterly and shook his head. "It clearly didn't work."

"Well, no, but what did happen?"

Zero rubbed at his brow. "I don't understand... I stepped into the arch and woke up on my back."

Honey wiggled her nose and shot a look to the back of the stage. "The white light pulsed, and coils of silver crackled around the arch. The one on the platform exploded, and this one looked like it was gonna, but then a figure appeared."

"What do you mean?"

She craned her neck out and sniffed. "A man appeared in this arch. He smacked into you—"

Zero got to his feet with a growl. "A stage invader! Sabotage, I bet Apollo had something to do with it."

She frowned. "I'm not sure."

Honey gestured to the back of the stage and Zero sneered in the direction.

He pointed to the shadowed area. "You see him?"

Honey's lime eyes shimmered, and she nodded. "Yes. I see him."

"Come out here now!"

The man in the darkness didn't move, and Zero tapped his foot to the floor.

"I don't recognise him," Honey whispered. "And he smells odd."

"I don't care how he looks or how he smells. He ruined my grand moment, and I will make him pay—"

"Wait, he's coming out."

Zero puffed in a furious breath through his nose and exhaled slowly. Honey angled her shoulders up ready to pounce, and her fur stood on end in offence.

"I—I don't know what's going on."

Zero narrowed his eyes. "What's going on? You've ruined my moment, now come into the light, so I can see the face of my enemy."

The man left the safety of the darkness but kept his distance. "Enemy?"

Zero didn't think it was possible to dress blander than his striped suit, but the man wore a plain charcoal shirt with no embroidery or pattern. His trousers didn't sparkle or shine, and his shoes were matt black.

"Who are you?" Zero growled.

"I don't know where I am. Is this some kind of joke?" the man said, gripping his face.

Zero shot a look to Honey, who lessened her aggressive stance.

"No one's laughing," Zero muttered.

"I—urm. I don't know what happened...maybe it was something I ate, maybe I'm dreaming."

"You jumped up on stage and overloaded my machine."

The man shook his head. "I didn't—I don't know what happened. I was at the club, and then...and then I got pulled in."

Zero shook his head and took a step closer. The man ran his hand though his chestnut hair, not even a strand of glitter sparkled at the movement. Not just his clothes were bland, but his face and hair too. The man's eyes were wide and unfocused, and he swayed on his feet.

"How much have you drank?" Zero asked.

He shook his head. "Nothing. I swear."

Zero approached, and the man retreated. "Do not play games with me. Now tell me your name."

"Logan, my name's Logan."

Zero sneered at the name. "Well, Logan, I hope he pays you well for destroying my life."

Logan recoiled and sunk back into the darkened area of the stage. Zero turned and marched back to Honey.

"Deal with him how you wish," he said, before continuing his march to the exit.

He hoped Logan would become accustomed to sharp claws in the next few minutes.

Chapter Two

Zero slunk out of the theatre and waited in the designated area for a car. Not all the audience members had gone, and many fingers were pointed his way. He snorted furiously and turned his back on them. Hundreds of cars zoomed through the sky, and Zero watched them dock at each flat. He had the longest wait being on the eight hundredth floor.

The car drifted down and floated beside him. He narrowed his eyes at Apollo's signature and scratched his nails across the name that mocked him. The metal didn't mark, and he cursed as he stabbed the button for the door to open.

Zero programmed his destination. The car rose from the ground and drifted through the sky to get to his flat. Zero stared glumly at the colossal buildings. All four of them towered high, and they kept the social area in the centre of the island in constant shadow. Forever night, people enjoyed spending time in the twilight zone, but Zero avoided the clubs and entertainment.

"Hello, sir, would you—"

Zero stabbed the social button with his forefinger to silence the machine. Honey enjoyed chatting to bots in the cars, but Zero didn't trust them. No doubt a whole database of the residents of *New Fretton* had been gained from the cars. All personal conversations, and secrets saved to be used as gossip or blackmail.

He removed his hat and dropped it to the floor of the vehicle with a huff. Eight years of work, destroyed in a single night by an oddly dressed stage invader. Logan. It was impossible to guess the man's age, and a sin to ask. His chestnut hair and eyes had been unusual for the residents of New Fretton. In fact, Zero had never seen anyone with both chestnut hair and eyes. He shook his head to fling the memory of Logan away.

The news of his failure would no doubt travel fast and he expected a backlash at work. He squeezed his head in his hands when he thought of all the jeers and laughs that would be directed his way. He hated his job as a picker-fixer, but it looked like that was all he was destined to be. Stupid Zero, thinking he could be an inventor. Stupid Zero forever in his ex-boyfriend's shadow.

A shimmering caught his eye, and he shot a look at the floating palace full of the rich and worthy residents. He longed to live there, wanted to be bathed in luxury and craved by the attractive life-forms of the island.

Zero huffed at his knees and clenched his fists until they had climbed too high to see the palace and its sparkling lights.

The car docked in his flat and announced its arrival with its annoying buzz. Zero shoved at the door and climbed out with a grimace. He shut the car with an unnecessary slam and hugged his arms around his body.

The front door scanned his hand before allowing him entry.

He left the flat in a mess, believing it would be the last time he would be inside it on the eight hundredth floor. He thought he'd be in the floating palace, sporting a gold medallion around his neck, with the emerald-haired man keeping him company. No such luck, and Logan was to blame.

Zero went to his bedroom and flung himself down on the mattress. The machine immediately started massaging his tense shoulders.

"I want to sleep," he said.

The rollers and probers stopped moving.

"Of course, sir."

A high-pitched sound rang out, and Zero felt his eyes droop and his muscles relax.

"No dreams," he whispered.

"No dreams, sir."

Zero didn't wish to relive his failure and humiliation and trusted the flat to wake him if he ventured into the REM sleep stage. He sagged into the bed and allowed sleep to wash his troubles away.

*

Zero woke to the flat chirping, and the bed vibrating in time with the alarm.

He groaned and stretched out his limbs. "What is it?"

"Honey is at the door, should I let her in?"

Zero nodded and rolled off the bed. He stomped into the living room and awaited her arrival. He hoped she had brought some drink to wash away his depression. He'd need a whole flood worth to cure himself permanently by drowning, but one or two bottles were a good start.

Honey walked in with her head lowered and her eyes tracking the floor. The lack of bottles in her paws alarmed Zero more than her reluctant shuffle.

Zero exhaled through his nose, then widened his eyes and glared at her.

"Shit, you didn't kill him, did you?"

Honey lifted her head and narrowed her eyes. "'Course I didn't kill him."

Zero rubbed at his chin in thought. "I sure hope you scratched him up, scared him a little..."

"I didn't need to do anything. He was already terrified."

"Good—"

"Zero...you need to talk to him."

He smirked and turned away. "Talk to him? I doubt we'll ever see him again now."

Honey scratched her ear and took a step back. "The thing is... I didn't know what to do with him."

"What does that mean? He's not here, is he?"

She raised both her paws in surrender and backed away. "Kinda. But I can't get him out of the car."

Zero moved towards the dock window with a sigh. The car floated inside with its door open.

"Just programme the stupid thing to take him home."

Honey shook her head. "He has nowhere to go."

Zero flung his head back and growled to the ceiling. "Fine, I'll do it."

He stomped out of the room and opened the door to the dock. Inside the hovering car Zero could see the man huddled in a ball. He muttered words Zero couldn't hear and rocked back and forth.

"Oi, you there. Logan. Where do you live?"

Logan lifted his head and gazed at him. "Not here."

"You don't say," Zero muttered, rolling his eyes.

"I—I don't live around here, I don't even know where I am."

Zero exhaled heavily though his nose. "You're intoxicated and need to sleep this off."

"I haven't had a drop. I swear."

The car beeped, announcing it was due to be called away to another residence. The door began to close, and Logan's eyes widened.

"It will take you back to the ground and you can sober up the—"

Logan launched himself from the car and collided into Zero. They stumbled back and fell to the floor with a thump. In a tangle of limbs, Zero cursed and shoved Logan away.

Honey stood over them with her lips tilted in a smile. "This gonna be a habit with you two?"

Zero huffed and got to his feet. "What was that?"

Logan looked up at him with wide eyes. "I—I don't wanna go back down there. There's too many cat-people..."

Honey raised her eye-arch. "He keeps calling me a cat person."

"Cat person?" Zero said.

Logan got to his feet and pressed himself to the wall furthest from Honey. "Yeah, she's a speaking, upright cat."

Zero shook his head. "We do not know of these 'cats' you speak of. This is Honey."

"She even has a cat name."

Honey narrowed her eyes. "I can't tell if you're insulting me or not."

Logan swayed his hands in front of his body. "I'm not, I'm not!"

Zero squeezed the bridge of his nose. "As I was saying, this is Honey, I am Zero. I'm sure you're familiar with Apollo, how much did he pay you to pull that little stunt?"

Logan shook his head. "I don't know any Apollo, and I told you what happened. I was by the vanishing door, and this white light started and pulled me in. Then I was on a stage, in front of loads of weird looking people."

"Weird?" Zero said. "You're calling us weird, what is weird?"

Logan waved his hand. "You're less weird than everyone else."

Zero squinted and scrunched his nose. "What does that mean?"

"Means you look normal-ish."

"Normal. Normal! I've never been so offended in my life."

He turned to Honey with wide eyes. "You hear that? He called me normal."

"Well you did dress down today." Honey smirked.

Zero stomped into his bedroom and threw his suit jacket on the bed. He attacked the buttons of his shirt and flung it at the floor. Never in his life, had someone told him he looked normal. Flamboyant, eye-watering, striking. Those were how he liked to be described, but normal would not do.

He brushed his hands along his many suits and pulled out a glittering indigo blazer, with complementing waistcoat. He dressed hastily and slipped into some pulsating bronze shoes. He shoved on his hat and added a maroon handkerchief to the top pocket of his blazer. The last thing to go with the outfit was a cane, which he twirled as he walked out the bedroom.

Honey had moved to the sofa, but Logan hadn't joined her or ventured further into the flat. He kept his back pressed against the wall and had difficulty pulling his eyes off Honey.

"How about now?" Zero said.

Logan flashed a look at him. "You're still normal in comparison."

Zero banged his cane to the floor. "First, you ruin my invention, then, you come into my flat uninvited, and now you insult me."

Logan pressed his hands together. "No, I'm sorry okay, I just have no idea what's going on."

Zero rolled his eyes and turned away. "Whatever. I'll call you another car."

"Wait," Honey said beckoning Logan towards her. "Tell Zero what you told me."

Logan didn't move any closer, and his terrified eyes followed the movement of Honey's paws.

"Oi," Zero huffed, "you gonna speak or what?"

Logan pulled his gaze from Honey and attached it to Zero.

"Sorry, this is mad. This place is like something from a film, and I don't know how to handle it."

Zero glanced around his flat. "Not any film I've seen."

"No, I meant out there," Logan said.

He moved to the window and pointed at the sky. Zero followed him and took in the view.

"Still the blandest film I've ever seen. Where's the action? The smells, the tastes and the sounds. That is just the sky. Maybe you're hallucinating."

Logan sighed and leaned forward. He recoiled fast when his head went through the force field.

"What the hell?"

Honey moved to steady him, but he launched forward and Zero caught him before he fell through the window.

"Right, you need to sit," he said and led Logan to the sofa.

"None of this is possible. This is some messed up dream I'm having."

Zero squeezed the bridge of his nose with a nod. "Perhaps. The best cure for messed up dreams is sleep."

Logan nodded then frowned. "What?"

Zero huffed and held out his hand. "Come on, I've got a nice comfy bed you can rest in."

"You'll let me sleep in your bed?"

"Believe me, I'm not thrilled about it, but I can't let you leave a messy splat on the pavement eight-hundred stories below."

Logan reached for his hand. "Thank you."

Zero led him into the bedroom and flicked his head towards the bed. Logan removed his shoes and climbed on the mattress. He lay down, facing the ceiling with the same panic-blown eyes he had when looking at Honey.

"When I leave the room, send him to sleep."

Logan frowned and turned his head to check the space around the bed. "Who you talking to?"

Zero huffed then closed the door with a firm click and waited for the flat to work its magic.

A minute later when he swung the door open, Logan lay asleep on the bed.

"Right, let's find out who you are."

Zero preferred seeing him relaxed and snoring softly than verging on a cardiac arrest. He didn't know what Logan had taken, but it hadn't affected him positively.

"Maybe Apollo didn't pay him to sabotage," Zero said over his shoulder, "more an unlucky coincidence."

Honey appeared behind him and they peered down at the odd man on the bed.

"Have you ever seen someone who looks like him? No patterns, no embroidery, chestnut hair and eyes," Honey asked.

"No, not in New Fretton."

Honey cocked her head. "I mean he's kinda cute."

Zero rubbed his chin and studied the man in his bed. He had a caress-craving jaw, kissable lips, and soft looking hands, but Zero was distracted by the dull clothing, and his bland hair.

"He's cute in an odd way," Zero concluded.

"He smells odd too."

Zero's inadequate nose couldn't detect a smell from the distance, and he didn't fancy shoving his nose in Logan's hair.

"Whatever. Let's see if he has his name card on him."

He began patting the peaceful man's legs, hoping to find his card of information. He felt a rectangle in the man's pocket and slid it free of his tight trousers.

It was not what he sought, but an odd black rectangle with a picture of a bitten apple on the back.

"He said it was his phone, whatever that is."

Zero placed the rectangle on the bed and continued his search. He tugged harder to retrieve a thicker square. He rubbed his fingers over the soft material with a look of wonder.

"What is it?" Honey asked.

Zero shrugged. "No idea."

The square package opened, and inside was an assortment of coloured plastic. He pulled out one of the rectangles and frowned. He had never seen an identification card like the one in his hand.

"Logan Turner. Born 7th of September and lives in London."

"London?" Honey said, "You mean *New London*."

Zero shook his head. "Just says London."

He ran his fingers over Logan's age again and realised he had mistaken the two for a four. "2000...not 4000...7th of September 2000."

"What?"

Zero twirled the card in his fingers and showed the information to Honey. "Look at his date of birth."

"2000...maybe the four got scratched or rubbed off."

Zero slid out more cards, and dropped each to the bed repeating, "year of birth 2000."

"What are you saying?" Honey asked.

"I'm saying he's not from around here. He's from two thousand years ago."

Honey's pupils shrunk into black lines. "Wh—what?"

"Seems I didn't create a transportation device, but a time machine."

Honey pressed her paw to her face, but Zero still heard her gasp.

"What do we do now?"

Zero pursed his lips, then clapped his hands. "Well, I don't know about you, but I need a drink."

He strolled from the bedroom with Honey following behind.

Chapter Three

Zero unscrewed the bottle and gave it a sniff. He pursed his lips before offering the bottle to Honey to smell.

She wrinkled her nose and narrowed her eyes. "I wouldn't if I were you."

Zero huffed and slid the bottle to the back of the cupboard. "No drink for me."

"You know you could just throw that out?"

"I could, but that's rather too much effort for me."

Honey flicked her head back. "The recycle chute is right there."

Zero shrugged. "Exactly, too far, besides if I leave it in there long enough it might get toxic enough to kill."

Honey hissed and flashed her teeth.

"Not for myself, but maybe if I ever get Apollo in here again."

Honey shook her head. "We need to decide what do to with Logan."

Zero huffed and moved to the sofa. "We let him sleep for now."

"And then what?"

"Then we get him a car back to the ground, and he goes on his way."

Zero dusted his hands together in case his words weren't enough for Honey. She stared at him. Her eyes turned to slits as she hissed with her teeth on show.

"You pulled him through time. Created a time machine."

Zero sighed. "Yes, quite amazing, but it exploded, I can't get famous from it when the damn thing is broken."

"I don't care about you getting famous. He is here because of you."

Zero rolled his eyes. "I am not taking in stray life-forms. He'll be fine once he settles in."

"Do you know anything about where he's from?"

"You know full well I don't and nor does anyone. No one knows what life was like before the nuclear war, and looking at him, I don't think we're missing anything from his century."

"He freaked out when he saw me. When we left the theatre, he almost ran onto the magnetic lines, I had to pounce on him to stop him and force him into the car. He will not survive here."

Zero sighed and pinched the top of his nose. "Yeah, well, he's not my problem."

Honey flicked her claws out. "He is your problem. You brought him here."

"He broke my machine, so excuse me for not being overly concerned."

"Your machine failed. You can't abandon him. He is your responsibility."

Zero snorted bitterly. "I thought today was going to be my day. I thought the crowd would stand and applaud and marvel at my genius. I thought I would be escorted to the palace and be given a flat even bigger than Apollo's. I'd get a medallion that everyone would want to see and caress, even Apollo would beg me to hold it—"

Honey lashed out at his leg. Not hard enough to break skin, but it got Zero's attention.

"Stop it, just stop thinking about yourself! You've seen Logan, he's frightened half to death," she said.

"Then we need to frighten him that half more."

Zero gasped when Honey's claws sunk through his trousers. "You need to get him home."

"It took me almost ten years to make that machine, and years longer to plan it. A few seconds and Logan destroyed it."

"He didn't destroy it. Your design failed, your invention failed, and with its failure it dragged someone else into our world. Someone who is confused and overwhelmed. Who seems to trust you more than me."

Zero drew his eyebrows together and huffed. "Normal, he called me normal. How insulting."

"I don't think he meant it as an insult. You've seen the way he looks at me, he's scared, but when he looks at you he's less so."

"What would you have me do?" He threw his arms up in exasperation.

Honey retracted her claws and settled beside him. "Fix the machine."

"Fix the machine? You say it likes it's *easy*. You saw how burnt out it is, and you know how long it took me to make."

"We have to try. We have to get him home."

Zero flicked his chin out towards the bedroom. "And what do I do with him in the meantime?"

Honey frowned and looked out the window. "Keep him safe. I don't know what will happen if the elite find out about him. They could experiment on him, use him for entertainment, hurt him for being different."

"Stop being dramatic. He is nothing special, and they wouldn't believe he was from the past anyway. They would think he's broken and fly him off to the recycle planet."

Honey shuddered. "We can't let that happen to him either."

"Would make things easier," Zero muttered.

He knew she had heard by the twitch of her ear, but she didn't swipe him. Instead, she rubbed her paws on her cheeks and chattered her teeth together. Zero hated seeing her so glum and sighed at his hands.

"Fine. For now, I will keep him."

She stopped stroking her face and smiled. "He'll need food and water."

"I'm sure I can handle that."

"He can't be left alone, and he'll need company."

Zero waved his hand at the flat. "He's not alone, and they will have riveting conversations."

Honey shook her head. "Not an A.I., I meant you. He almost fell out the window earlier. The flat won't be able to stop him doing something stupid like that."

"Right, well, you take him then."

"He's scared of me, besides this is your mess."

Zero flung his head back into the sofa. "Fine. I will attempt to take care of him."

"Not attempt but will."

Honey's pupils retracted, and she forced down her brow in a menacing expression. Zero rolled his eyes then nodded, and Honey's face relaxed and she appeared her friendly self again.

"Now, I'm late," she said and sprung from the sofa.

"Late for what?"

Honey turned to him and smiled. "My date."

"Date?" Zero said. "How many is that? Five this year."

"Eight, actually."

Zero shook his head in disbelief. "Eight dates, think of all that time you could've spent becoming rich and famous."

Honey exhaled slowly from her nose. "I know eight might be a lot, but I value my time spent with Rae more than the pursuit of success."

"That's just...odd," Zero said, scrunching his brow.

Success was the ultimate goal of one's life. Wars had been fought and lost over the need to find success, but Honey never spoke about her dreams and goals. She spoke about Rae with a floaty voice and dilated pupils. Zero had only ever seen people react like that when they bragged of money and fame. It was strange.

"How many dates did you and Apollo have?"

Zero clacked his tongue to the roof of his mouth. "Two in five years."

"An—and did you enjoy them?"

"The whole time I was thinking of my teleportation machine, and he was thinking of a solution to the floating car. I don't think we spoke."

Zero couldn't even remember what restaurant they went to, or what Apollo wore. He did remember he picked a flattering jacket, with flashing white hem and glittering tassels.

"Oh…I enjoy hearing Rae speak and talking to her."

Zero rolled his eyes. "Yes, but you also enjoy chatting to the cars, the lights, the flats, and the buildings."

"They're less prickly than you."

He sighed and hunched forward. "I'm sorry, Honey, it's just not the day I thought it would be. Go enjoy your date."

Honey pressed the button on the wall to call a car to the flat. "Be nice to Logan when he wakes."

"Nice? I don't know the meaning of the word."

"Please, Zero. We need to help him. Explain about our century and ask about his."

"Why the hell would I want to know about his?"

Honey huffed and tapped her foot to the floor. "It's polite."

The car arrived outside the flat, and Zero waved her away. "Go, have sex and food."

"Fun and conversation and laughing," Honey said.

"Yeah, whatever…"

Zero watched as she climbed into the car and drifted from his view.

He sunk back into the sofa and huffed at the ceiling. "What the hell do I do now?"

"Well, sir, I could load the news hologram."

"Hell no!"

He didn't wish to see a news update when he knew he would be the top story.

Zero huffed and got to his feet. He moved towards his bedroom and opened the door to see Logan still peacefully napping. His lashes fluttered as Zero crept closer.

Not only were the strands on his head chestnut, and those of his eyebrows, but his eyelashes too. Zero sat on the mattress, and Logan rolled onto his side towards him.

Zero stilled, then bent down and sniffed at his hair. He couldn't identify the subtle smell, but it didn't repulse him, in fact he kept breathing in his scent to become familiar with the smell of a twenty-first century man. It was almost nice. He didn't have the sweetness of Honey, but it was still pleasant to draw into his nose.

Logan's rhythmic breathing stopped and Zero leaned back.

Logan's eyes were wide open, and his bottom lip trembled.

"I didn't mean to wake you. I was just sniffing you."

Logan whipped his hand through his hair and shuffled away. "What the hell?"

"Don't worry, it's standard practice here."

It wasn't, but there was no way he was about to admit it. He blamed Honey for repeatedly commenting on Logan's different smell.

Logan leaned up on his elbows and looked around the room. "I'm—I'm still here."

"Yes, and I guess I'm to blame for that." Zero gestured to the door. "Come on, we'll talk out there."

Logan followed Zero out the bedroom at a distance. He curled his fingers around the door frame and peered around the living room. Zero knew he was searching for Honey.

"She's not here," he said, and Logan's fingers relaxed. "Now sit. Are you hungry?"

Logan stopped clinging to the doorframe and moved into the room with his arms wrapped around his body. He walked hesitantly towards the sofa and perched on the edge.

"Urm—no, not really."

Zero huffed and ruffled his hair. "Well, I am."

He moved to the kitchen and searched the drawer for a favourable food pouch. He nodded his head at the one labelled cave fruits and joined Logan on the sofa.

"What's that?" Logan asked.

Zero waved the pouch. "Food, as I said."

"Looks like cat food."

"Is that an insult or a compliment?"

Logan shuffled, and it took a few seconds for him to answer. "Compliment. It's a compliment. Looks tasty."

Logan pressed his lips together and glanced away while Zero opened his meal. He squeezed the contents into his mouth and the effects were instant. He sighed in pleasure at the taste and felt some of the weight of the day lessening. Not to the same extent alcohol affected him, but food still eased tension from him.

"What is this place?" Logan asked.

Zero pursed his lips and glanced around the flat. "The pickers' tower. Depending on your status as a picker you're closer to the ground. This is the eight hundredth floor. I think you can work out that's low status."

Logan frowned. "Surely that's high status?"

Zero huffed and shook his head. "Listen here. Today had been an absolute disaster, and to make matters worse, I have you to look after. Don't irritate me or I'll fly you back to the ground and leave you there."

"Please don't. I'm sorry. I didn't mean to irritate—"

Zero sighed and gripped his head. "No, it is me who should apologise. I just don't know what I'm supposed to do with you."

Logan bit his lip, then released it and spoke. "How about you tell me what's going on?"

"I guess that's the logical place to start. I think you have been pulled into my timeline via the transportation arch. The year is 4021. The question is, what year have you come from?"

Logan rubbed at his head. "2021. I was at the club, drinking away my sorrows—"

"Ah, so you were drunk?"

"I sobered up pretty damn quickly when I found myself on stage being gawped at."

"You're twenty-one," Zero said, eyeing the man next to him.

Logan nodded. "And you?"

It was rude to ask, one of the most offensive questions to come out with, but Zero sighed in defeat.

"I'm twenty-eight, but as a rule don't outright ask anyone. You wanna know their age, you got to be sneaky about it."

"How did you know mine?"

"The cards in the strange pouch you carry."

Logan patted himself. "My wallet?"

"Is that what it's called? It's on the bed."

"Got my ID in it, and my bank cards."

Zero frowned. "Bank cards?"

"For money, you don't get money for working?"

Zero waved his hand at the flat. "We get accommodation, electricity, food, drink, and tokens for evenings out."

"Oh," Logan said, dropping his gaze.

"Look. I'm going to do my best to fix the machine and send you home, but it's gonna take a while. You just have to deal with our century till you're back in your own."

He chose not to tell him it might take years, in case Logan threw himself out the window.

Logan shuddered. "Are there more cat-people?"

"You mean like Honey? Yes, thousands, but they're not called Cat-people. Her race is referred to as Furists. There are different races, but we are all life-forms."

"Life-forms. Got it."

"And stop being afraid of Honey, she's the nicest, kindest life-form in the city."

Logan swallowed loudly. "Sorry, just a shock. I'm not used to seeing cats so big, and standing on two legs, and talking."

Zero pressed his thumb and forefinger into his temples. "She's called Honey."

"Right, yeah, I'll say sorry to her next time."

Zero nodded. "Good, and I've got work tomorrow. I don't want to leave you here alone in case you fall through the window, or get sucked into the recycle chute, so you'll be coming with me. If we've got time afterwards, we'll start on the machine."

"Okay, I'll help you, and then you help me," Logan said.

"Something like that."

Logan glanced around the flat with a frown. Zero observed him for a few minutes before sighing.

"What is it you're looking for?"

"A TV."

"What's that?"

Logan waved his hand at the wall. "Like a big electronic screen that shows programmes, soaps, documentaries, and the news."

The flat responded at the programmed buzz word and the hologram of the news report appeared in the room.

"Stop!" Zero yelled.

The hologram froze, but Zero still saw the picture of himself and the word failure branded across his image.

"Shut it down."

The hologram faded, and Zero huffed.

"What did you fail?" Logan asked.

"I failed at life," Zero replied. "Being a success is all that matters, and I failed."

He felt Logan's gaze on the side of his face but didn't turn to him.

"Can you tell me more about this century?"

Zero huffed and raised his head to the ceiling. Teaching Logan would take hours, and all he wanted to do was collapse back into bed and sleep until it was time for work.

"Can you prepare two pouches of water please?" he asked

Logan's mouth popped open as if to speak.

"Of course, sir."

Logan threw himself back and dug his nails into the cushions. The sofa responded at the cue. The rollers in the backrest moved to massage and the cushion they sat on released a subtle electric current to sooth their muscles. Zero didn't react, but Logan yelled and fell to the floor.

He gave the sofa an accusing look. "What the hell was that?"

Zero rolled his eyes. "It's gonna be a long day…"

Chapter Four

Logan listened intently to Zero's explanations of the century. His complexion paled, but he didn't faint and Zero thought that was a success. The idea of different islands didn't seem different to Logan's time, but then Zero explained they floated on the ocean, tunnels led down to the crust, and huge caverns had been built to grow food. Logan pulled an odd expression, and Zero continued. Each island was self-sufficient, and every life-form apart from the elite had to work. Life-forms could move to other islands but had to prove their worth before they were accepted. Logan nodded in understanding, and Zero thought there was hope for the man out of his time, all until he asked to use the toilet.

It was normal practise, every living creature had to excrete waste, but then Logan repeatedly asked for toilet roll.

At first, Zero froze, mind spinning with the idea of a rolling toilet. How was anyone supposed to excrete waste if the thing moved? After Logan explained through the door, Zero was even more disgusted. People of the twenty-first century wiped themselves and didn't have a button in the wall that cleaned their intimate areas.

"You see the scarlet tile on the wall?" Zero said to the edge of the door.

"Erm—I think so."

"Press it."

Zero tapped his foot on the floor, waiting for the machine to take care of Logan's problem. He heard a squeal and a thumping sound. Zero tried to rub the smile off his face, but it stubbornly wouldn't leave.

"You better not be laughing."

"'Course not," Zero said once he composed himself. "No toilet roll as you put it, but it does a thorough clean."

"Some warning about the spraying water would have been nice."

Zero snorted. "Where's the fun in that."

The next morning, Zero climbed into his overalls with a huff. The amber didn't suit his hair, or his eyes but his request for a different colour went unanswered. During the week, they weren't individuals but part of the workforce, and needed to dress accordingly.

He turned to Logan who sat at the table. The amber complimented his hair and eyes, but the hanging jaw wasn't so appealing.

"Just eat the damn thing," Zero said.

Logan held the food pouch higher. "I thought in the future we would stop eating from packets and containers."

"Sorry to disappoint you, but no. Now, eat it."

Logan sighed and tore the corner of the pouch. He rested it between his lips and then squeezed the contents into his mouth.

Zero watched until Logan pressed the pouch flat before raising his eyebrow. "Well?"

"Not as bad as I thought."

Logan smiled, and Zero's stomach fluttered. He rubbed the odd reaction away and shook his head.

"Now, do you remember what I told you? You're a friend from Far Away."

"Yeah, far away...but what's the exact place?"

Zero pinched the bridge of his nose, sensing another headache. "That is the name of the planet. You're from Far Away, and you're visiting for a few months. You need to work for the right to live here, but they're always looking for picker-fixers so that's not a problem. Don't stare at anyone—"

"No matter how odd they look."

Zero huffed and shook his head. "No one here looks odd expect for you, so you might be on the receiving end of some curious looks, but all you gotta say is—"

"I come from Far Away."

"Exactly, I doubt anyone here's been there, so we're good, and when we finish, we'll head to the theatre and see what we can salvage."

Logan bobbed his head. "And fix the machine."

Zero turned away. Only people who had never made a complex piece of machinery would assume fixing it would be easy. He had no idea how bad the damage was and didn't want to give more false hope.

"We'll see what we can do. Now come on, car's waiting."

*

The leers began as soon as Zero stepped on the underground tram. People shuffled and knocked their elbows into each other when finally one of the rabble spoke.

"So how was your day off?"

Zero turned to Decimal and sneered. All three of his eyes were on Zero and they each blinked out of time. The sound infuriated him more than his nasally voice.

Decimal flicked his chin out. "Well?"

Zero pressed his teeth together and hissed through them, "My day off was fine, thanks."

"Fine? Who you kidding, all of us saw the news? Getting above your station again, you're a picker-fixer, and when you embarrass yourself you embarrass all of us."

Zero sighed and lifted his head. "Suddenly my horrific failure has a bonus."

One of Decimals eyes moved to study Logan and then the other two followed. "And who are you?"

"I'm far away."

Zero resisted the urge to smack his hand to his face and shuffled instead.

Logan shifted foot to foot and recovered. "I mean I'm from Far Away, and I've come to work here for a few days?"

Zero subtly shook his head.

"A few weeks," Logan said, and Decimal frowned.

"What's your name?"

"Logan," he said.

Decimal cocked his head and hummed.

"Well, Logan, I'm Decimal, and I'll give you a friendly bit of advice. Stay away from Zero. He's an embarrassment to the island, to our work force, to humanity."

The rest of the workers in the tram grumbled their agreement, and Zero sighed.

"I think anyone who takes advice from you is a grade A moron."

The eye in the centre of Decimal's head widened and bulged dangerously close to falling from its socket.

"How can you call me a moron?"

Zero waved his hand by his face. "I used my brain, my voice box, and my mouth. Very low IQ you have."

Decimal flared his nostrils. "You were the one who stood on the stage and gathered hundreds of the elite to watch you. You were the one to make ridiculous claims, and undermine Apollo, our hero. Your invention didn't even work, it did nothing but prove once and for all you are nothing just as—"

"My name says, yeah, I got it."

"I don't think you do. You are nothing, and its time you accept it. All you can be is an efficient picker-fixer. That is your purpose. That is your role this century. You are not worthy of being remembered."

Zero swallowed uncomfortably and turned away. Decimal didn't say anymore, and the tram fell under a heavy muteness.

It docked, and the other workers formed a queue to get out. Zero stayed where he was until the last of them had left. He sighed and flashed a look at Logan.

"The good news for you is no one cares that you're here, they barely even noticed. They're too angry at me."

"He had three eyes..."

Zero frowned. "Yeah...and?"

"You said about the furists, and the cold-blooded but didn't mention anything about a three-eyed race."

Zero rolled his eyes and huffed. "Decimal is Human, he voluntary had an eye attached. It's art, now, come on."

Zero plodded to the door, and Logan's softer steps followed. They pushed through the doors into the cavern, and Zero rolled up his sleeves ready for work. He paused and turned when he heard a gasp from behind him.

Logan stood with his mouth hanging open and his eyes rounding like Decimal's.

"What?" Zero asked.

"The—this place."

Zero turned back to the cavern with disinterest. "Surely you had crops in the twenty-first century?"

Logan moved closer and waved his hand. "Not like this."

There was nothing special about the cavern they stood in. It looked the same as hundreds of others. A mile high, mile long field, lit by specialised lamps. The plants grew from the ground, from the walls, and from the roof. It was a box of colour, that smelled fresh and earthy.

"But there's no sun down here," Logan said.

"Sun? Plants don't need the sun. Why do you think such nonsense? They get nutrients from the lights."

"Where I'm from crops grow on the surface."

Zero snorted. "Sounds ridiculous, who has enough space for crops up there?"

"We have fields, woods, parks, forests—"

"Yes, well, you're not there now, are you, and I'm telling you, there's no foliage on the surface."

"No trees?"

Zero scratched at his head. "What is a tree?"

Logan pointed at the closest plants, spindly and drooping with beans. "Kinda like these but huge, with a thick trunk and branches, and you can climb them, can attach a rope and swing on them."

Zero prided himself on being able to imagine and create concepts in his mind. But a tree, it sounded too farfetched. The crops had unstable stalks and there was no way they could support heavy weight. The growing fruits and vegetables had them bowing over in defeat.

"Enough with the fantasy, let's get to work."

He walked into the field with Logan at his side.

"These vines grow all these different fruits?"

Zero nodded. "Yup, their all specific to each fruit and vegetable, and they're separated into areas. The vines all look the same but grow different fruit dependant on where they are."

"So, you pick all these crops?"

"Ha! Yeah, right. Good one."

Logan drew his eyebrows together. "What do you do?"

Zero sighed. "I fix the picker machines. They have a habit of breaking down."

"Oh."

Zero tapped his foot on the metal track running parallel to them. "The pickers run on these lines. Very efficient, very fast. They have to pick the plants clean every day."

Logan gasped again, but this time Zero didn't turn to him. He waited until Logan recovered enough to speak.

"You have fresh crops every single day?"

"Yes, the food is transferred to the factory, and made into our food. Does that not happen where you're from?"

Logan nodded, and Zero relaxed. At least there was something that lasted through the millenniums.

"It's a much slower process in the twenty-first century."

Zero rolled his eyes. "Don't tell me, you pick it by hand."

Logan drew his eyebrows together and shook his head. "Urm—not everything..."

"Oi, Zero!"

He stilled at the hiss of his name but didn't turn. "What?"

"There's a picker broken down at the top."

Logan spun around and recoiled at the sight of King behind them. Zero snorted before finally turning to face his boss.

"Let me guess, you want me to go up there."

King bobbed his head patronisingly slow. "Yes, yes I do. With any luck, you'll fall, and the island will be free of you."

"I was contemplating jumping, but now you've said that, I'll make sure I survive that little bit longer."

King's scales darkened, and his forked tongue slid through his lips. "Stay up top, all those break downs will be yours today."

Zero forced his face into a delighted expression and smiled. "Sounds good to me."

King hissed and looked at Logan. "And you—wait who are you?"

Logan's skin had blanched, and his pupils were mere pinpricks. Zero didn't think he was capable of answering and did for him.

"Logan," he said.

"Where's his ID card?"

Logan didn't respond until Zero kicked his ankle. His hand shook as he showed his plastic card.

King grabbed the small piece of plastic and grimaced. "What the hell is this?"

Zero flicked his chin at the card. "He's from Far Away. That what's their ID cards look like."

King dropped the card as if burned. "Far Away. That strange planet."

Zero nodded. "Yeah, he's seeing if he can make it on Earth."

King scanned Logan's appearance and breathed heavily through his nose. "No chance. Take him to the top with you."

Zero saluted and ushered Logan away. His feet were reluctant to move but after a firm push from Zero he staggered, then retreated fast from King.

"Remember I said not to stare?" Zero said.

"Yeah—but he looks like a snake, a snake."

"Snake? What is a snake?" Zero said, drumming his fingers on his forehead. "They're race is the cold-blooded. I told you about them."

"I thought you just meant they weren't very friendly."

Zero snorted. "They're not friendly. They're arseholes, and King gave me a suicidal job."

"Is it dangerous working at the top?"

Zero lifted Logan's chin with his hand until he faced the roof.

"What do you think?"

"Surely, there's safety measures, cables, and harnesses."

Every time Logan opened his mouth, he confused Zero more. Another headache began to form, and he rolled his thumb on his temple.

"Nope, no whatever you said. You and me, a mile in the air. Let's get on with it."

Zero patted his thigh and walked, and after a moment of paralysis Logan followed. They walked over to the wall of the cavern and Zero hit the button for a pod. Zero watched it travelling towards them using the same track as the pickers. Its door slid open for them to get inside and Zero turned to Logan with his eyebrow raised.

"Well?"

Logan stopped staring at the ceiling and jolted when he noticed the machine next to them.

"All you seem to do is jump in fright."

Logan narrowed his eyes. "Screw you."

Zero had no idea what the words meant, but he was happy to see an expression other than terror on Logan's face.

*

The fix wasn't difficult. The vines of the grapes had tangled in its wheels, and all it needed was to be cut free and restarted.

Logan was reluctant to step out onto the extended platform. He clung to the seat in the pod, with his head lowered, and his eyes scrunched shut.

"You're not scared again, are you?" Zero asked with a smirk.

"Shut up!"

He smiled at the aggressive tone. Seeing Logan frightened unsettled Zero in a way he had never felt. It was annoying and made his stomach feel tight. Anger was far more favourable, and Zero intended to keep him that way as a distraction for both of them.

Zero walked along the platform, and it retracted behind him. He hit the button inside the pod to start the picker and it whistled past them.

Logan continued to scrunch his face and rock back and forth on the seat.

"Sitting like that, you look like you're having the world's most painful shi—"

The pod beeped to announce another breakdown at the top, and Zero sighed.

"Here we go again."

Logan relaxed after the third job. He didn't move outside of the pod, but he did lift his head and snarled words Zero didn't understand. A line appeared at the top of his nose when he growled, and Zero didn't know why that small crease of skin had his interest. The phrase "oddly cute" formed in his mind.

"Why are you so horrible?"

That word Zero did understand, and he turned to Logan with a frown. "I'm not 'so horrible'. I'm just teasing you a little."

Logan stood and pointed his finger at Zero. "I didn't ask to be here. I don't want to be here, so quit calling me scared."

"But you are scared," Zero said with a smirk.

He walked out onto the platform and turned back to Logan.

Logan's nostrils flared, and his eyes darkened a shade. "Shut up!"

"You're scared, and my teasing has made you angry. That anger displaces your fear. Look at you, do you even realise you've followed me onto the platform?"

Logan's feature softened, and he glanced over the edge. He looked back to Zero with wide eyes, but they were absent fear.

"There's no wind."

Zero frowned. "Why would there be?"

Logan stared at the plants hanging from the ceiling; he looked left and right with an awed smile.

Zero turned and began analysing the picker machine that called for his help. He removed the front panel and glanced inside to see a blockage.

"Ah ha," he said.

"What is it?" Logan asked.

Zero smiled when he realised Logan had moved closer to see. He reached inside and pulled the banana out.

"Don't want this getting stuck in unnecessary places."

Logan glanced down at the banana and then laughed. His happy expression, and pleasant sniggering affected Zero more than the fear. His stomach fluttered, and he quickly glanced away.

Zero forced a cough and waved the banana for Logan to take.

"What should I do with it?"

The top of the banana had been mangled by the machine, and Zero shook his head.

"Shove it in the pod, and we'll put it in the recycle chute on the way out."

Logan licked his lips and Zero moved his gaze away with a curse.

"Can't I eat it?"

"It's half crushed and hasn't been processed yet."

Logan unpeeled the banana. "It's only the top, rest looks fine."

Zero shook his head. "It hasn't been processed yet."

Logan ignored him and took a bite. It was Zero's turn to jump back alarmed. People didn't eat bananas that way; they didn't eat any food raw. It had to be processed.

Logan finished the banana with a satisfied hum.

"How are you feeling?" Zero asked.

He was half tempted to hit the emergency button on the pod, but he refrained when Logan didn't collapse or turn the colour of death.

"Good. It's like torture being surrounded by all this

fresh smelling fruit."

Zero nodded. "Yeah, does make you kind of nauseated."

"No, I meant it makes me hungry."

"The smell of raw fruit makes you hungry?"

"Yeah," Logan said, like it was the most obvious thing in the world.

"You're odd," Zero said as he turned back to the machine to reattach the front panel.

"Thank you for removing the banana," the machine said.

"No problem."

Chapter Five

The last call for help that day came from the grape picker line. The pod stopped next to the machine in trouble and when Zero saw it was the same picker he helped that morning he sighed. The platform extended and instead of walking hesitantly behind him, Logan walked at his side.

"Two break downs in one day," Zero muttered.

"Is that bad?" Logan asked.

Zero nodded. "Yeah, means it might be on its last wheels."

The picker called out for help and Zero walked over to it.

"Do-do they feel pain?" Logan asked.

Zero's laugh died in his throat when he noticed Logan's worried expression. He hated that he wanted to sooth his fear, hated that Logan affected him at all.

"They don't feel anything. They added the voices to motivate us to get to them faster. It's never nice to hear a distressed shout."

Logan nodded, but lines of concern continued to mark his brow.

Zero removed the front panel of the picker and it fell silent. He flicked a look back to Logan and noted he no longer seemed traumatised once the screams for help ended.

The wheels were tangled again, and Zero lasered them free.

Logan plucked a grape and rubbed it between his thumb and forefinger.

"That's really disturbing," Zero said.

Logan placed the grape in his mouth and bit down hard. It crunched, and moisture dripped from his lip. Zero forced his gaze elsewhere and inwardly cursed at his interest in the strange man. It couldn't be sexual attraction, there was no way his head could be turned by such an odd-looking man with no fashion sense.

"Throw me one and I'll catch it in my mouth."

Zero frowned. "What?"

Logan nodded, and his lips lifted in a smug smile. "I'll catch it like a seal."

"A what?"

"A seal," Logan said as he flapped his hand. "Just throw me one."

"I don't want to touch them if I can help it."

Logan lifted an eyebrow. "Why are you scared?"

"Not scared," Zero said, reaching for the vine.

He plucked one free and held the detached grape for Logan to see. "See, not scared."

"Okay, now throw it at me."

Zero gripped the grape in his palm and threw it hard and fast at Logan. It smacked his eye, and he yelped, cupping his face. He swayed, and Zero rushed forward to steady his wobble and pull him from the mile drop.

"Thought you said you could catch it like a sea-eel, stupid," Zero growled.

"A seal, not a sea-eel, and I can when you throw it right, that felt like you were trying to knock me off."

Zero wiped his fingers on his uniform and shook his head. "I threw it like you said."

"A gentle throw. Underarm, that's what I meant."

"Gentle throws? A throw is a throw."

Logan stopped rubbing the heel of his hand in his eye socket and blinked in quick succession.

"How's it looking?"

Zero held Logan face and stared into his watering eye. On closer inspection the shade of chestnut was slightly different to the hair of his head. Zero couldn't describe the colour. It was a mixture of russet and chestnut.

"Zero?"

"Sore," he said, "a bit sore but should be fine."

"Good to know, don't wanna lose an eye."

Zero shrugged. "You could get a new one, happens all the time."

Logan laughed, but Zero hadn't meant for it to be funny. He stroked his thumb along Logan's cheek bone amazed at the softness of his skin. Their eyes met and Zero quickly withdrew his hand.

"Enough games. I'll fix this, and we can start work on getting you home."

Logan nodded and dropped his gaze to his shoes. There was a definite blush growing on his cheeks, and Zero's own face heated in response.

Grapes vines had wrapped around the pickers inner circuits, and when Zero poked his head in further, he noticed it was empty of fruit.

He frowned and removed his head.

"What is it?" Logan asked.

Zero squeezed his temples. "It hasn't picked anything all day. Definitely not good."

He untangled the vines and flicked his head back to the pod.

"You wanna press the scarlet button for me? It will send the picker back to the ground."

Logan nodded and hurried down the platform. He turned to Zero and bit his lip.

"What is it?"

"The scarlet button, right?" Logan asked.

Zero narrowed his eyes. "Yes, that's what I said."

Logan lifted his lips in a brief smile and disappeared inside the pod. Zero stepped back from the picker to avoid being smacked in the face by it when it rushed past.

Working with Logan hadn't been as irritating as he imagined. In fact, several times he had massaged his face to remove a stubborn smile. Logan wanted to know all the fruits, and although him sniffing at them had been strange to watch, it had made Zero's insides feel light and fluttery.

The picker clunked, and Zero waited for it to move out of his view. It didn't whizz past like expected but dropped down onto the platform. The impact knocked Zero off his feet and he only just managed to cling on to the edge of the pod. The platform buckled under the weight of the picker, and Zero watched with an open mouth as it plummeted towards the ground.

Zero's fingers ached from pressure, and he scrambled for a better grip. He heaved himself inside and curled panting on the floor. He winced at the loud crash below and kept his eyes shut.

"What was that?" Logan asked.

Zero opened his eyes slowly and stared at Logan. "You trying to kill me!"

Logan recoiled. "What you talking about?"

Zero pointed out the door. "Was that revenge for throwing that grape at you, hey?"

Logan opened his mouth and his chin shook but no words followed.

"You detached the picker," Zero growled.

"The scarlet button," Logan said, pointing at the control panel.

Zero jumped to his feet and grabbed Logan's overalls. "I said scarlet, scarlet. That is vermillion."

"Vermillion?" Logan whispered.

Zero released him and turned to the door. "What the hell have you done?"

"You said it was on its last wheels, to get it to the ground."

"Last wheels, last everything now. It can't be repaired if it's in pieces, and what if it killed someone?"

Logan paled, and slid down the side of the pod. "Killed someone."

Zero didn't have time to worry about Logan's emotional state when he neared a heart attack himself. He rubbed at his chest to calm his thumping heart and breathed as slow and deep as he could. The speaker in the pod crackled, and an unmistakable howl of Zero's name filled the silence.

"Yes, King," he said and closed his eyes.

"Get your arse down here."

"On my way."

He hadn't died from the fall, but that didn't mean he was escaping the underground cavern alive.

*

The pod stopped at the bottom of the ascent and a crowd of workers stood to greet them. They shouted insults and shook their fists in a suggestive manner. Zero ushered Logan behind himself, if it was to end in a fight, he didn't want the man out of time experiencing his first cold-blooded bite.

King stood with his arms folded and his tongue lashing.

"What the hell! You destroyed a picker, damaged our crop, and put the lives of your fellow workers at risk."

Zero pressed his hand to his heart. "An innocent mistake."

Kings eyes narrowed. "Innocent, there's nothing innocent about you. You're fired."

Zero hung his head and gawped at the floor.

Fired from a job as a picker-fixer, the lowest job in the world. The day before he had thought he would climb to great heights and move into the floating palace, but he was being forced out of the underground, unworthy of even that menial job.

"Now get out of my sight, or I'll let this lot tear you apart."

Zero swallowed uncomfortably at all the angry eyes attached to him. All three of Decimals eyes bugged from his face, and his lip twitched with pure fury.

"Wait!" Logan shouted, "It was me. I pressed the wrong button. He said press scarlet, but I hit another one. A vermin-vermined...I don't know...another colour."

"You think I'm going to believe that?" King hissed.

"But it's the truth."

King's scales darkened, and Zero knew he was preparing to strike. Zero grabbed Logan by the arm and tugged him back sharply. King's eyes snapped to Zero, and he launched forward with his mouth open and fangs extended.

Zero didn't have a chance to defend himself while holding Logan at his back. King pressed his fangs in his neck. He winced at the sting of the poison and ground his teeth together. The moment was over in a few seconds, but the burn of fire started immediately.

"Now get out," King kissed, licking his fangs.

Zero nodded, unable to speak and pulled Logan towards the tram that led to the surface. The wound burned, and his eyes filled with pained tears, but he'd be damned if he let King and the others see him cry.

The door of the tram slammed shut, and he collapsed to the floor holding his neck. Logan kneeled beside him and rubbed Zero's arms. It had taken Zero most of the day to remove the fear from Logan's face, but it returned in full force.

"He bit you. He can't bite you."

Zero pressed his lips together not to scream and nodded.

"But he can't bite you."

If his eyes weren't swimming in water, he would've rolled them. Instead he tightened his fists and tensed his muscles to ride out the burn.

"What do I do? Do I call an ambulance, do you have ambulances?"

All Zero wanted was for Logan to shut up, but he couldn't tell him in case his pain vocalised and filled the tram. He didn't reply, hoping Logan would get the hint.

"What-what do I do? Are you going to die?"

Zero squeezed his eyes shut to block out Logan's visual panic.

He jolted in alarm when Logan's head pressed into his shoulder, and his arms wrapped around him. A hug, Logan hugged him and Zero couldn't think of anything worse. He shuffled, but Logan tightened his grip and muttered sorry over and over.

The torturous sting stopped its climb and plateaued its burn. After ten minutes of being squeezed by Logan, Zero finally had the strength to push him away.

"Off of me."

"Are you going to die?"

Zero scrunched his nose and glared. "'Course not you idiot, its hurts that's all."

"I'm sorry, I didn't mean to get you fired. I didn't mean to get you hurt."

Zero breathed deep through his nose. "Did you do it on purpose?"

"What?"

"Hit the picker detach."

Logan shook his head. "No, 'course not. I had no idea. I hit the first red button I saw."

"Red," Zero growled. "Red? You hit the vermillion, not the scarlet like I told you."

"They looked the same."

Zero got to his feet and towered over Logan. "Don't be stupid, they look nothing alike."

He moved to the opposite end of the tram and sat down heavily. Logan didn't get up from the floor, he drew his knees to his chest and hugged his legs.

Zero quickly faced the window. He didn't want to feel any unnecessary unease. The bite to his neck hurt enough without his gut and chest squirming at the sight of Logan's distress.

The longer he spent not looking at Logan, the more his anger and resentment grew. Logan had ruined his teleportation machine, gotten him fired, and irritated King enough for him to strike forward with his fangs.

Even with the pain subsiding, he knew it would take weeks to heal. Logan, the human from another time was ruining his life. He hated him, a hatred to rival his feelings for Apollo.

The tram docked, but he didn't turn back to Logan. He strolled out and blinked in the sunshine. He waited for a car and could feel the presence of Logan behind him like a shadow but refused to turn to him.

"Don't leave me down here."

Zero grit his teeth. "I'm gonna call Honey, she'll send a car."

"No," Logan gasped, "I'm sorry, okay. We had fun today—"

"Fun? What use is fun? I am nothing, and that's because of you."

Logan's closed his fingers around his arm, but Zero shrugged him off. "Stay here, don't do anything stupid until a car comes for you."

"Please don't—"

Zero ignored him and climbed into the hovering car. He slid the door shut and avoided looking Logan in the eye.

Logan banged his fist into the car, but it lifted off the ground undeterred.

Zero sighed and dropped his head into his hands. Logan would be better off with Honey; he was certain of it. She had a high tolerance level unlike most of the inhabitants of the island.

A dark thought spun in his mind. Honey had told him Logan had almost walked on the magnetic line.

He flung himself towards the window and stared down at the figures below. It was hard to know which one Logan was, but there weren't any bright sparks coming from the magnetic line.

Zero's thumping heart didn't slow, and he rubbed over the organ with a frown on his face. He had been worried for Logan, the only person he had worried about other than himself had been Honey, and even that was deemed strange.

Even with Logan out of sight, he still affected Zero.

"Stupid," he growled.

Chapter Six

Zero tapped the dashboard of the car and its lights brightened.

"How may I help you sir?"

"Call Honey from the west tower and tell her there's something waiting for a car outside the picker-tunnel."

"Yes, sir."

Zero tapped his finger on his knee as he waited for the car to respond. He didn't have to wait long before its overly joyous voice sounded again.

"She's requested to speak to you."

Zero nodded slowly, he had expected that, and instead of allowing verbal contact between them, he sighed. "Denied."

"She insists, sir."

He snickered. "Bet she does."

Zero stabbed the off button to silence the machine. He knew Honey wouldn't leave Logan, knew she had a weak heart when it came to unfortunate life-forms. She would hate him, and he would expect a claw to his face the next time they saw each other, but it was worth it to be free of the troublesome Logan.

Zero imagined him waiting in the square below. Eyes wide, and chin wobbling with fear. The visual churned his gut, and he shifted in the chair, tapped his foot to the floor, and grit his teeth, but the image wouldn't fade.

He closed his eyes and pictured the crowd at the theatre. They shook their heads and shot him disgusted looks after his failure. He thought about the other picker-fixer workers. They stared at him with equal levels of anger and embarrassment. Logan had been responsible. Zero used the humiliating memories to push the last remains of guilt away.

He climbed from the docked car and strolled into his Logan-free flat.

Fired from his job as a picker-fixer. He didn't think he could feel any more embarrassed, but it kept coming. Zero sighed and yanked on the drawer that held the food pouches. He counted twenty pouches and predicted he could ration himself to two a day. That gave him ten days to find a job or apply to join another island. It wasn't enough time for the island to forget his double humiliation, and he suspected his disastrous theatre performance had been projected on other islands, if not other planets.

Zero flung his head back and stared at the ceiling. He didn't want to leave *New Fretton*, but once his rations ran out, he would be kicked off the island. If he couldn't find another one to join, he'd be shipped off planet.

He shuddered at the thought and smacked his lips at the sudden stomach-churning taste in his mouth. Those who couldn't work, or those who were criminals were sent to the recycling planet. Once people got sent to that place, they didn't come back.

The imagined dirt of the planet had him itching and desperate to escape his work clothes.

Zero's wardrobe full of luscious outfits called to him, and he rushed in the bedroom to change out of his hideous work-overalls. One positive of being fired, he would never have to where garish amber again.

Zero froze when he saw the neatly folded clothes on the bed. No sparkles, or tassels, but just as eye catching when they belonged to Logan. He ran the back of his fingers against the soft fabric and clutched the T-shirt and lifted it higher. He twitched his nose, tempted to breathe the unique scent of Logan into his lungs.

He caught himself at the last moment and growled.

Zero grabbed Logan's clothing and rushed to the recycle chute. He waved goodbye as they vanished into the darkness, then dusted his hands together. Logan wasn't his problem anymore, but Honey's.

The amber overalls followed Logan's clothing, and Zero sighed in pleasure when he climbed into his burgundy suit with gold lapels and buttons. He ran his hands along his collection of cravats before he selected one the same silver as his hair. He spun his hat in his fingers and placed it on his head with a firm push.

He walked out and sunk into the sofa with a sigh. His usual after work activities were either tinkering with his teleportation machine or finding an attractive life-form to engage in a quick burst of pleasure. He could do neither and patted his hands to his thighs and clacked his tongue.

He didn't dare switch the news hologram on, convinced it would be his face projected in front of him with failure branded across it again.

"Can you send me to sleep?" he asked the flat.

"Of course, sir. Do you want dreams this time?"

Zero shook his head. "No, no dreams please."

The orbing ring sounded in the flat and Zero's eyelids drooped. He sagged into the sofa with a sigh, but before he faded into unconsciousness an image of Logan, sad and confused pulsed in his head.

*

Zero woke to the flat ringing and apologising. He blinked the room back into focus and noted the blackened sky outside. He had slept longer than normal, but he didn't feel refreshed.

"Sorry, sir, Honey's at the door."

Zero groaned and shook his head. "Not happening."

"She asks to speak with you."

He huffed and rolled his shoulders. "Fine, I'll speak, but she's not coming in."

"Zero!" she hissed, "Open the door."

"Not gonna happen."

Zero took off his hat, ruffled his hair then placed it on top again. Honey panted and released a distressed noise that made him frown.

"Logan's in trouble..."

The uncomfortable fizzle in his stomach returned, and he swallowed awkwardly. The reaction itched his skin, made him shudder and roll his wrists. No movement quelled the heaviness in his gut, and he sighed.

"He's not my problem."

"Please, Zero. I don't know what to do with him."

Zero huffed and got to his feet. He paced back and forth, but that didn't loosen the coils of his insides. The only way to relieve the tension was to allow Honey and Logan into the flat.

He buttoned his jacket and moved to the door. "Fine."

The door slid open, and Honey struggled inside with Logan's arm thrown over her shoulders. Zero rushed forward and held up his other side. He still wore the bright amber overalls, but his hair was no longer fluffy in appearance but damp and flat.

"What happened?"

Logan's head lolled forward, and his feet dragged on the floor. They heaved Logan onto the sofa, and he muttered words Zero couldn't decipher.

"I thought a drink would cheer him up, and it did at first. He started laughing, and he relaxed. He was even calling me Honey, not cat."

Logan leaned forward and grabbed his head in his hands as he groaned.

Zero steadied him and flashed a look at Honey. "Then what happened?"

"He got confused and scared again when he looked at me."

It was not uncommon for alcohol to affect people that way. Zero didn't understand Honey's concern. A dreamless sleep was all Logan needed.

Zero huffed, looking down at the curled over man. "How many did he have?"

"One."

He whipped his head up to face her. "One?"

"Yeah, it all happened so fast. He kept saying he felt sick, but I don't know what that means."

Zero shook his head. "I don't know either."

He crouched in front of Logan and tried to pry his hands away from his face.

"Logan, how do you feel?"

"Like you care."

Zero rolled his eyes. "No need for dramatics."

Logan peeked through the gaps of his fingers. Zero frowned at the blood-shot appearance of his eyes. His black pupil had expanded till only a narrow ring of iris remained.

"I think you need to sleep."

Logan lurched to his feet and Zero flailed and fell backwards.

"I don't need sleep. I need to get out of this place."

Zero jumped to his feet and straightened his lapels. "The doors there—"

"I need to go home," Logan said, swaying on his feet.

"I can't get you home. The machine is broken. You need to accept you live in this time now."

Logan shook his head. "I can't, I have friends, and a family. I—I want to see them."

"Well, tough."

Honey pressed her hand to Zero's chest, and he retreated a few steps. Never had he been knocked over in his own home, and he seethed with humiliation.

Logan fixed his eyes on Zero. "You're so selfish. You only care about yourself—"

"Of course, I do! That is how it is here. I want to be successful, and since you arrived my life has come apart, and my dreams are now unreachable. If I'm not successful, I won't be remembered, I won't mean anything, and I would have failed at life."

Logan curled his lip and shook his head. "You think you're the only one to fail, the only one to humiliate yourself and not be the person you want to be. Get over it and accept it, like I've had to."

Zero puffed his chest out and matched Logan's furious expression. "I don't care of your failure. I care of mine. You are nothing."

The words were sour in his mouth, and after he said them, he dropped his head. He didn't mean them, but he hadn't been able to stop from vocalising the fleeting thought.

"Logan, I—"

"No, you're right. People expected me to be someone, but I am nothing. They probably don't miss me—probably happy I'm gone."

Zero swallowed uncomfortably and his fingers twitched with the need to reach for Logan. He didn't know what he would do if he did, a hug was uncharacteristic of him, but in that moment, he felt the need to give one. Honey moved first, wrapping her furry arms around Logan's neck and purred to soothe him. Zero sagged and rocked back on his heels.

"That's not true. Of course, they miss you," Honey said.

Logan sniffled and wiped his hand across his eyes. He lifted his head and gestured to the room. "Everything has turned to shit."

Zero recoiled and glanced around the flat. "I think you're mistaken."

"No, I'm not, it's all shit."

Zero narrowed his eyes. Logan was clearly hallucinating, but still Zero felt insulted being told his home was a cesspool.

"I think you need to lie down," Honey said.

Logan bobbed his head and followed obediently into the bedroom.

"Apparently the bed is free of shit then," Zero muttered.

The door closed, and Zero lashed out and kicked the sofa.

"May I suggest using your punch bag, not the sofa," the flat said.

"If I wanna kick the sofa, I'll kick the sofa."

He didn't strike it again but spun around and threw himself back into the cushions. The door to the bedroom opened and Honey sneaked out. She flicked her head to Zero who sighed and lifted his chin.

"Send him to sleep. No dreams."

"Yes, sir."

Honey moved closer, and Zero offered her a weak smile. Her eyes narrowed, and her lips pulled back until her teeth showed.

"You left him down there alone."

Zero shrugged. "I knew you would send a car for him."

"What if I didn't? No one knows who he is. He would be sent off planet."

"Probably the best place for him."

Honey's claws flicked out and she hissed. Zero held his hands up to appease her.

"Easy—"

"You will help him," she demanded.

Zero shook his head. "He's made me a laughing stock, got me fired—"

"It's not the first time you've been fired, get another job."

He took the hat off his head and brushed away the imaginary dust on the top. "No one's going to employ me. Not now. I've run out of options here."

"Here?" Honey whispered.

She retracted her claws and sat beside him. Her gaze pierced the side of his face, and he felt compelled to say more.

"I'm going to have to move again, start somewhere else. It's that or I run out of rations and I'm transferred off planet to die."

Honey gasped and covered her mouth with her paw.

"I don't want you to go off planet."

Zero shook his head. "Me neither, could you imagine this suit getting dirty?"

Honey laughed and knocked her shoulder into his. "What are we gonna do?"

"What can I do? I've got ten days' worth of food, and then I'll have to move on."

"What about Logan?"

Zero squeezed his head and slid his foot on the floor. "I don't know…"

"You've got to help him get home."

"It took me years to make that machine. You're asking me to remake it in ten days."

Her ears twitched, and she shifted closer. "I'm asking you to try."

"I don't want to get his hopes up. It's better that he accepts he's here for the long-haul than think he will get home."

Honey pressed her paws together and pleaded with her rounded eyes. "Please, can you try to do the impossible for me?"

"Fix the machine. It's not that simple—"

"No, not that," she said shaking her head. "Try to stop being selfish and think of it from his point of view. He doesn't belong here. He wants to go home and the only person he remotely feels comfortable with keeps trying to be rid of him."

"I'm not like you. I can't care about others. I don't even know how to."

Honey licked her lips and leaned closer. "You care about me."

Zero nodded. "Yeah, but you're my anomaly, my small margin of error."

"Make that error a little larger, and maybe you'll find out it's not an error at all."

Zero opened his mouth to dismiss her words, but her eyes pleaded with him to agree. Life-forms had a responsibility to themselves in the forty-first century. There was no emphasis on caring for others and Zero liked it that way, but Logan needed an ally; he needed someone to care.

"Fine," he said and glanced towards the bedroom door. "I will try to stop being selfish and to get him home."

Honey leaned forward and licked his cheek. "Thank you."

Chapter Seven

Zero yawned and stretched out his limbs. It was the second night he had spent on the sofa, and after being unable to drift off himself, he used the flat's sleep frequency to force him under.

He stumbled up and made his way to the food drawer. He planned to eat two a day and last ten days in the tower block before being forced out. Logan complicated the plan. He had no food rations or any tokens to trade.

Zero sighed and picked a grape flavour pouch. He didn't bother sitting at the table. He split the corner and eased half the contents into his mouth. He folded the foil over and hid the half-eaten packet at the bottom.

He faced the ceiling and spoke in a whisper, "When he wakes, tell him to pick a pouch."

"Of course, sir."

Zero nodded to himself, then his rumpled sleeves caught his attention. He sighed and ran his hands up his creased suit. He hadn't wanted to wake Logan, which meant he slept in his suit. The luscious material no longer sparkled. It dulled and Zero huffed at his flagging appearance.

He shot a look to the bedroom door and shook his head. "Call me a car."

"Yes, sir."

Zero strolled to the sofa and stooped down to get his hat. He pushed it down on his hair, grateful that it wasn't in disarray like his clothes. As long as he was seen at head height, no one would notice his less than perfect outfit.

"The car has arrived."

Zero nodded and made his way over to the dock. "When he wakes, tell him I've gone to the theatre. He is welcome to stay up here or come and join me. It is up to him."

Zero didn't wait for the flat to reply. He exited his front door and climbed into the waiting car. He promised Honey he'd try to fix the machine, and he owed it to the man dragged from his timeline.

The car dropped, and Zero pressed his hand to his stomach at the sensation. The unease passed, and he looked out the window at the bustling town below. Zero spotted some amber overalls and ducked even though they couldn't see him inside the car. Decimal walked along the pavement with his rabble of three-eyed companions. They moved off in the direction of the underground tram, and Zero released the breath he'd been holding. He had to get to the theatre with as little humiliation as possible.

Zero tapped the side of the car, and the door slid open. He stood, brushing the dust from his trousers. The eyes of the remaining life-forms in the square stopped and stared.

He should have ignored them, but instead he twirled on the balls of his feet to face them. He bowed forward with his hat in hand.

"Morning."

No one greeted him back, and he straightened with a huff. "Bit rude, isn't it?"

"No one wants to speak to you."

Zero dropped his gaze to the young cold-blooded. "Except you it seems."

"I didn't want to..."

Zero pressed his forefinger to his head. "Well, you must've done, otherwise words would not have come from your mouth."

The youngling hissed, and his scales darkened. "Nothing but an incompetent failure."

Zero waved his finger. "Interesting double negative. Your Dadda teaching you big words, but not how to use them."

"My Dadda will sink his fangs into you, just like King did."

The pain in Zero's neck prickled at the mention of King, and he resisted the urge to rub the wound. The youngling smiled as if he knew pain reverberated in his neck.

"Pleasure talking to you," Zero muttered, then he turned and made his way up the street to the theatre.

The gaze of other commuters settled on him, but he didn't engage in any further conversations. The stupid youngling had practically bested him in a war of words, and he didn't wish to add to his mountain of embarrassment.

The grim front of the theatre made him grimace. He had wanted to spruce it up, brighten the colour scheme and add strobing lights, but he'd traded ten years' worth of tokens for the place and had nothing more to give. He pressed his hand to the door for scanning, then shoved with his back straight and his shoulders squared. As soon as the doors shut behind him, he hunched forward and released a long-suffering sigh.

Silence hummed around him in the colossal room. He ran his hand along the backs of the chairs and made his way towards the stage. Lingering dust, and the scent of fried wires had him nearing a sneeze. He caught himself at the last minute and huffed at the tiny triumph. It didn't last long as soon as he felt the itch passed. It returned in full force and his sneeze echoed around him.

"Lights," he said.

The room responded, and the bulbs in the ceiling flickered and stuttered. They didn't bathe the space in a vibrant white, but a dull rust.

"Welcome, Suuuuur—"

Zero sighed at the haggard building and lifted his hat from his head. He threw it towards the stage and watched as it skidded along the debris covered surface.

One arch stood tall with its wires dangling, and the other was mere stumps on a platform.

Honey had told him the high arch had blown first, and there was little left of it, but it wasn't necessary. Logan had appeared through the arch still standing.

He heaved himself up to the stage and swivelled his legs around. He reclaimed his hat then dusted the edges. He shoved it back down on his head and nodded at the task in front of him.

The metal panels of the arch had melted, and the circuits were misshaped from heat. He had traded meals and tokens for parts to the machine, and without a job he knew he'd be unable to get more. He had to salvage all he could.

"Right," he said, slipping his suit jacket off and rolling his sleeves.

The first thing he needed to do was strip it back to its wooden frame and then repair and replace all the components. Zero yanked away the panels and threw them in a pile. Metal clanged and crashed as the pile grew higher.

"Sir there's..."

He stilled, waiting for the theatre to finish but it didn't. "Never mind then, useless building."

Zero turned back to the littered stage and drummed his forefinger on his chin.

"Hey?"

Zero startled at Logan's voice and shot a look at him. He raised his eyebrow when he saw the clothing Logan had chosen. The navy suit complimented his hair and eyes, and the velvet material sparkled in the light. He matched the suit with a black shirt with lace trim. A top hat would've completed the look, but Zero couldn't expect him to get it right on his first attempt.

"I look stupid, don't I?"

Zero pressed his lips together and replied, "You only look as stupid as you feel."

Logan narrowed his eyes with a snort. "Thanks for clearing that up. I feel ridiculous and must look it too. I couldn't find my clothes."

"Ah, about that. I threw them away."

Zero waited for anger to descend on Logan's features, but he only shrugged and clambered onto the stage.

"You're not upset?"

Logan shook his head and grinned. "Not really."

Zero blew a breath through his teeth. "I damn well would've killed someone if they threw one of my suits away."

Logan waved his finger still smiling. "I know how to irritate you now. Don't mess with the suits."

"Exactly," Zero agreed, and bowed his head and spoke to his feet. "I'm sorry about yesterday."

"You were angry with me, I get it. But I didn't mean to press the wrong button."

"Can you really not tell the difference between scarlet and vermillion?"

Logan shook his head. "They're both red."

Zero narrowed his eyes. "And what of my suit?"

"It's reddish brown."

"Burgundy," Zero corrected, "my hair, my eyes?"

He lifted the top hat from his head and ruffled his strands.

"Silver," Logan said.

Zero grinned. "Good, least we got that colour in common."

"And your eyes are purple."

"They are a shimmering mauve."

Logan flapped his hand. "Mauve is a type of purple."

"Must be a very simplistic world you live in."

"We don't do stupid things like put two red buttons next to each other."

Zero shook his head and turned back to the machine. He had torn most of the metal cladding from the wood, leaving a naked frame to start from.

"The-the wood," Logan said.

"It's really rare. Some old frame. They found it when digging the caverns. I dunno how it survived."

Logan pressed his hand to the arch. "It's a door."

Zero frowned and wiggled his hand in the empty space. "Not sure how doors work in the twenty-first century, but there's no sliding mechanism, or opening one."

Logan laughed and ran his fingertips up the wood. "It's a doorway. I recognise it."

Zero rolled his eyes. "Think that one drink you had is still affecting you."

"No look," Logan said. He crouched down and pointed to the carved symbols at the bottom. "I did this, they're my initials."

Zero dropped to his knees and studied the marks on the wood. They were jagged and uneven. He had despised the marks and took great pleasure in covering them.

"I did this when I was eight. My dad went crazy," Logan said.

He crawled to the other side of the arch. "And here, you see that scuff mark. I threw my shoe and hit the doorway."

"Why were you throwing a shoe?"

Logan drew his eyebrows together in thought. "I don't even remember now, but my dad wasn't happy."

Zero scanned the arch and lifted an eyebrow. "Bit of a grand door to have in your home."

"Wasn't in our home. It was at the club. The magic club my dad owned. It's a vanishing door."

Zero rapped his knuckles to the wood. "Feels pretty sturdy to me."

"The door itself doesn't vanish, but what passes through it does."

"It vanishes things? How sinister that your dad owned such a thing, was he not tempted to push you through it?"

Logan shoved at his shoulder, but there was no malice to his expression. "You walk through it and disappear and reappear through a smaller door at the opposite end of the stage."

Zero staggered back a step and glared at Logan. "What did you say?"

Logan ran his hand fondly up the wood.

"It's a vanishing door. A magic trick."

Zero waved his hand and shook his head. "You said, you walk through and then appear in a different doorway."

"Yeah, to the eye that's what happens," the awed expression fell from his face and his eyes darted around the stage. "Wait, Honey said you had two arches...you were performing the trick?"

Zero lurched forward and gripped both Logan's shoulders. "You know how to do it? You know how to transport a living thing. Tell me the secret, please."

Logan chuckled and quirked his eyebrow. "A magician never reveals his secrets."

Zero shook his head manically. "I will do anything you want. I swear to you, just tell me how to do it. How do I disappear myself and reappear myself?"

Zero's voice shrilled with need, but he didn't care. Logan held the key to transportation.

Logan's eyes widened, and his chin bobbed. "It's a trick, a magic trick."

"I don't know of this magic you speak, but please tell me how. I found a way to break down atoms and put them back together perfectly in one arch but reforming them in the opposite one was my downfall. I succeeded a few times but couldn't accurately transfer an object."

"I—it's a magic trick. It's not real, you just make the audience believe it is."

Zero took a step back and tightened his face. "What?"

"No one from my time has really disappeared and reappeared somewhere else instantly. It's not real. That's what magicians do, they make the impossible seem possible. It isn't though, it can't be done."

The adrenaline that surged in Zero's body stilled. "You lie to your audience. You make a mockery of them?"

He turned away from Logan and rubbed at his chin. The twenty-first century was nothing but deceitful and demeaning. Anger rose sharply in Zero's chest and he turned back to face Logan.

"You humiliate and deceive."

Logan backed away with his palms up.

"No, the audience knows it's a trick, it's not real. They come to be fooled."

"Your world of magic makes no sense. It's insulting to the great inventors of my time."

"It doesn't need to make sense, its entertainment, that's all it is," Logan whispered, lowering his head. "Guess that means magic doesn't last through the centuries."

"And so it shouldn't. What a pointless activity."

"It wasn't the activity, or the mechanics of the tricks, it was how it amazed the audience that made it special."

"You know what would be amazing, huh? If this stupid thing had worked in the first place and rebuilt my body above the stage. That is amazing, not your trickery. It is utterly pointless."

Logan lifted his head and balled his hands into fists. "It is not pointless. I love magic, and I loved watching my dad perform each night."

Zero studied Logan intently. The whites of his eyes had pinked, and his irises shimmered under an extra layer of moisture. He was usually inept at spotting sadness, but he suspected Logan was upset.

"I'm sorry… I didn't mean to make you unhappy. It's obvious you care for your dad and will defend his honour."

Logan rubbed angrily at his eyes and spoke to the arch. "I know you didn't mean to. You don't understand the time I'm from, but my dad was a magician, the town's hero, and I'm proud of what he achieved, even if it equates to nothing in the end."

Zero bowed his head and bit his lip. He knew he should say words of comfort, or assurance, like Honey would've, but nothing came to him.

"Magic dies with time," Logan whispered.

Zero swallowed uncomfortably. "Looks that way."

Logan rubbed the heel of his hand into his eye socket and sniffed loudly.

"I've never heard someone speak so fondly of their dad. It is not done in this century," Zero said.

"Why not?"

Zero shrugged. "At ten, we begin our adult life and don't hear from our parents again. When they die, we're notified, and their possessions are exchanged for tokens. The only thing I have of my dad's is my top hat."

"What about your mum?"

Zero frowned. "I assume she's still alive, but she doesn't live on earth."

"I couldn't imagine living that far from my mum. I see her every day..." Logan paused, then whispered. "Saw her every day."

He sniffed loudly then dropped down at the edge of the stage.

"Where you going?" Zero asked.

Logan didn't stop, but he slowed his stride. "Back to the flat...it will let me in, right?"

"Yeah, it will let you in."

He disappeared through the double doors and Zero stared after him. Honey's words echoed in his mind. He had to stop being selfish and see the world through Logan's eyes. Clearly magic meant something in his time, even if Zero thought the idea of it was useless.

He sighed and began picking his way through the pile of metal. He didn't know what "love" was but could tell it was important to Logan. He had to try to get him back to the time of magic, back to his town, and back to his parents.

Chapter Eight

Zero hoped Logan's mood would improve, but the next few days passed without them even talking. Zero worked on the machine while Logan stayed in the flat, and when he finished and returned home, Logan shut himself in the bedroom. Zero enjoyed solitude, but not when someone else hovered in the next room. It unsettled him and made his skin itch.

"So, have you applied to move to any other islands yet?" Honey asked.

Zero shook his head, and she narrowed her eyes.

"You need to, Zero, otherwise..."

He waved his hand. "I'm focusing on Logan first, then I'll deal with that."

"Don't leave it too late," she hissed.

"That depends on Logan, the quicker I can help him, the quicker I can figure out where I'm to go next, but I find him distracting and confusing."

"Is this still about the magic?"

"Magic," Zero spat. "Pointless trickery."

"You need to see it from his perspective," Honey said.

Zero scoffed and shook his head. "It's a little hard when humans of his time like such stupid things."

"It's not stupid to him."

Zero waved the brush in his hand and leaned forward. "Whatever, you're not here to talk about Logan, what's going on? Why am I brushing your fur?"

Honey turned and looked up at him from between his legs. She twitched the corners of her mouth into a smile. "I'm going on another date with Rae."

Zero twirled his finger for her to turn and resumed detangling the copper fur of her nape.

"Jesus Honey, you're addicted to her like people get to alcohol and mushroom pouches? Maybe you should seek medical help."

Honey swiped her paw at his leg, but he managed to dodge her claws with a shuffle.

"Being with her makes me happy, you wouldn't understand."

He shook his head. "No, I don't. Success is what we should aim for, happiness will follow once we become important."

"There must be more than the need to succeed. This...me and Rae. It feels like something."

"Good sex?" Zero offered.

He didn't move his leg fast enough and her claw's dug through his trousers into his leg. "Okay, okay."

She relaxed her paws and placed them in her lap. "I think spending time with someone who enjoys your company is just as important as success."

Zero rolled his eyes and clutched the brush in his grip. "Society lets us secure our food, our water, and warmth by rewarding us for work, then they give us security with our homes. After that we strive to improve ourselves as individuals and then finally, we achieve our full potential and become worthy of being remembered. That is what we are taught, that is how we live—"

"You missed one out."

Zero whipped his head towards the bedroom. Logan stood in the door frame with his shirt untucked, and his hair messy. Zero resisted the urge to rush over and tuck his shirt in, but he couldn't stop the unconscious twitch of the hairbrush. He coughed and dropped it on the sofa.

"What do you mean?" Honey asked.

Logan stepped into the room and flicked his chin at Zero. "You were quoting Maslow's hierarchy of needs."

"My teachers name was not Maslow," Zero muttered.

"It's a pyramid. Physiological needs, then safety needs, followed by self-esteem and then self-fulfilment, but you missed one."

Honey shook her head. "No that's all—"

"You missed love."

Zero shot a confused look at Honey who responded with the same doubtful expression. Logan had used the word to describe his dad, and magic, but Zero had no clue what it meant.

"Love," Zero said, "what is this love, is it as deceitful as magic?"

Honey elbowed his calf, and he cursed as he rubbed the aching flesh.

Logan huffed to himself and moved his gaze to the window. "No one knows what love is here? That makes a lot of sense, actually."

"Come on then," Zero sighed, "spit it out and enlighten us."

"There are different types. It's a feeling, caring, can be between a child and a parent—"

Zero flapped his hand. "Yes, parent's care for their children, and once they turn ten, they moved to a different island and start again. That is as far as care goes, it's a necessity to nurture a child into society."

"It's not just children, its friends, family, lovers. Love is caring for someone else more than you care for yourself. It an intense feeling...of belonging, of valuing someone and having them value you in return. You feel it in your chest, in your heart when you look at them."

Zero collapsed back into the sofa and laughed. "Sounds like nonsense, don't you agree, Honey?"

She didn't reply, she stood and took a step closer to Logan.

"Yes," she said. "I—I feel it in my body, a floating feeling when I am on the ground."

Zero shook his head. "That's atmospheric pressure from the sudden descent."

"No, I only get it when I look at Rae. When I spend time with her, it's like nothing else matters."

"When you spend time with her, you're usually drinking, don't mistake alcohol symptoms for this ridiculous concept," Zero said.

Logan curled his hands into balls and breathed heavily from his nose. "It's not ridiculous. It's important in my time. People want to find someone to spend their life with, to have security and comfort. The knowledge that you are not alone in this world."

Zero pointed at the window. "There are millions of life-forms out there right now, is your population really so sparse?"

Logan flung his head back and growled at the ceiling. "It's a feeling, a feeling that you belong with someone, that you want to be with them, look after them, make them happy."

"If you waste all your time on caring for someone else, how do you have time to fulfil your potential? It's a sacrifice, and not one where I can see a reward."

Honey rushed to the sofa and pressed her paw to Zero's mouth. He struggled, but she flicked out her claws in a threat and Zero stilled.

"In your time, all life-forms feel that way?"

"A lot of humans do. We fall in love, and live together, and some of us have kids."

Zero yanked Honey's arm away and stood before she could cover his mouth again.

"Love has no part in reproduction. Sexual intercourse is what creates new life. Society works out a match, and a new life-form is born."

Honey frowned and bobbed her head. "That is true..."

"Some people only want to have children when they fall in love, some people only have sex when they're in love," Logan said.

"Unless society wants a new-life form, sex is only for pleasure."

The distracting dent appeared at the top of Logan's nose. Zero turned away and shook his head.

"I guess you are one of these people that need "love" to have sex," he mumbled.

Logan stamped his foot to the floor. "I am."

Zero chomped on his tongue and ignored the churning in his stomach.

"Then this century isn't for you. There is no deceitful magic, and no pointless love. I for one am happy we evolve to be free of such meaningless concepts."

"Zero!" Honey hissed.

He turned and clutched his forehead. "Enough, I don't wish to argue anymore. You are from your time, and I am from mine. It is not your fault you exist in an obsolete world."

"Screw you!" Logan yelled and stormed back through the bedroom door.

Zero turned to Honey with wide eyes. "What did I do? I told him it wasn't his fault."

He expected Honey to agree with him, but she picked at her claws with a far-off expression. Zero moved closer and clicked his fingers in front of her eyes.

"Hey Honey?"

She blinked up at him. "What?"

"Please say you're not thinking about 'love'."

Her lips lifted into a smile and she ducked her head. "It doesn't sound like such a bad thing."

"It sounds stupid, and until this mystical feeling arrives, you can't even have sex."

Honey narrowed her eyes and flexed her whiskers. "He said some people don't have sex until they fall in love, not all of them."

"Whatever, it's still stupid."

She lifted her lips and unleashed her teeth-showing smile.

"What the hell is that look for?" Zero asked.

"Does it bother you that he won't have sex with you?"

Zero blew a breath through his teeth. "Haven't even thought about him in that way. He's far too irritating."

She snickered into her paws then raised her head. "I don't believe you."

"Right enough, off with you. Go on your date."

Honey bounded across the room with her smile still intact. Zero ushered her towards the dock with the waiting car.

"Go, go on, go have lots of love-free sex with Rae."

Honey winked at him. "I'm gonna tell her I love her."

Zero smacked his hand to his head. "She will think you're crazy and stop seeing you."

"No, she won't," Honey said, still grinning.

She climbed into the car and when the door slid shut relief filled Zero at not having to look at her happy face any longer.

The empty room prickled with the uncomfortable feeling somebody was close by, and Zero couldn't relax. He knocked on the door, before remembering it was his bedroom and barged in.

Logan didn't acknowledge Zero's dramatic entrance. He lay curled on his side, with his back to Zero.

"I'm sorry for losing my temper."

There was no response, and Zero grimaced in the silence. He darted a glance through the door, and turned his feet in the direction, then he shook his head. He didn't wish to spend another afternoon with Logan confined to the bedroom, and him restless on the sofa.

He perched on the edge of the bed. "I'm not used to the things you speak of. They are uncomfortable to imagine."

Logan rolled on to his back and stared Zero in the eye.

"Is it really so uncomfortable to imagine caring for someone more than yourself? Surely, you've had a partner, a boyfriend or a girlfriend?"

"Boyfriend? What is this?" Zero said.

"Someone you spent time with and were intimate with them regularly. You enjoyed their company."

Zero hummed. "Maybe."

Logan leaned up on his elbows. "Right, and you must've cared for them. Wanted them to be happy."

Zero glanced away. He despised looking back on his relationship with Apollo. His weakness slapped him in the face. The caring Logan spoke of, was flawed.

"It's overrated."

Logan narrowed his eyes. "But you care for Honey?"

"'Course I do."

"And she loves someone. Don't you think she'd appreciate you being happy for her, rather than mocking?"

Zero pinched his nose hard. "You need to be careful what you introduce here."

"How could adding love be a bad thing?"

"In the time you live, how do people express love?"

Logan drew his knees up and wrapped his arms around them. "Spending time together, people kiss, they hold hands, they laugh and hug, and use their words to express it."

"You must've noticed we don't behave like that here. There's no hand holding, or hugging. That is for a mother and a child to express, not two adults. If Honey goes out there and starts shouting about love, and kissing everyone, there will be consequences."

"Like what?"

Zero shrugged. "No idea, but there will be. It's unusual that she and Rae have been on that many dates. She needs to be careful. Society doesn't like change unless it's the successful kind."

Logan breathed heavily through his nose. "I don't like this time."

"I don't like your time either. Let's agree on that and move on."

"Okay, fine, let's get the machine fixed, and then we'll both be happier."

Logan climbed off the bed, and Zero's eyes tracked the creases and wrinkles of his shirt.

"What?" Logan asked, flicking his fingers over the material.

Zero grit his teeth. "Nothing, nothing at all."

"So, we going down to the theatre or what?" Logan said.

The darkened sky loomed beyond the window. "You wanna go now?"

"Yeah, quicker we fix it, the quicker I go home, and you're free of me."

Zero ignored the "we" and bunched his lips, then nodded. "Yes, that does sound good," he strolled to his wardrobe. "Just let me pick out a hat and a cravat and we can go."

Logan gawped at him, and Zero chose to believe it was a gawp of amazement.

Chapter Nine

"Increase lights." Zero sighed.

The theatre flashed, then gradually the lights functioned more efficiently and lit the area. They had passed through the blinding twilight zone in a daze. The social area of *New Fretton* never saw the sun, but the vibrant lights and the signs on venues pulsed in their vision.

Logan curled over with his hands on his knees. "How can any of you see out there?"

Zero shrugged. "You'll get used to it."

"I hope not."

Zero clicked his heels together then strolled down the aisle to the stage. "Come on."

"So...what have you got to do to fix it?"

"Oh, is it back to you instead of we now?"

He didn't turn to Logan but heard him huff.

"The idea is quite simple really. Everything is made of atoms, electrons, neutrons, and protons. The machine pulls them apart simultaneously and rebuilds them at another location. That is what it is supposed to do anyway."

"Well, it didn't."

Zero rolled his eyes. "Quite obviously. When the second arch failed, it must've linked with a suitable other...what do you remember?"

Logan rubbed his chin. "Heat. The door got hot, and then there was blue and white light, floating in the centre. I reached for it, and it yanked me through. I landed on top of you, thought I'd killed you."

Zero raised an eyebrow. "So concerned you ran off and hid at the back of the stage..."

Logan flared his nostrils as he glared at Zero. "I didn't know what the hell was happening."

Zero raised his hand and Logan quietened.

He climbed up onto the stage and toed the discarded metal. "I don't know why it happened. I don't know why it made a channel from my time to yours, but the light is what happens when it's ready to break atoms apart. It must've broken you down and put you back together here."

Logan swallowed uncomfortably and patted his torso. "It pulled me apart?"

"Yes, a nanosecond. So brief a moment it didn't even register in the human mind."

"Still doesn't sound very nice though, does it?"

Zero shook his head. "Not nice, magnificent. My best bet of getting you home is to recreate the machine and hope it links with the arch in your timeline."

"Right. So how do you do that?"

"Lasers."

Logan widened his eyes. "What do you mean lasers?"

Zero waved to the pile of unsalvageable material. "That's how it works. Sixty lasers working against each other to pull the components of an atom apart. All evenly spaced, all evenly balanced."

"You're gonna shoot me with lasers." He gasped, rushing back a few steps.

"No, no, no...you're going to walk into them."

Logan paled, and his chin bobbed. "Wh-what?"

"I need to rebuild all the lasers from scratch, position and balance them. Then I'll practise on objects till I'm confident it will be able to put a human back together. The last bit is hope, we have to hope it will remake the channel and send you back. Otherwise who knows where or when you might end up."

Logan bent his knees and dropped to the floor. "This sounds like the worst plan ever."

"It's not the plan that's bad but the timing. I don't know if I'll be able to fix it, but I promised I'd try."

"What about that bit?"

Zero turned to where Logan pointed. "Ah, that's the transmitter. It looks intact but will need power and have to be lined up at the right coordinates again."

"Coordinates?" Logan asked.

Zero waved his hand. "The point is, that part is irrelevant until we fix all the lasers."

He moved away from Logan and chose a piece of metal that didn't look too distorted. The first thing he had to do was cover the wooden frame in a conductive material. He had taken great care covering it the first time, believing its image would be beamed on news holograms through-out the worlds. He buffed up the metal till it reflected its surroundings perfectly. The joins between pieces had been invisible to the naked eye, and he selected bronze rivets to decorate it. It had been a work of art, one worthy of being broadcast in every life-form's home.

Zero shook his head and got to work. It wasn't about him anymore; it was about getting Logan home. He bolted panels to the top of the arch first, then the inside before he moved his attention to the outer wood.

Each time Zero spared Logan a glance, his head had drooped lower, and his arms had wrapped tighter around his knees. No one in the forty-first century displayed their worry so obviously, and Zero shuffled with unease at the affect it had on him. He usually enjoyed silence, but the lack of conversation irritated him, and he needed to end it.

"Hey?" he shouted.

Logan glanced up, but no smile greeted Zero's. "What is it?"

"You wanna hold this piece while I nail it?"

Logan darted his gaze off the stage, then climbed to his feet with a sigh. He joined Zero and pressed his hands to the metal.

"Like this?"

"Yeah, keep it real still. All the pieces have to touch or else it'll break the circuit."

Logan did as Zero told, but there was no emotion to his face, and he pressed his lips together.

"So, this magic—"

Logan rolled his eyes. "Don't."

"I wanna know about it... Tell me some of the deceptions?"

"Tricks, they're called tricks."

Zero bunched his lips and nodded. "So, teleportation is one of those tricks, what else?"

Logan turned away, and Zero was sure he wouldn't answer, but then he looked back, and a smile twitched his lips.

"There are small ones, and big ones."

Zero drew his eyebrows together. He didn't wish to know of any small tricks, he wanted to hear of the big ones the twenty-first century humans went wild for.

"Big magic please."

"Okay, there's one with a cabinet, and it can disappear and reappear people."

Zero slapped the arch. "That's what I could do with this, take atoms apart and reform them."

Logan shook his head. "No, okay that was a confusing example. There's a trick where a magician saws a woman in half. Her torso and head in one box and her legs in the other, then they fix her back together again."

"Limb replacement, they have that in this time too. Saw a leg off, get a new one grown for you in the hospital. It costs a lot of tokens, but it can be done fast."

Logan frowned and bowed his head, then he straightened and wagged his finger. "Mediums, the spirit box."

"Explain."

"The magician ties himself up and sits in a box. The door shuts and a spirit appears, messes with the box, makes noise, and when the door opens the magician's still tied up. He hadn't moved, it was the spirit he conjured."

Zero shook his head. "How is that a trick? Everyone knows ghosts exist."

Logan took a step back. "What?"

"Yeah, they got so fed up of people trying to contact them, society signed a contract. No more disturbing the dead for us. Anymore?"

Logan shook the shock from his features. "How about levitation? Making things float through the air."

Zero laughed and flicked his head towards the doors. "You must've noticed the cars."

"I'm starting to understand why magic didn't survive. You can do all the things a magician claimed to." He lowered his head and eyed his shoes. "I get why you think it's stupid now."

Logan stopped pressing on the metal and moved to the edge of the stage and sat with his legs dangling over the edge. Zero couldn't see his face, but his shoulders hung, and his head bowed. The odd sensation in Zero's gut became dominant, and he shifted from foot to foot thinking of something to say.

"You're forgetting you have one over the forty-first century," Zero said.

"What's that then?"

"Your magicians made people believe they could teleport. That reality still doesn't exist in my time."

Logan turned slowly. A smile grew on his lips, and Zero copied his expression. In that moment his broken dream didn't matter, cheering up Logan did. Never had failure felt so good.

Zero clapped his hands. "I think I've done enough for now."

More people had congregated in the square, and a recognisable tuft of amber fur caught Zero's attention. He pressed his hand to Logan's chest, and he stopped and looked in the direction Zero pointed.

Honey moved unsteadily on her feet, and her eyes were half closed. Rae walked beside her with her lips split into a huge smile. Her turquoise scales seemed to pulsate and rivalled the brightness of the lights they passed under.

"She's-she's a snake person," Logan whispered.

"A cold-blooded," Zero corrected.

Honey's ears twitched, and she turned slowly towards them. She waved her paw and rushed over with Rae close behind.

"This is the one I was telling you about," she said, pointing at Logan.

Rae fixed her gaze on Logan. "The one who calls you a cat."

Honey nodded. "Yeah, that one."

Logan didn't speak, he retreated two steps and hid behind Zero's back.

"He did call you a cat, but now he calls you Honey," Zero said.

Rae flicked her tongue out to taste the air. "And what would he call me?"

Zero snorted. "A snake most probably."

"A snake? What is this, does he insult me?"

Zero shook his head. "No, he doesn't insult. He's just confused."

Rae withdrew her tongue and nodded.

"How was your date?" Zero asked.

He rolled his eyes when smiles bloomed on both their faces.

"Good," Honey said, and she laughed into her paw.

"It can't be that good, you're still down here."

Rae stuck out her tongue and narrowed her eyes. "We're about to get a car to mine actually."

"I hope Honey hasn't scared you off with any unheard-of words beginning with *L*."

Rae's scales darkened in confusion, and she shook her head. Zero snickered, flicking a look back at Logan.

"Ah, there it is," Rae said.

Zero closed his eyes with a sigh. He knew she had seen the mark to his neck. The high collars of his shirts were only effective at certain angles.

"Yes, there it is..."

"It still hurt?" she asked.

He shook his head. The bite ached, but only when he turned his neck or when someone reminded him.

"His belly's bigger than his bite."

Rae grinned. "That is probably true. From what I hear, he wasn't aiming for you, but him hiding at your back."

Logan shuffled and hesitantly stepped forward. "What?"

"You tried to blame dropping a picker on confusing the colours, when their difference is as clear as night and day."

Logan scanned the square they stood in and shrugged. "Night and day. It's confusing in this time."

Rae hissed and shook her head. "Should've let King strike him, taught him some manners."

"He is fine," Zero said giving Logan a reassuring grin. "Not his fault if King has no sense of humour."

"He dropped a picker from the roof. That is not a sense of humour."

Zero shrugged. "Would've been funny if it landed on him."

Rae rocked back and bared her fangs. "I can give you another bite to match his."

Honey pawed at her and whispered words Zero couldn't hear.

"Relax," he said, "I like the symmetry, but I don't want another of those bites."

Rae relaxed her stance, and she and Zero shared a nod of understanding.

Honey's drooping eyes sharpened, and she stood straight. She had seen something over Zero's shoulder, and he turned to see what had her so alert.

Apollo moved through the crowd. He bowed, he smiled, and waved his hand to the adoring public. His gold suit gleamed in the light of the twilight zone and round his neck hung his huge medallion.

"Who is that?" Logan asked, "He looks like an over polished Oscar."

"I hope in your century Oscar means excrement."

Logan laughed, and Zero's lips twitched into a smile.

Apollo paused when he caught sight of them. His smile changed from friendly to smug, and he lifted his shoulders and strolled over.

"Zero."

He gritted his teeth at the mocking tone before replying with a tired, "Apollo."

"You having a fun night?"

Zero rubbed at his chin in mock thought. "It was fun until about thirty seconds ago when you arrived."

"Don't be bitter," Apollo said.

"I have every right to be bitter."

Apollo sighed. "Who's your companion?"

Logan stepped forward. "I'm Logan, from Far Away."

He introduced himself perfectly just how Zero had told him, but for some unknown reason he stuck his hand out in front of him. Apollo quickly smacked it away with an expression of outrage.

"Don't you dare try to take my medallion. You are the one King spoke of, the human that took him for a fool."

"King is a fool," Zero said.

Honey muffled her laugh in her paw, but Rae hissed at her side.

Apollo shook his head. "No, the only fool of this town is you, Zero. You humiliated yourself in front of the public, and the residents of the floating palace. Then you get fired from your job as a picker-fixer and bitten by King."

Zero rolled his eyes. "Thanks for listing my failings. I was unaware of them until now."

Apollo chuckled darkly and brushed his hand through his long hair.

"You are not worth remembering for the years to come, but watching you try your hardest and fail has been most entertaining. It would be disappointing for that to end so soon."

Apollo opened his jacket and reached deep inside. He dropped a hand full of tokens to the ground, followed by another, and another. Zero had never seen so many before, and when he shot a look at Honey, her eyes were wide, and her mouth hung open.

"This should keep you on the island a little longer, and when you run out, come to the palace. I'm sure you can do something for me worthy of a token or two."

Zero couldn't stop the shudder that rattled him. Apollo tipped his head back and laughed. He turned and continued his awed stroll through the square.

Zero dove down and grabbed a fist full of token with the aim of imbedding them in Apollo's head.

"Wait!" Honey said, gripping his arm.

She flicked her chin towards Logan, and the fire in Zero faded. He could trade the tokens for food, and more days in his flat. More time for him to fix the machine and help Logan get home.

He sagged in her grip and nodded. The four of them gathered up the tokens in silence. He never envisioned he'd be scrapping tokens off the ground in desperation, but there he was, dirtying his knees and wrinkling his suit. Zero could feel Logan looking at the side of his face, trying to connect their gazes, but he refused him.

Chapter Ten

Zero woke in his bed and blinked slowly at the ceiling. For a second after waking, he thought the past few days must have been a horrible dream, but a turn of his head brought a whiff of the pillow below. It held a hint of Logan. The memories of his failure and humiliation sparkled to life and he groaned.

He hadn't spoken to Logan on the drive back, and as soon as they docked, he strolled through his flat into his bedroom and closed the door. Logan had whispered his name on the other side, but Zero hadn't replied. He had asked to be sent to sleep, and the flat responded to his wish.

Zero sighed deeply, rolled to the edge of the bed and stood. He hurried into the bathroom and asked the cubicle to perform a thorough clean. His skin reddened, and his feet itched with the intense heat, but he endured it to be free of the grubbiness he felt after speaking with Apollo. Once the wash had finished, the fans in the cubical dried him till not a patch of dampness lingered on his skin. He ruffled his hair, stroked his chin to test his stubble level, then asked the cubical to laser the hair away.

He stood still with his eyes shut, and the lasers performed a close cut. He brushed his fingers over his newly smooth jaw and nodded his approval. He closed his eyes and breathed through the water streaming down his face. A panel opened in the wall, and a nozzle poked out. Zero considered it for a few seconds, then held his hand underneath. The lubricant filled his hand, and he pressed his forehead to the tiles and dropped his hands down his body. He touched himself, ran his hand firmly along his erection in a familiar rhythm. An image of Logan filled his thoughts, and he groaned, tugging harder. The tingle of orgasm grew, and he rocked his hips imagining he was driving into Logan. He finished, basked in the sensation for a few seconds, then punched the wall at his stupidity.

The wardrobe slid open with a shriek, and the sparkle and shimmer of the clothes lifted Zero's lips in a half smile. He ran his hand along the glamourous collection before selecting a jade suit with gold trim and a black cravat. The trousers he chose were charcoal in colour, with UV lights down the seams. His trusty hat completed the look, and as he pushed in down on his head. His confidence grew.

Zero turned to the full-length mirror and smiled at his reflection. Clothes were the one thing the public couldn't take away from him, nor society. They were his pleasure, his pride, and he spun on the spot to marvel at his style.

Logan yawned from the sofa when Zero strolled into the room. He struggled up on his elbows and swung his feet to the floor.

Zero bowed his head. "Morning."

Logan wrinkled his brow. "Morning...about last night—"

Zero waved his hand. "Let's not speak of it, it's a new day, and I intend to use it."

Logan sunk his teeth into his lip and stood abruptly. "I wanna say I'm sorry."

"You don't need—"

"I kept saying you're selfish, and you're not. You've taken me in, and I lost you the job, broke your machine. You took that bite from that sna—cold-blooded for me, and then I found a half-eaten pouch and asked the flat how much you've been eating, and you've been eating less for me."

Zero narrowed his eyes at the light above him, and the flat flicked with unease. "It shouldn't have told you that."

"I'm sorry for calling you selfish," Logan said.

"You are right to do so. I am selfish, but with you, I'll try my best not to be."

"And I won't cause you anymore trouble."

Zero rolled his eyes and laughed. "That, you cannot promise."

He turned and tugged the drawer open. He selected a carrot and mango pouch and wrinkled his nose. Not his favourite flavour, but there were worse. The pouch below stared up at him and he grimaced before flicking his gaze back to Logan.

"Carrot and Mango or spinach and mushroom?"

Logan hummed, and Zero started to regret asking.

"Spinach and mushroom."

Zero grinned and turned sharply. "Great."

They sat side by side on the sofa squeezing their breakfasts into their mouths. Zero raised an eyebrow when Logan finished first.

"What?"

"You really like spinach and mushroom."

Logan nodded. "In an omelette it's the best."

"An omelette?"

"Eggs...from chickens."

Zero dropped the pouch from his lips. "A what?"

"Chicken, it's a bird...you have birds right, lots of feathers and they fly in the sky."

Zero recoiled and stared at Logan accusingly. "Nothing but the cars fly."

"You're kidding, right? You don't have any birds, or animals?"

Zero shook his head. "Nope."

Logan shook his head and rubbed his chin. "Then you don't have meat?"

"Oh, we do. That's where Honey works, the meat factory, but you have to trade tokens for meat, precious stuff."

"But you have to have animals for meat."

Zero shook his head with a chuckle. "We don't have these animals you speak of. The meat is grown, like the fruit and vegetables. There're great cubes of it, all different flavours."

Logan shuddered. "That sounds weird."

"I imagine I'd think animals were just as weird if I knew what they were."

Logan bowed his head with a hum, his lips twitched but no words followed.

Zero finished the remaining mouthful of carrot and mango as he turned to Logan. His face was creased with confusion, and Zero rolled his eyes.

"What is it?"

"That man…"

Zero sighed and exhaled slowly through his nostrils. "You mean from last night, Apollo?"

"The man dressed in gold, you and him?"

"Yeah, we were intimate regularly…as you put it."

Logan stared down at his fidgeting hands. "It didn't work out."

"Evidently," Zero said, turning away.

"But you're still hung up on him?"

Zero frowned. "Hung up?"

"I mean, you still like him in that way."

"Oh, no. The sex was average, nothing special. I'm more annoyed about his success than anything else."

Logan sagged and huffed at his lap. "'Cause that's all you care about, success."

Zero studied him intently, then shook his head. "No, success is important, and I crave it, of course, I do, but with him it's different."

"What do you mean?"

Zero shook his cravat to loosen the neck of his shirt. "You asked whether I've ever cared about someone other than myself, and yes I have. I cared for Apollo, and at one point I cared about him more than my desire to be remembered. That is why I know that caring is overrated."

Logan leaned closer and flicked his chin in encouragement. "What happened?"

Zero squeezed the bridge of his nose and curled forward.

"Please," Logan whispered.

He exhaled and offered Logan a weak smile.

"The cars we used years ago were unreliable. They overturned, they attracted and repelled each other and caused accidents. Apollo wanted to fix the design, solve the problem, but he struggled. I stopped my work on the teleportation machine and helped him, and together we discovered if the cars were round, the magnetic field would flow evenly around them. They could get A to B without any problems. Apollo became famous, with no reference to me. He moved into the floating palace with all the other elite, and I was thrown away like a used food pouch."

Silence lingered, and Zero raised his head poised to ask the flat to fill it with music, but Logan spoke quietly.

"I'm sorry he treated you badly."

Zero waved his hand. "Don't be, it was a lesson, that's all. It's better not to care for others, than care and have them discard you."

Logan shook his head. "He's one man, it's doesn't mean they're all like that."

Zero snorted. "Yeah, they are here. It's everyone for themselves, and that's the way it needs to be to keep striving forward. That is the way I need to be."

He looked at Logan, but his eyes were downcast, and his brow had wrinkled in confusion. Zero patted his knee and stood to button his blazer.

"Now, time to fix a way to take you backwards."

Logan got to his feet, but his troubled expression didn't shift. "Will you wait for me while I wash...and shave?"

Zero nodded and watched as he disappeared into the bedroom. He appeared twenty minutes later dressed completely in black. Even his hair seemed black in its damp state. His jaw was smooth and absent of hair.

Zero pointed at the wet strands on his Logan's head. "It will dry you if you ask it too."

Logan didn't reply, he continued to frown fiercely and Zero sighed.

"Come on, let's get to it," Zero said.

During the drive Zero drummed his fingers on his trousers to fill the silence, and once landed, he clacked his tongue on the roof of his mouth. Logan drifted behind him, footfalls so soft they couldn't be heard and clothes not swishing as he walked.

Zero pushed through the door and turned to him. "What is it?"

Logan shrugged and passed him. "Nothing."

"It's not nothing, I can tell by your face."

"It's just... I get why you hate the idea of love."

Zero rolled his eyes. "I hate it because it is stupid."

Logan shook his head. "You hate it, because you got your heart broken."

"What are you talking about," Zero said patting his chest. "My heart is functioning perfectly thank you."

"I mean, he hurt you emotionally, and you don't want to feel that hurt again."

Zero stabbed his finger in Logan's direction. "I'm not going to feel like that again. I won't make the same mistake. It's a lesson and I've learned."

Logan shook his head and walked towards the stage. "You're impossible."

He jumped up and rapped his knuckles to the shiny arch.

Zero hurried forward with a hissed, "Careful."

"What can I do?" Logan said.

Zero waved his hand at the pile of rubble. "You could put all that in the chute."

He expected a protest, but Logan smiled in reply and started hauling the pieces of metal into his arms. Zero moved to the opposite end of the stage and huffed at the tangle of wires.

"Here we go again," he said to himself.

Making the arch the second time around was simpler than the first. For years he experimented, designed different prototypes that failed miserably, and scalded his fingers until the tips turned a permanent coral. The arch had been the most successful, and he played with spacing the lasers, giving more energy to some and seeing the effects. Only when he spaced them evenly, angled them correctly, and supplied the machine with enough electricity did he have any success. He had to rebuild again, which meant making sixty lasers and wiring them to the arch. It was a lot to do, and with the tokens Apollo had thrown to him, it was a job that needed to be done in four weeks at most. It bordered the impossible, but he didn't want to admit it aloud.

Zero had just finished the first laser when he heard Logan gasp from the across the stage.

"What is it?"

Logan stood and lifted the small box in his hand. "It's my pack."

Zero twisted his face. "You're what?"

Logan grinned, the biggest one Zero had seen and his stomach skipped at the sight.

"My pack of cards."

Zero gently placed the first laser on the stage and strolled across to see what had lit up Logan's face.

"They were in my back pocket when I got pulled through. My cards," Logan repeated.

He opened the small box and emptied the contents into his other palm. The small rectangles were the same size as identification cards but held no information other than a number and a symbol.

"There...?"

"To do with magic, and games," Logan said still grinning.

"Oh."

Zero tried to hide his disappointment but knew he had failed when Logan's face sagged. He walked back across the stage to start work on the next laser.

Zero started on the second laser, but noises from the other side of the stage hindered his progress. There was a flicking sound, but each time Zero turned to catch what made the noise, he didn't see anything different. Logan sat cross-legged with the cards in his hand, eyeing them curiously.

Logan noticed Zero and raised an eyebrow. "What?"

"Nothing," Zero said. He turned only to hear the odd swishing sound again.

"What is that?" he said, abandoning the coil in his hands.

Logan nodded at the cards. "Just playing with them."

Zero dusted his knees and moved closer. "Show me."

The cards moved between Logan's hands with no use of magnetic fields. They flowed from one to the other, and back again.

Zero dropped down to the stage opposite Logan. His jaw hung, and he scanned the cards twirling in Logan's hands.

"Again," he said.

Logan held the group of cards in one hand, with his thumb against the top corner and the heel of his hand supporting the bottom. The cards bowed, and shot across the space, passing through air in a continuing flurry. No magnetic fields, just the skill of Logan's grip.

"That's-that's amazing," Zero said, swallowing audibly.

Logan shook his head. "It's not."

"Can you do others?"

A blush formed in Logan's cheeks and he nodded. "Yeah—I can try."

"Please do," Zero said with a nod. He crossed his legs to mirror Logan's position and waited patiently.

Logan fanned the cards out and flapped them to create wind, then he twirled them with ease between his fingers. He moved them with a staggering ease, and the cards blurred with the speed.

"Outstanding," Zero said, "show me more."

"I-I can do a card trick."

Zero narrowed his eyes. "These are tricks?"

"No, but I can do one if you want."

"I'm not sure about these tricks. I don't like to be deceived." Zero rubbed his chin, then nodded. "Okay, show me one."

Logan unleashed another stomach tickling smile, and Zero shuffled awkwardly to ride out the sensation.

The cards were shown to him, and he studied them in detail. Logan explained what the symbols were, the colours of the card, black and red. Zero would've described it as lava, but he didn't want to argue with Logan when he smiled so freely. He explained about jokers, queens, kings and aces, and then he fanned the cards out.

"Now pick a card. Any card. And hold it to your chest so I can't see."

Zero did as told and peeked down at the two of diamonds. "Okay...now what?"

Logan arranged the cards in one solid lump again before angling his head away. "Now place it on top."

Zero did, and Logan immediately began moving the cards, sliding one after another, slotting them into each other, and moving his card deep within the pack. Zero watched in fascinated, amazed that Logan didn't look to his hands once but continued to stare at the back of the theatre while he worked.

"Now, what happens?" Zero asked.

Logan flashed a smile as he spread the cards along the stage. All the cards faced up, except one that was upside down with the backing on show. Logan tapped the hidden card with his eye crinkling and cheeks rounding.

"This, this is your card." He leaned back and nodded down to it. "Turn it over."

Zero flipped the card onto its back and gasped at the two of diamonds. "How did you—but you mix them up?"

Logan gathered the cards up with a soft laugh. "Magic."

"Tell me how."

"No, that will ruin your amazement."

Zero bunched his lips, then nodded in acceptance. "Can-can you do it again?"

"If you want me to."

Zero nodded eagerly.

Logan repeated the card magic again, and Zero gasped the same as the first time. He thought that the two of diamonds might have been a lucky guess, but Logan picked the eight of clubs, the queen of hearts and the ace of spades. The fast movement of Logan's hands made Zero gawp, as did his beaming smile and his blushing face. Logan's cheeks grew a deeper scarlet each time Zero complimented him and told him of his astounding talent. Zero enjoyed Logan blushing, and smiling happily, he didn't know why but it made him feel like smiling too.

"It's not that amazing," Logan said, face closer to terracotta than peach.

Zero blew a breath through his teeth. "Don't be modest, it's incredible, just watching your hands move and the cards within them is mind boggling. If this is magic, I understand why twenty-first century life-forms enjoyed it."

Logan tapped the cards to the stage. "This isn't considered that amazing. It's the big tricks that get the attention, the showmen and the dangerous stunts. This is nothing in comparison."

Zero shook his head. "Don't belittle yourself. It has astounded me. You said your dad does magic? You've taken after him."

Logan swallowed and dropped his gaze. He opened his mouth, then snapped it shut and shook his head.

"This was the first trick he taught me. My sister didn't have the patience, my mum wasn't interested, but I liked watching my dad."

"Now, you can do it too it seems."

"His tricks were even better."

Zero scoffed and shook his head. "I doubt that."

"No, they were. He could do small magic, big magic, the classics and some he made up on his own. A true magician, and people travelled to see him. They bought his drinks, got his autograph and they looked at me expecting me to be the same, just as good..."

Logan trailed off and faced away, and the drop from happiness to sadness gave Zero emotional whiplash.

"What is it?" Zero asked.

"Nothing...I'll do it one more time if you want?"

"One more time," Zero agreed.

Logan performed the same trick, but when he laid the cards out on the stage, there wasn't one upside down.

Zero sagged and offered Logan a small smile. "It happens to all of us."

"I guess so...wait..."

Logan reached forward and brushed his fingers against Zero's top hat. When he pulled back, the correct card was held between his middle and forefinger.

Zero snatched the hat off his head and shook it. "How did you...?"

Logan returned the card he named joker to the pack. "A magician never tells."

Zero smiled and Logan smiled back.

Chapter Eleven

Zero fixed seven lasers in seven days. Logan grinned happily at the progress, but Zero sagged and sighed. He hadn't revealed just how many lasers he had to fix before they could even start testing. Logan might've believed they only needed ten, and Zero didn't want to shatter the illusion.

They took turns sleeping on the sofa or in the bed, and Zero happily discovered Logan enjoyed the opposite flavour combinations to him. There was only one that Zero had to concede defeat and hand to Logan. Strawberry and banana, but Logan seemed to sense Zero's disappointment and offered him half the pouch. The human addition to his flat wasn't as irritating as expected, and he found himself watching the news less and listening to Logan more. The twenty-first century sounded like the oddest of places, and not a place for a man like Zero.

"Need more," Zero said after the eighth laser.

Logan nodded. "Eight's good though, right?"

Zero hummed and turned back to the pile of wires.

The flicking of Logan's cards distracted him, and he peeked over to him hoping to catch Logan shuffling. Zero had seen the card move over and over, but the amazement didn't fade.

Logan showed him a new trick or "card manipulation" every day, and the task of fixing the machine was lost under the desire to be astounded.

"So how many lasers do you need?"

Logan had finally asked the dreaded questions, and Zero swallowed awkwardly.

"More."

"Yeah, but how many exactly? Ten, twenty?"

Zero rubbed at his tight throat and shook his head. "More than that."

He heard Logan get to his feet, and step across the stage. "Tell me."

Zero sighed. "Sixty, I need sixty."

Silence followed, and Zero clacked his tongue to fill the theatre with some sort of noise.

"How long have you got before you're removed from the tower block?"

"I've traded the tokens, we've got about three weeks."

"Oh."

Zero turned to Logan and gave him a sympathetic smile. "I'll do my best."

"I know you will."

Logan bowed his head and toed at the stage. "I guess my card tricks have been a distraction."

"They're amazing. I enjoy watching them, and you," Zero said.

Logan widened his eyes and rocked back on his heels. "Th-thanks."

Zero coughed awkwardly and removed his hat from his head. "It's hot in here, isn't it?"

"It's the same as it always is," Logan said.

Zero turned back to the laser he was working on. "Anyway, I need to carry on…"

"Yeah. No more tricks, until you've made half."

Zero snapped his head back. "What?"

Logan laughed lightly and tapped the pack of cards on the back of his hand.

"I won't do any more card tricks until you're halfway."

"But…that's not fair."

Logan slid the pack into his trouser pocket. "It's motivation."

"It's cruelty," Zero scoffed.

Logan laughed and retreated across the stage. Zero kept his eyes on him until he drifted into the shadowed area at the back.

"Where are you going?"

"You said me, and the cards were a distraction."

Zero shook his head. "No, you said that."

"Whatever. I'm hiding both so you can focus."

Zero glared into the darkness and huffed. "What, so you're gonna stay over there and watch? You can go back to the flat if you want."

"You like watching me, and my magic, and maybe I like watching you and your tinkering."

Zero's skin prickled with heat, and a quick swipe of his face confirmed the blush in his cheeks.

Before his humiliation at the theatre he got attention from many life-forms, but none had made his face heat and clothes feel too tight. The Logan unsettled him, and he didn't know why or how to cure himself. Sex was off limits, which left him floundering to find something to retaliate.

"Right," he said, rolling his shoulders, "back to the task."

He fixed three lasers that day, motivated by the promise of more magic tricks, and the need to see more smiles lighting up Logan's face.

They strolled out of the theatre into the twilight zone, and a bundle of amber fur immediately headed towards them.

Honey stopped in front of them, flashing a look at

Zero then Logan, then back again.

"You meeting Rae?" Zero asked.

Honey nodded eagerly. "Yeah, we're going to have a drink a Swoshies."

Zero bowed with his hat. "Have fun."

She gripped his arm and he straightened. "Wait, why not come with us?"

"I don't have any tokens," Zero said, gesturing to himself and to Logan.

"I know Kitty who runs the place, she'll let us in for free."

"Why would she do that?"

Honey wriggled her nose. "Last time I was there I sniffed out a meat cube that was about to go bad."

Zero squeezed the bridge of his nose. "Then take Rae."

Honey yanked at his arm and he yelped. "I am, and I want you and Logan to come too."

Zero shook his head. "I don't think it's a good idea. We've managed to keep his presence here on the low, but if he goes hallucinating again, he'll draw attention to his oddness."

Logan huffed and knocked his shoulder to Zero's. "What are you talking about?"

Zero didn't wish to embarrass him and waved his

hand to move the conversation along.

"It doesn't matter. Thanks for the offer, Honey, but I think we'll go back to the flat."

Honey blinked at him, twitching her whiskers before fixing her gaze on Logan. "You wanna come to Swoshies?"

Logan shuffled and coughed awkwardly. "I don't know what it is?"

"It's a bar. They serve alcohol. Not a good idea," Zero said.

"Oh, it was a bit of a disaster last time I drank," Logan whispered.

"Exactly," Zero said, steering Logan towards the car zone.

Honey waved her paw. "We know your limit now, a sip is probably enough for you, like the younglings."

Zero rubbed at his mouth to stifle his laugh, but Logan saw and narrowed his eyes.

"You know what... It sounds like fun."

Zero gawped at him. "This isn't a good idea."

"No," Honey said, "it's the best idea. Come on."

*

The indigo lights of Swoshies pulsed, and the scent of sweaty fur wafted from the door. Rae waited outside, she smiled and flicked her forked tongue out when she saw

Honey.

"Wasn't expecting you to be here," she said, narrowing her eyes at Zero.

He looked pointedly at Logan. "Trust me, wasn't my idea."

Logan raised a tentative hand. "It was mine."

Honey licked Rae's face, and an amused hiss escaped her lips.

Zero rolled his eyes. "Don't do that in the street, at least get in there first."

Honey clapped her paws together and strolled to the door, arm in arm with Rae.

"Honey," Zero whispered, glancing behind himself, "don't draw attention to yourself."

Logan followed Rae and Honey, and Zero groaned before trailing behind him. The scent of sweaty fur tickled his nose, and he glanced around the tables before smacking his lips together in distaste.

"Can practically taste them."

Honey turned to him sharply. "What was that?"

"Nothing, just complimenting the décor."

Honey nodded at the projections on the walls. Famous Furists of the centuries, all in their prime. The most famous of the Furists, Whiskers, had his image above the bar.

"Who's that?" Logan asked.

The surrounded table stopped their chatter and showed their daggered teeth. Logan shot backwards and pressed himself to Zero's chest. Honey bristled, and Rae darkened her scales and whipped her tongue out in lashes. Zero delved his hand into Logan's pocket then held up his ID.

"Relax, Logan's new here," Zero shouted, "He's from Far Away."

The hostile Furists shared looks of pity, then relaxed, and turned back to their conversations.

Zero smacked Logan's ID on his palm before handing it back. "Never forget this, it's quite literally a lifesaver."

Honey blinked till her pupils turned from slits to circles and smiled at Logan. "That is whiskers," Honey said, pointing a claw above the bar. "He was the first Furist to travel to Earth over a thousand years ago."

"You weren't created on this planet? In a lab or something?" Logan asked.

Honey glanced at Zero for help, but he shrugged in reply.

"The Furist planet became unstable, and six explorers set out to find a new planet to sustain us. Whiskers returned, but the other five didn't. He had found earth, and an agreement was made between the remaining humans and the furists. If it wasn't for

Whiskers, we'd all have died out."

Logan nodded. "Whiskers."

"Yes."

Honey flicked her chin out at the huge hologram. Whisper's pewter fur and ash-coloured stripes were rare among the furists. Honey had experimented with stripes but favoured the natural look of her amber fur and bronze nape.

"But...Whiskers," Logan muttered.

He studied the hologram and wrinkling his nose.

"Over here," Rae said.

They followed her low tone over to the far end of the bar. Honey shuffled along the bench and pressed to Rae's side. Zero and Logan sat opposite with a healthy distance between them. Kitty brought over the drinks and smirked when she linked eyes with Zero.

"Great. My humiliation still hasn't blown over."

Rae shook her head. "You should hear what they say about you at the water purifier."

He huffed, and too a huge gulp of his drink. Logan raised his glass to his lips, and Zero gripped his arm.

"Not too much yeah."

Logan tutted. "You're not my dad."

"'Course I'm not, but I'm sure your dad would appreciate someone looking out for you."

Logan dropped his gaze and pressed the glass into

his bottom lip. Zero cursed himself for mentioning his dad, no doubt his mind had filled with the desperate desire to be home and back with him.

"I'll get you back to him," Zero promised.

Logan didn't lift his eyes. He gulped a mouthful of drink and shuddered.

"You learned anything interesting about the twenty-first century?" Honey asked.

Zero whipped his head back to check no one had glanced over. "Easy Honey."

She pressed her paw to her mouth and widened her eyes. "Sorry."

"I think he's starting to like aspects of Far Away," Logan said, and blinked with one eye.

Honey stared blankly. "What?"

Logan banged his hand to his head. "When I said Far Away, I'm talking about where I'm really from."

He performed the one-sided blink again and Zero pointed at it.

"Right, that...that's definitely from Far Away. We don't do whatever that is here."

"It's a wink."

"Well, we don't do that here."

Logan turned back to Honey and patted his chest. "I think Zero likes what he's learned about where I'm from."

Honey arched her brow. "Oh...I get it now, do tell."

Zero sighed and linked eyes with Logan. For weeks, Logan had painted a picture of the past in his mind, not bland, but beautiful in a way the forty-first wasn't. There was variety, not through-out the hard to reach galaxy, but on earth. Different landscapes, different climates, and a variety of species that filled it.

Zero leaned over the table and licked his lips

"They have foliage on the surface. Can you believe that? And not the skinny plants of the crops, but huge. Logan said you can venture deep inside and not see another human for days."

Both Rae's and Honey's eyes widened, and Logan sniggered.

"He told me of life-forms called animals, hundreds, thousands of different types. He said his favourite is an elephant. A creature with two huge noses and a long ear."

Logan laughed and shook his head. "No, it's got two huge ears, and a long nose called a trunk."

Zero waved his hand at the minor mistake. "There's birds, creatures that fly through the sky, faster than any car, and the sea, he said the sea has its own animals, swift swimming creatures more efficient than our underwater vessels."

Rae leaned back and darkened her scales. "How do you know any of this is true? He could be making it all up."

Logan recoiled. "I'm not."

Honey clicked her claws on the table. "Wait, you said I looked like a cat, and Rae like a snake. What are they?"

"They're animals," Logan said with a smile.

Rae leaned forward. "And the cat and snake, what are they like? Do they have relations in your time?"

Logan scratched at his chin. "Erm, not really. If anything, a snake would probably eat a cat."

Rae hissed and narrowed her eyes. "Eat a cat? What kind of monsters are you to eat other life-forms?"

The tendons in Logan's neck tugged sharply, and his lips quivered with no reply.

"He showed me magic," Zero said quickly.

Honey relaxed her angry expression and twitched her nose. "Magic? The thing you said was idiotic."

"Yeah...but then he showed me."

Rae huffed and glanced away. "Sure, he did..."

Logan tugged the pack of cards from his pocket and placed them on the table.

Rae lashed her tongue towards them. "What are they?"

"Cards," Logan said, "For a magic trick."

Honey and Rae shared a doubtful look. Zero slapped his hand to the table, and they jolted back in surprise.

"Pause the roll of your eyes. Watch and see."

He flicked his head in encouragement, and Logan began his hypnotic mixing of the pack. He fanned them out and waved the cards towards Honey.

"Pick a card, any card."

Honey blinked and shot an unsure look at Rae and then Zero. "You want me to take one of the rectangles?"

"Yes," Logan said, "take it and hold it to your chest, don't let me see what's on it."

Honey snatched one out and pressed it to herself.

"You know what it is?" Logan asked.

Honey shook her head. "No."

"Take a look, you're allowed to see it, but I'm not."

Honey peeled the card from her chest, and both she and Rae stared at it.

"Now, put it back on the top of the pack," Logan said.

Honey placed it down tentatively and then straightened in her seat fast. Logan shuffled the cards, before laying them on the table. He tapped the upside-down one, and Zero couldn't help the grin that spread his lips.

"Now, turn it over," Logan said

Honey flipped it and stared, but she didn't react with any surprise. Zero rubbed his head in confusion and looked to Logan.

"Is-is it your card?" Logan asked.

Honey flashed a look down at the card, then up to Logan again.

She smiled and rounded her eyes. "No idea, but it was amazing."

Zero groaned and dropped his head to the table.

"Honey," he mumbled, "you're supposed to remember the card."

Rae clapped her hands slowly and bobbed her head. "Yes, it's the same card. Impressive."

Honey scrunched her paws and twitched her whiskers. "I missed it, show me again."

*

Logan performed the trick five times, and each time more customers crowded around the table to watch. They gasped and mumbled words of wonder. The amazement made Zero feel good, and he puffed his chest out proudly. He patted Logan's shoulder each time he successfully performed the trick, and they shared a smile.

Logan blushed at the praise and shuffled closer till the healthy gap between them no longer existed. Zero could tell the furists intimated Logan, but he nodded in reassurance and Logan continued to dazzle the customers with his skill.

Rae's scales flushed a vibrant turquoise, but she didn't smile or gasp like the rest. It was the biggest compliment anyone could get from a cold-blooded, she glowed brighter than the neon sign above the door.

"Even Rae enjoys a bit of magic," Zero said.

"It's entertaining, I'll give him that."

"It's incredible," Honey shouted.

Zero raised his glass and saluted Logan's talent. "He sure is."

He downed his drink and stood abruptly. Logan gripped the thigh of his trousers and stared up at him with panicked eyes.

"Where are you going?"

"The toilet," Zero said. He tapped Logan's cheek. "I'll be back in a few minutes, you're in your element right now, no need to get scared."

Logan narrowed his eyes and released Zero's leg. "I'm not scared."

"Good." Zero brushed his thumb against Logan's cheekbone, "I don't like it when you are."

Chapter Twelve

Zero ruffled his hair before rubbing the skin of his under eyes. He hadn't slept long enough, and a shadow of tiredness had appeared. It was made worse by his mauve irises that seemed to compliment his flagging appearance.

He flattened his shirt and rearranged his top hat before strolling back into the bar.

The crowd that had gathered around the table had returned to their own, all except one furist that had taken Zero's seat. His fur shone in the light, and at certain angles it looked navy, not black. Both Rae and Honey appeared uncomfortable in his presence, but Zero couldn't see Logan behind the bulk of the furist.

"Excuse me," he said, "That's my seat, thanks for keeping it warm."

The furist didn't appear to hear, he continued to tower over Logan who was still hidden beneath the furry life-form. The purring noise unsettled Zero and he shuffled and huffed. Furists only purred like that when they were looking to seduce.

Something hot and tight coiled in Zero's insides, and he gritted his teeth.

"Felix, that's enough," Honey snapped. "He said he's not interested."

Zero glanced at Honey with wide eyes, then smacked his palm to Felix's back. "Get away from him, you great idiot."

Felix straightened with a grumble and turned to Zero slowly. He bared his teeth, and Zero rolled his eyes.

"Off with you."

Felix sprung up, and Zero stepped back with an audible gulp. Felix stood tall, and wide, and snarled at Zero with his hair on end. One of his teeth had snapped off, but Zero didn't think it would be a bite that killed him, more a crushing.

"How dare you interrupt," Felix hissed.

Zero resisted the urge to raise his hands to placate the irate furist. He stamped his foot to the floor and pointed his finger.

"I do dare when your advances aren't welcome."

He angled his head around the bulky Felix, and spied Logan, wide eyed, and blanched. It was a relief to see him frightened, and he hated himself for his internal sigh. He couldn't think of anything worse than seeing Logan turned on by the seven-foot-fur ball that was Felix.

"That's my seat, and I want it back," Zero said.

"Are you sure it's the seat you want back or your companion?"

Zero pushed his chest out and stood on his tiptoes. "Both."

Felix scratched at his whiskers and shot a look back to Logan. "We could have fun together. I'll make you feel good."

The tight coil in Zero's insides twisted in a knot, and a fierce anger overtook him.

"Ha!" Zero barked, "Yes, I'm sure he wants to get squished by your massive bulk and smothered by that musky fur of yours."

"Zero!" Honey hissed.

Rae chuckled into her palm and glanced away.

Felix clicked his claws out and turned to Zero with menace creasing his fur. "You better watch that tongue of yours, or I'll rip it out."

Zero pretended to yawn. "Are we done here?"

Felix spoke over his shoulder, but his eyes stayed on Zero's. "When you're done with this embarrassment, come find me. I'll make you feel better than he can."

Felix pushed forward with a powerful stride and knocked Zero off balance. He caught himself on the edge of a table and winced. Once he was sure he could hide the pain on his face, he turned, and blew a kiss at the snarling Felix.

"What the hell are you doing?" Honey said, digging her claws into his arms. "Starting on Felix like that, he could've killed you."

"I thought it was brilliant," Rae said, and her turquoise scales confirmed her words.

"I couldn't have him rubbing himself all over Logan, could I?"

Honey shook her head. "He would've got the message and left."

"Well he wasn't getting it fast enough," Zero snapped.

Logan shuffled along the bench and glanced up to Zero. "Can we...go back to the flat now?"

"Of course," Zero said, "let's go."

He lifted his hat and bent his back in a goodbye to Rae and Honey and hurried Logan towards the door. Felix watched them intently, and just before the door slid closed behind them, Zero smiled smugly and performed the one-sided blink.

They didn't talk on the walk to the cars, and they didn't speak on the ride to the flat. Zero's nostrils flared with the scent of Felix. It was obvious he had rubbed his cheeks on Logan, a signal to all other furists that he was off limits, and Felix wanted to bed him.

The thought irritated Zero, and he tightened his hands into fists. He didn't know why he cared, why the thought of Logan seduced made him shift uncomfortably and cock his jaw.

A tickling sensation made him glance down at his hand, and he saw Logan's fingers rubbing his straining skin.

Zero relaxed and sighed deeply. "I'm sorry."

Logan shook his head. "Thanks for…looking out for me."

Zero pressed his lips together and nodded.

"He came over and started sniffing me. I asked him to stop, but it was like he didn't hear."

"He didn't hurt you, did he?"

"No, just rubbed his face to mine, and licked me."

Zero curled his hands again and cracked his neck left and right. "I should've punched him."

The rage inside rattled his bone's, and he tapped his foot to the floor of the car to distract himself.

"As Furists go, he's not a bad looking one."

Zero's stomach plummeted, and he shuddered at the thought of Logan and Felix. The anger gave way to an emotion he didn't know. He wanted the rage back, not the despair that rendered him speechless. He hadn't experienced the internal squirm before, both his lungs and heart seemed to derail before continuing as normal.

Zero wanted to escape the car and put some distance between him and Logan. He couldn't even look towards him.

"Seems I should've left you to it," he snapped.

Logan tried to unfurl his hand, but he resisted. "Wait, I was joking, joking. I don't think he's attractive."

"Good looking, and attractive, Felix is doing good for himself."

"I said I don't find him attractive. I was trying to be funny, thought you'd laugh."

Zero frowned and tightened his hand. "I don't find it very funny hearing of who you'd be willing to sleep with."

"I don't wanna sleep with Felix. Bad joke. I'm sorry. He's not my type, none of the furists are, nor the cold blooded."

Zero loosened the coils of his fingers, and Logan clutched them in his.

The car docked, but neither of them moved.

They stayed in their seats, and over the course of twenty minutes, Zero started to grip Logan's fingers in return. He didn't know what they were doing, but it didn't feel bad holding on to Logan. Their fingers slipped together, and Zero gazed down at them with a frown.

"Do-do they do this in the twenty-first century?" he asked.

"Yeah. It's holding hands, it's a sign of—"

"Please don't say love."

Logan chuckled. "A sign of affection. A sign that we care."

"Caring isn't good."

Logan squeezed him. "Yeah, it is. You care about me. I know you do."

Zero grimaced. "Is it caring, or am I just not being selfish?"

Logan shook his head, and the adorable dimple appeared at the top of his nose. Zero bit the inside his cheek and glanced away, but he didn't stop holding Logan's hand.

"You protected me from Felix's advances, that's caring."

He didn't know if he had, didn't know why he had become so irritated at Felix's sloppy seduction technique.

Zero pulled his hand from Logan's. "Was I protecting you, or could I just not stand the thought of him, having you? Was I being caring, or selfish?"

Logan bit his lip and turned away. Zero knocked his fist into the side of the car and the door slid open. He climbed out and stared at his hands wanting to still feel Logan's again. He huffed and marched across the flat.

"You were being caring," Logan said.

Zero raised his hand and tilted it one way and then the other. "Maybe, maybe not. Maybe both. I don't know. I find a lot of this stuff between me and you confusing. It'd be best for both of us if I don't think about it."

Logan joined him on the sofa, thigh to thigh, and Zero quickly shuffled along to the end.

"I want you to think about it," Logan said.

"Why? At the end of all this you go home, and I stay here. Why change me, or how I think when it will amount to nothing?"

Logan leaned back and tilted his head to the ceiling. The scent of Felix escaped the flesh of his neck and Zero grimaced.

"You might want to have a wash."

Logan jolted forward and pressed his hand to his neck. "What? Why?"

"You reek of Felix. He's marked you."

"Marked me?"

Zero nodded. "Yeah, warning off any competition."

"Didn't warn you off though. He's double the size of you and you stood up to him."

"Let's just blame the alcohol."

Logan laughed and got to his feet. "I better go wash then."

"Please do."

Zero swivelled and brought his legs up on the sofa. He shuffled down to get comfortable, then removed his hat. Logan watched from the bedroom doorway. He knocked his knuckles on the frame and darted his eyes.

"What is it?" Zero asked.

"I was thinking. Instead of us taking turns on the sofa, we could both sleep in the bed. There's enough space."

Zero rubbed his chin. "I don't think it's a good idea."

Logan frowned. "Why not? There's plenty of room, I promise to stay on my side of the bed. We can even top and tail if you want."

"Top and tail, what's that?"

"Where your heads by my feet, and mines by yours."

Zero wrinkled his nose and huffed. "That sounds disgusting. I don't want to breathe in your feet."

Logan rolled his eyes. "Then we sleep side by side."

He had only slept with other life-forms as an after-sex ordeal and vanished as soon as his partner had fallen asleep. Apollo had been the worst, he tightened his arms around Zero, and escaping the clutch became a skill.

"I—we could try it."

Logan smiled brightly, bit his lip and disappeared into the bedroom. Zero cursed and flung himself back.

That smile, that was a reason why it was a bad idea, along with the protectiveness he felt, and the desire that sizzled. He rubbed fiercely at his face and tried not to imagine Logan lying next to him. He already sniffed the pillow to catch Logan's scent, and reacted strangely inside and out whenever he smiled, but lying beside him, it was sure to be torture.

It didn't seem like much time had passed, when Logan slid the door open a crack, and poked his head through. "So…I'm gonna go to sleep now, you coming?"

Zero stood with a sigh and dragged his feet across the flat. He squeezed through the gap of the door to be immediately flawed into muteness by Logan.

He stood in nothing but a shimmering silver pair of boxers, Zero's boxers. He had assumed Logan wore his underwear, and hadn't questioned it, but he gawped at the sight, and quickly swallowed the excess saliva that had filled his mouth. Logan's flesh was palest at his throat, and his nipples were small, and coral in colour. It was uncommon for men of the forty-first century to have body hair; that was saved for the furists. Logan had chestnut swirls that travelled down from his bellybutton into the boxers. Zero gulped and tried to rub the heat in his cheeks away.

"Sorry, I can put a shirt on if you like," Logan said.

Zero couldn't speak, he shook his head and began to undress. He arranged his clothes on their designated hanger and slotted them into the wardrobe for it to clean and iron.

When he turned, Logan whipped his head down and coughed awkwardly. Zero had caught him watching and lifted his eyebrow as he took in Logan's complexion. Logan's cheeks were flushed, and he hoped it was a symptom of arousal, not embarrassment at Zero's body. Zero may not have been as bulky and tall as Felix, but he did take care of himself, and his job as a fixer-picker had given him muscles, particularly in his stomach and arms. Logan flashed a glance up, and Zero noted his eyes were darker than usual. He wasn't repulsed much to Zero's relief, but on some level liked what he saw. They were both attracted to each. A perfect match to engage in sexual intimacies, but Zero knew they couldn't.

"Just going to freshen up before bed," he said and walked as casually as he could into the washroom.

He pressed his head to the wall and panted. He started his repetitive counts of ten to calm his body down. On the twenty-eighth count, he finally had enough composure to wash. He climbed into the shower for a blast of cleanliness, then asked the cubicle to clean his teeth with the dental laser. The nozzle in the wall extended, but pent up and frustrated, Zero didn't need any help. He dealt with the throb between his legs in record time before asking the cubicle to wash and dry him.

When he walked back into the bedroom, his stomach flipped at Logan snuggled in the bed. Duvet up to his neck and looking like he had been eaten by the mattress, Honey's description of odd-cute echoed in his head.

Zero slipped in beside Logan, and they both stared at the ceiling without talking, or moving a millimetre. Even their breathing seemed hesitant, and after a minute, Zero begged for it to end.

"Send us to sleep," he said, and he'd never been more relieved to hear the high-pitched frequency coming from the walls.

Chapter Thirteen

The odd sleeping arrangement continued, but Zero found a way of lessening the awkwardness. He ensured Logan went to bed before him, and whenever he returned, he was too tired to care whether Logan lay awake or asleep. He spent so long working on the machine, he collapsed nearing unconsciousness onto the bed. He couldn't feel uncomfortable in that state, he couldn't even take off his shirt or remove his shoes. When he washed, he touched himself thinking of a fantasy scenario with Logan, but appeared in the living room fresh-faced, not giving anything away.

A few times he had woken in the night and observed Logan beside him. His stomach and heart fluttered, and he frowned at his bodily functions. He hadn't been affected like that with Apollo, or any of his other partners, but with Logan his chest felt warm and spacey. He quietened his own breathing just to hear Logan's and subtly drew his comforting scent into his nose.

Zero woke when something beneath the duvet gripped his fingers. His rampant heart slowed when he realised the only person who could've touched him was Logan. His eyes were shut, and his chestnut lashes fanned out on the skin beneath. His lips were pressed together, and he breathed softly through his nose. Apollo had been a mouth-breather, and a snorer, but Logan puffed away quietly and barely made a sound.

Logan's fingers tightened around Zero's, and he responded and squeezed back. Logan didn't stir, his fingers seemed to react out of impulse, and they continued their odd finger tugging game. Then Logan wriggle his fingers through Zero's, and they held hands like they had in the car.

Logan's breathing didn't change, and he didn't fidget. A smile lifted the edges of his lips, and Zero stared in fascination. The hand holding increased his mood, even when asleep. How such as simple thing could have such an effect was beyond Zero, but he didn't want to stop holding hands.

Logan shuffled closer, and Zero stiffened, closing his eyes to fake sleep. He cracked one open, and then the other. Logan hadn't woken. He pressed his forehead to Zero's arm and tucked his chin under the duvet. For the first time in years, Zero didn't request being sent to sleep, he stayed still and listened to Logan's soft breaths until he drifted off all on his own.

They were no longer holding hands when he woke for the second time.

"Stupid," Zero muttered and rolled out of bed.

He flexed his fingers, but there was no evidence the moment had occurred. The flesh of his arm didn't confirm or deny either. He picked a suit and strolled into the washroom.

"I said no dreams," he growled at the ceiling.

He didn't hear the flat's reply; the showers hiss blocked it out.

In three weeks, he had made twenty-eight lasers, two away from seeing a magic trick, and thirty-two away from making any real progress. He glanced down at the remaining food pouches, enough for a comfortable week, or two weeks at a stretch.

He sighed and slit one open. Apple and raspberry. The sweet taste declogged him of his depressive thoughts, and he asked the flat to call him a car.

The arch stood centre stage, catching the stray beams of light. The twenty-eight lasers had been attached but hadn't been angled. He needed to have all of them before he began directing the beams. Logan believed once the sixtieth one was done, that was it. Zero would switch on the machine, and he'd walk through into the arms of his dad, but it wasn't that simple.

Fixing the lasers was one thing, but he still had to test them and after that; he had to line up the transmitter again. There were risks to testing the lasers. Many times, Zero had blown himself across the stage or ended up with a piece of shrapnel in his chest. Forty-first human's blood clotted near instantly, and his body reproduced any lost in a matter of minutes, but Zero wasn't sure what would happen if Logan got hurt.

Zero shuddered, then clapped his hands together. He couldn't mope around, he had to at least try.

Logan appeared a few hours later, dressed in a black blazer and fuchsia trousers. Each stride of his legs made the material glow, and his cheeks turned the same vibrant colour.

"I didn't realise they did that."

"Vibration technology, each time your feet hit the ground, the light particles react and pulse."

Logan stood still and looked down at himself. "It's ridiculous."

"Don't you go insulting my clothes," Zero said lifting an eyebrow, "or I won't fix this machine."

Logan snickered and clambered up on stage. The outfit pulsed with the movement, and Zero had to blink in the darkness of the back of the stage to regain his sight.

"I think I blinded a few life-forms on the way here," Logan said.

Zero waved his hand dismissively. "If they're that damaged, they can buy new eyes."

Logan scanned the arch counting each of the lasers. "Two away from a trick."

Zero lifted the laser he had finished in his hand. "Actually, only one away now."

Logan rocked back on his heels. "I better go practise." He gestured to the stage, and then the ceiling. "Is there not a curtain?"

Zero strolled across the stage and lifted the force field remote from its holder. He clicked the button, and a fluttering curtain appeared and split the stage horizontally.

"Perfect," Logan said with a smile, "can't have you seeing how the magic's done."

Zero cocked his head and returned to the arch. Logan disappeared behind the curtain but could still be heard tapping and scraping. Zero had no idea what the noises meant, but he couldn't wait to find out.

He dusted his hands together after the thirtieth laser had been attached and wired to the arch.

"I'm ready for the trick," Zero called.

The force field faded, and Logan stood on the opposite side with a shy smile spreading his lips. He moved forward and sat cross-legged on the floor. The pulsating light of his trousers stopped, and Zero rubbed at his eyes before joining him. He copied Logan's positioning and left a gap between them for the cards to be laid out. His stomach fizzled with excitement, and a laugh bubbled in his throat. He thankfully held it in, but he couldn't stop the huge smile from taking over his face.

Logan placed a stack of cups on the stage, and three, what looked like, fur balls.

"Are those—are those Honey's?"

"I asked if I could use some of her fur to surprise you. She was a bit freaked out but gave me a whole bag full in the end."

Zero looked doubtfully at the balls of amber, then nodded for Logan to continue. He didn't reach into his pocket for the cards at all, and Zero sagged.

"Oh."

Logan frowned. "What do you mean 'oh'?"

"Nothing, carry on...show me what you can do with Honey's fur."

"I have three cups, one red, one green and one blue, and I have three orange balls."

Zero would've used different words to describe the colours, but he didn't argue.

Logan placed the cups upside down in a line on the stage. One amber ball was placed on top of the red cup in the centre, and then he stacked the two others on top.

Zero huffed. There were far more entertaining games to play with balls than balance them on cups, and he wasn't talking about the make-shift fur ones.

Logan smacked his hand on top of the stack of cups and then slowly removed them. The fur ball wasn't sandwiched between the cups but had passed through the red one and appeared on the stage.

"How did you?"

Logan chuckled. "There's more."

He placed the red cup on top of the ball, then balanced another fur ball on top. He stacked the rest of the cups, then tapped his palm on top of them. When he removed them one by one, the second furball had joined the first on the stage.

"You made them pass through the red cup? How?"

Logan tapped his nose. "Wait there's more."

Logan covered the two balls with the red cup, then he picked up the final ball. Zero thought he was about to see the same trick again, but Logan didn't stack all the cups. He placed the final ball on the top of the blue cup before dropping the green on top.

Zero held his hand up and Logan stopped. The red cup had two balls beneath it, and the other ball was trapped between the blue and the green cup. Zero rubbed his chin and wondered what would happen next. He predicted the trapped ball would drop to the stage beneath the blue cup just as the others had with the red.

"Can I continue?" Logan asked.

Zero nodded and drummed his fingers to his chin.

The trapped ball didn't drop to the stage, and it was no longer trapped between the blue and the green cups. It had joined the first and second ball and rolled out when Logan lifted the red cup.

"How the...? How did you? You passed it through the cups? You teleported it?"

Logan shook his head. "No, I told you, it's magic."

"It's not possible," Zero said.

He reached for each cup in turn and studied the bottom, probing it with his forefinger. They were completely solid. He rolled Honey's fur balls in his hand, even sniffed them be certain Logan hadn't drenched them in some dissolving agent, and then he placed them on the stage, and gasped.

"Amazing! To get them to pass through and drop to the stage, incredible."

Logan pressed his lips in a tight smile, scratching his head. "Yeah...pass through..."

"I thought the card tricks were good, but this is something else."

Zero clapped his hands together and smiled at Logan.

A blush crept up his cheeks, and he sunk his teeth into his lip. "Thanks."

"Remarkable."

Logan clutched the back of his neck and grimaced. "As I said before, it's not that—"

"Don't you dare," Zero said, leaning across the space between them. "What you can do is mind-boggling, and don't you let anyone tell you different. I am stunned, and that doesn't happen often, if ever."

Logan lowered his head and studied his hands. "Yeah, right."

Zero reached for Logan and lifted his chin. "I mean it."

Logan's chestnut eyes met Zero's mauve ones, and the room dissolved to insignificance around them. Zero didn't stop holding Logan's face, but brushed his thumb along his smooth cheekbone.

"Amazing," he whispered.

He wasn't sure if he was talking about the trick, Logan himself, or both, but his heart beat fast and his breathing came in rushes. Zero's fingers drifted under Logan's jaw, and he felt Logan's hammering pulse, the same rampant speed as his. Logan's chest rose and fell with exaggerated breathing, and his pupils expanded.

They stared at each other with a mysterious force pulsing between them, and only when Logan's gaze dropped briefly to Zero's lips, did Zero stand and break the moment.

"Better get back to it," he said.

He dusted his hands together and resisted the pull of Logan's eyes. When he next turned, Logan had retreated to the darkness of the stage.

Chapter Fourteen

Zero perched on the edge of the bed and tapped Logan's face. He wanted to leave him to sleep for longer, but excitement bubbled in his body and he was eager to get going.

"Come on, busy day."

Logan groaned and rubbed at his eyes. "A busy day, watching you work and not being clever enough to help."

Zero gently pinched his cheek and pursed his lips as he spoke.

"Aww, aren't you a grumpy one this morning."

Logan covered a yawn with his palm. It was the same palm Zero had been drawing patterns on while they lay in bed. The hand holding had become a regular thing that neither of them mentioned. A few times, Logan had actively sought his hand before asking the flat to send them to sleep. Zero didn't know why he enjoyed it, didn't know why he woke when their fingers untangled, and could only get back to sleep when they linked again.

He blinked out of his thoughts when Logan tugged the duvet tight around himself.

"I'm comfortable and warm."

Zero tutted, stood, then ripped the duvet away. "How about now?"

Logan gasped and curled into a ball. "Jesus!"

"My name is Zero, this Jesus better not be an ex of yours."

Logan laughed, but Zero didn't find it funny at all. He clapped his hand together as hard as he could. Logan moaned at the noise and covered his ears.

"Now, come on. I need your help today."

"My help?"

Zero rolled his eyes. "Yes, that's what I said. I've grown bored with lasers after the forty-ninth. We're having a change of scenery."

Logan shuffled up on his elbows and widened his eyes. "Where are we going?"

Zero smiled and leaned close to see Logan's reaction.

"The recycle yard."

"Recycle yard?" Logan repeated.

He collapsed back onto the pillow and flung his arm over his eyes.

Zero frowned. "That was not the reaction I was expecting."

"What did you want me to do, jump out of bed and dance around the room?"

Zero rubbed his chin and thought about it. "That would've been nice. I enjoy the recycle yard. All broken down machinery, wires, rivets, components." He smacked his lips together. "Look I'm practically salivating."

"You're so weird," Logan muttered.

"Anyway, I need your help."

"What possible help will I be?"

Zero counted each point on his hand. "The lookout, the motivation, the carrier, and the cute arse to walk in front of me down the narrower paths."

Logan laughed. His face froze, before turning serious. "What do you mean lookout?"

"I need you to keep an eye out for Hummer."

"Who—what is Hummer?"

Zero rubbed at his straining throat. "Well, he's a cold-blooded that guards the recycle yard."

Logan blinked up at him. "Guards it? So, we aren't allowed there?"

"Not strictly speaking…"

"What will happen if he finds us there?"

Zero waved the question away. "He won't."

"But if he does."

"You don't have to worry about Hummer. He's a scrawny, four-foot cold-blooded. He's ancient, with poor eyesight and next to no hearing."

Logan relaxed and nodded. "And what do you need there?"

"A distributor. My other one exploded, I need a new one for when we're ready. Thought it would be a nice change, a chance for you to see more of this world."

Logan glared at him. "You want me to see more of this world, and your first thought was the recycle yard."

Zero nodded with enthusiasm. "Exactly that."

*

High powered security fences surrounded the yard, and Hummer roamed the area inside. He was not the four-foot pushover Zero had described. Even Rae shifted uncomfortably at the mention of his name. Thankfully Logan didn't have a clue of Hummer's brutal reputation.

Logan sighed. "There's an alarm. We step through those lasers and it'll go off."

Zero cocked his eyebrow. "Alarm? What is an alarm?"

He leaned down, picked up a discarded bottle and threw it towards the beams of light. They sliced the bottle in half, and both pieces clattered on the ground the other side.

Logan backed away and positioned himself behind Zero. "It'll cut us in half."

"We're a bit bigger than the bottle. It will cut us in quarters."

Logan dropped his forehead to Zero's back and muttered a word he didn't know. He reached over his shoulder and patted Logan's hair.

"Relax, I'll sort it."

"How?"

Zero yanked a device from his pocket and waved it. "This beauty disrupts a current, got me into all sorts of places but will only be of use for a few seconds."

"This is such a bad idea."

Zero blew a breath through his teeth. "Relax, quit being scared and keep a look out."

Logan scanned through the fence, cocking his head and squinting to see further. Zero pressed his lips to withhold a laugh. Logan wouldn't have to squint to see Hummer. Zero was certain Logan would faint at the sight, maybe even the sound of him.

Zero unscrewed the panel in the ground, wired in his little black box, and the fence flickered. He quickly removed it, stood, and tugged Logan's hand.

"Now!"

They rushed through, and the fence flashed up again as they landed on the dirt. Logan stared wide eyed at the fence and then the decapitated bottle.

"That could've been us."

Zero tapped his chin, contemplating. "I for one am not made from plastic. Could've been cut to pieces, but we weren't."

"How can you be so calm? It's almost like you're enjoying this."

He brushed the dirt from his trousers and smiled. "I am. This place always brings back memories."

"Near death ones?"

Zero nodded. "Oh yeah, when I was ten, I wasn't quite quick enough. Lost two of my fingers."

Logan stumbled forward and grabbed Zero's hand. "No, you didn't."

Zero pointed at the pale line's cut across his little and index finger. "Remember I said they grow them easily?"

Logan shuddered. "That must've hurt."

"It did, but I still came back the next day."

"You're mad."

Zero shook his head and smiled. "No, I was a young adult, this place had everything I needed to start inventing. I scavenged, I build simple robots and dreamed of creating something worthy of remembrance." He dropped his head and scuffed his shoe on the ground. "Wasn't meant to be though."

"There's still time, though, right? After I'm gone?"

"Maybe."

Zero flicked his head to the stacks of machinery and then started to walk with Logan by his side.

The piles towered on either side of them: old hologram units, projectors, meat containers, pickers, old wardrobes, faulty cars, and air conditioning units that were used to ventilate the towers.

"What happens to all this stuff?" Logan asked.

"In the end, it will be flown to another planet and dumped."

"That's horrible."

Zero shrugged. "It's the way it is. Not nice, but there's nowhere else for it to go. How do you deal with waste in the twenty-first century?"

Logan turned his head. "Dig huge holes in the ground and bury it."

"Ah. Perhaps our methods are equally bad."

"The planet, no one lives there right?"

Zero swallowed uncomfortably. "There was no native species to that planet."

Logan exhaled slowly. "Good."

"What we're looking for should be around the next corner."

He clapped his hands together at the pile of water-purifying units.

"This is what you want?"

Zero nodded. "Yeah, the best distributors. The electricity must pass through the water evenly to purify it. It's perfect for the lasers, if one laser isn't balanced, the atoms will rupture."

"Then what happens?"

"Cell combustion. For a living thing...immediate death."

"Oh, well that's lovely."

Zero chuckled and tapped the unit. "That's why we need the best, and I'll test it before I try it on you."

"Good to know."

He pulled the set of screwdrivers from his pocket and began removing the first unit's panel. He grimaced when he saw the state of its insides.

"Not this one."

He moved onto the next, which had its distributor intact. "You're the look out."

Logan nodded, and Zero climbed inside the unit. He unscrewed the distributor as quick as he could and climbed back out.

He showed the circular device to Logan. "What a beauty..."

"Is it?"

Zero swung the drawstring bag off his back and lowered the device inside. "This thing will ensure you don't end up as vapour."

*

They clambered across the rubble towards the path. Zero gripped the string of the bag to feel the weight of the distributor, then smiled. The day had gone better than expected, and Logan smiled at his side, pointing to various piles of rubbish to ask what they were.

Zero could see the perimeter fence when he heard the first rattle. He slapped his hand to Logan's chest, and he stopped. The rattle sounded again, and Zero took a step back, encouraging Logan to do the same.

"What's that?" Logan whispered.

Zero quickly shushed him and grabbed his hand. They moved as stealthily as they could back the way they came. The noise seemed to lessen, and Zero sighed in relief.

All until Logan tripped on the shell of a picker.

Zero spun around, grabbed Logan's hand and yanked him to run.

"What the hell?"

Zero didn't speak, as he rushed the way they had come. A broken meat container caught his eyes, and he tugged Logan towards it.

"In here."

Logan jumped him, and pressed himself to the back, and Zero closed the door till only a slim line of the outdoors could be seen.

"What's going on?" Logan whispered.

Zero pressed his hand to Logan's mouth and tapped his ear to get him to listen.

The rattle came in waves and sounded nearer than before. The metal outside the container shivered with the sound, and the vibrating could be felt deep in Zero's chest. He swallowed and peeked out of the gap for any sight of Hummer.

The cold-blooded came into view, whipping his black as night tongue in the air. He stopped, and the rattle ceased. Only when he began walking again did the rattle continue. The noise bounced off the stacks of rubbish, and the vibrations knocked Zero's knees together.

Zero knew the exact moment Logan spotted Hummer by the size of his eyes. They bulged from their sockets, and he stared without blinking until they watered. Zero didn't remove his hand from Logan's mouth, he had felt him gasp and didn't know whether he would do it again.

Hummer stood eight-feet-tall, and at least three wide. His scales weren't small and intricate like Rae's but big and flaky. A huge crest surrounded his head, which caused the rattle when he walked. His eyes were as black as his tongue, and his fingernails were jagged and dirty. Not the harmless cold-blooded Zero had described at all. If there was a cold-blooded worthy of Logan's fear, it was the one a few metres from them.

Hummer turned, whipping his tongue towards each pile of rubbish. He flexed his face and yawned showing his impressive fangs. Life-forms had died from his bite, not from the poison gland, but the sheer size of his fangs could pass through a neck and out the other side.

Logan shivered, and Zero wanted to yell at him not to give them away, but the fear in Logan's face changed his mind. Logan didn't need to be scolded, but relaxed.

Zero leaned close to Logan's ear and whispered. "It's all right, he'll leave in a minute."

Logan trembled beneath Zero's hand, and he breathed through his nose in panicked rushes. Zero slowed his own breathing and forced his lips into a reassuring grin.

"It's okay."

The rattling began again, and the container they stood in quaked. Zero didn't say any more, he kept his face next to Logan's and waited. The rattle increased, and Zero was sure his brain grew dizzy with the sound and sensation. Hummer was right outside, and a deep breath through his nose confirmed his rotten scent. Hummer would kill them, he had every right to. Zero only hoped he'd put up enough of a fight to allow Logan to run, but then he remembered the perimeter fence, and Logan's fear of being cut in half.

The noise lessened, but Zero didn't move. He didn't trust his mind. He stayed close to Logan until Hummer was nothing but a buzz in the distance.

Zero dropped his hand from Logan's mouth and cupped his cheek. "He's gone."

Logan eyes were sore from unblinking, and his flesh had turned peachy to porcelain. The skin beneath Zero's hand felt cold to the touch, and he tapped Logan's face to get a reaction.

"Hey?"

Logan squeezed his eyes shut, and when they reopened, they weren't focused on the gap of the door, but Zero's lips.

He leaned forward and stopped a millimetre from Zero's mouth. They hovered in the moment, and Zero didn't know what to do.

Logan panted, and Zero was relieved he wasn't the only one struggling to breathe. The warmth in his chest expanded, down to his toes and up to his scalp, and the need to kiss Logan overwhelmed him.

He closed the gap and touched his lips to Logan's.

They weren't dry like the cold-blooded, or tickly like the furists. Logan's lips were soft and smooth, and by the gasp, highly sensitive. Zero let them seduce him and pushed harder until Logan pressed against the back of the container. His hands found Logan's face, and he held him still, stuck in two minds. He wanted to both devour and savour the moment. Logan's lips parted, and his warm mouth welcomed Zero's tongue. Logan moaned into the kiss, and his fingers found Zero's hips and clutched.

The sweetness to Logan's taste, the softness of his tongue and the gentle breaths that escaped him. Zero knew he'd never have another kiss like it, and the intensity of the simple touch terrified him.

Zero withdrew, and a sound escaped Logan that sounded close to a whimper. Zero brushed his cheek to Logan's and stared at the back of the container while he got his emotions under control. They stood with their faces pressed together and their rushed breathing filling the space. Zero didn't know the condition of Logan's heart but each beat of his felt like it rose in his chest, heading towards his throat to escape his lips as a bodily declaration.

Logan whispered by Zero's ear. "Not where I thought we'd kiss..."

Zero pulled back and shook his head in agreement. "No, I've always thought I'd start by kissing you lower..."

He laughed and expected Logan to do the same, but he didn't. Logan looked at him with his heated gaze and licked his lips.

Zero lowered himself back to Logan's lips, but before they could touch, the lust faded from Logan's expression and he narrowed his eyes.

"What is it?" Zero asked.

"That was not how you described Hummer."

He chuckled and leaned back. "Yeah, I might've lied a little..."

"A little?"

Zero sucked Logan's bottom lip into his mouth for a final taste before stepping backwards.

"Come on, he's gone. Let's get this distributor to the theatre."

He turned, peeked his head left and right, then beckoned Logan to follow.

Chapter Fifteen

Looks that lingered and small laughs filled the car ride back to the flat. Zero could see the promise of more kisses in Logan's eyes, and his stomach fluttered, and his crotch filled. They hurried through the front door and towards the bedroom with their hands linked.

"Sir, you have an urgent message from the palace."

All good feelings faded and Zero gulped and stopped his eager stride.

He moved away from Logan's bed-lust eyes and stood in the living room.

"Play it."

Apollo appeared in hologram form. He grinned smugly and brushed his fingers against his medallion as he spoke.

"It has been reported, that on the 21st of April, you dropped a food-picker from the top of the undergrown cavern. This resulted in a three-minute delay to the picker schedule. We have decided that you need punishment to set an example to other picker-fixers, and the younger generation. We have deducted five tokens. As you did not have any, we had to take the value from your food pouches. Look forward to hearing from you soon. Apollo."

Zero didn't wait for the hologram to fade, he rushed through Apollo to get to the kitchen.

He tugged the food draw open and swallowed uncomfortably at the remaining pouch. He wriggled his fingers, then reached for the broccoli and squash. As soon as he lifted it from the drawer, the lights in the flat changed from their warm gold, to a deep scarlet.

"What's that mean?" Logan asked.

Zero glanced at him.

"Zero?"

He crushed the pouch in his fist, then threw it on the table. He needed more tokens. He needed more time to fix the machine. The red lights signalled the end, the last day before he would be escorted from the tower block.

"Means I've got to call Honey."

He faced the ceiling and cleared his throat. "Call Honey, tell her I need her here ASAP."

When he turned back to Logan his eyes were wide and alert. "Why do you need Honey?"

Zero stared at Logan's feet as he whispered, "You're gonna spend the night with her."

"Why? Where are you going?"

Zero sighed and lifted his gaze. "To get more tokens. We need more time."

"Honey is on the way, sir."

Zero lifted his hat and bowed to the ceiling. "Thanks."

He pointed at the food pouch, and Logan eyed it with suspicion. "What is it?"

"Broccoli, and squash, it's all yours."

"We'll share it."

Zero rubbed at his queasy stomach. It wasn't the lack of food that had it bloated, but the thought of what he had to do to earn tokens.

"I'd rather go on an empty stomach."

"Go where?"

Zero huffed and strolled to the window. He glared down at the drop and spoke over his shoulder.

"I have to go to the palace."

Zero jolted forward at the slapping sound. He turned and dropped his eyes to the food pouch spilling on the floor. Logan's chin bobbed, and his lips quivered.

"Why?"

"Apollo said he would pay me a token, or two..."

It wasn't just Logan's lips that trembled, his whole frame seemed to vibrate, and his eyes didn't blink.

"For what? What will he pay you for?"

Zero pinched the bridge of his nose. "Don't make me say it. You know what he hinted at in the twilight zone. I didn't want it to come to this. I hate him, but I know he'll be true to his word, and I'll have more time to fix the machine."

"No!"

Zero staggered back at the shout, it wasn't a blush that coloured Logan's pale complexion. Anger and sadness changed his skin tone and filled his eyes with tears.

"I have no choice. It will give us more time. It's only sex."

"Only sex," Logan mumbled. "And I guess we only kissed, no big deal, doesn't mean a thing."

"Of course, it does," Zero yelled.

"Sir, Honey has arrived."

He spun around to face out the window. "Let her in."

"Please, Zero, don't," Logan gasped.

"It's only sex. It may hold more meaning in your time, but here it doesn't."

"But it means something to me!"

Honey purred in greeting, but it ended abruptly. "What has he done now?"

Zero turned to her with a frown. "I haven't done anything."

She flung her paw in Logan's direction. "Then why does he look like that?"

He didn't turn to Logan, knew his expression would be painful to see.

"I have to go to the palace to see Apollo."

Honey straightened her aggressive stance and looked around the flat. "You're on your last day."

"Exactly. I need to get more tokens, and he offered."

She twitched her whiskers and bobbed her head. "I understand, and you want me to keep Logan company while you're gone."

Zero pressed his hands together. "That would be great."

"Don't talk about me like I'm not here."

Zero refused to turn to Logan but watched as Honey did.

"He'll only be gone the night, and then he'll have more time to get you home."

Zero closed his eyes when he heard a sniffling from Logan's direction. He might've avoided looking towards him, but he could hear the despair in the wobble of his voice.

"I don't want him to do it."

Zero's gut tightened, and he flashed a pleading look to Honey to respond for him.

"But he needs more tokens."

Zero yanked at the collar of his shirt. "No time like the present, the car still there?"

Honey turned back to him and nodded.

Zero lifted his head and spoke to the flat. "Tell Apollo I'm on my way."

He strolled forward only to be blocked by a tearful Logan.

"That feeling you had when you saw Felix rubbing against me, I feel like that now. I don't want you to do this. I'm asking you not to go."

Zero shook his head and stared at the undone top button on Logan's shirt. "I'm sorry."

"I know there's something between us, something special. Don't snuff it out like nothing."

"Maybe it's best that it's snuffed out..."

Logan clutched his face and tried to connect their gaze, but Zero refused him and gripped his wrists. He gently eased Logan's hands from his face and flashed a look at Logan's chestnut eyes.

"Don't," Logan whispered.

"What's the alternative? They're going to throw us out of the tower block and make me leave the island. The arch is here, the only chance of getting you home is here, Logan."

Logan shook his head, and the movement dislodged the tears on his lashes. They splashed onto his cheek and ran down to his jaw. His irises were vibrant under the layer of moisture, and Zero found he couldn't look at them any longer, he could only stare at his shirt and watch as the material blotched with tears.

"I'll see you later," he said, slipping past.

Logan gripped onto his waist and tugged him back. "Don't do it."

Honey stepped forward and forced her way between them. "Let him go, he's doing this for you, to get you home."

"Honey will take care of you while I'm gone."

The arms around him loosened and as soon as they had gone, Zero missed them. They felt like the only thing holding his body together, and he staggered through the flat knocking into the table, and the door frame on the way to the dock. He climbed into the car without looking back.

"The floating palace," he said, and it reversed away from the flat.

The palace hovered four-hundred meters off the ground and had its own gold car to take visitors up to the elite. They were only allowed to visit the palace for a few hours and had to be invited. Zero brushed his hands down his suit and fixed his hair into position before pushing his hat on top. He puffed his chest out and strolled onto the hologram platform with all the confidence he could muster. The machine whirled and scanned him and when it finished mapping his physique, it spoke.

"Sir, who do you wish to speak to?"

The name Apollo stuck in his throat, and an odd squeak escaped him. He had to be invited in by Apollo but attempting to form the man's name left a sour taste in his mouth. Zero cracked his neck left and right and wiped his sweaty hands on his thighs.

"I...Ap..."

Logan's tearful face appeared in his mind, and he bowed as if winded. He rubbed at his chest, trying to ease the uncomfortable feeling but it wouldn't go.

"Sorry, sir, I did not catch that, who am I requesting contact with?"

Zero opened his mouth and his bottom lip shook. He thought of Logan's happy smiles, his dazzling eyes and his quick and nimble hands that he enjoyed holding. He thought of the kiss in the recycle yard, and the silent promise of more. He knew sex with Apollo would destroy the unknown energy that flowed between him and Logan, and the thought left him hollow and dizzy.

"Logan," he gasped.

"Sorry sir, there is no Logan at the palace."

Zero stepped off and huffed at his feet. He couldn't do it. He couldn't hurt Logan any more than he already had. He ran from the platform, until his thighs burned, and found himself in the twilight zone.

He couldn't have sex with Apollo, he couldn't earn any tokens and fix the machine. He had failed Logan.

The realisation crushed him more than his failed machine. His insides ached and compromised his steps.

He paused, turned, and slid down the side of a building till he landed on the concrete. The fear of the unknown bubbled inside him, and he drew his knees into his chest. What if he and Logan were forced off planet.

Zero rubbed at his face aggressively, and through the gaps of his fingers he caught a shimmer and a sparkle. He dropped his hands and stared.

He was responsible for the sparkle and shine, or more specifically his suit was. He had chosen a silver sequin blazer, with matching trousers. The silk shirt he had picked shone when he moved, and his shoes were polished to a mirror shine.

Zero stood, straightened his lapels and gawped at himself. He didn't have much, but he did own an impressive collection of suits.

An expensive, fabulous, *desirable* collection.

*

Zero's heart thundered beneath his rib cage. His feet knocked slowly against the pavement as he walked in a circle. He tapped the cane in his hand to the ground to create more noise and drew the curious looks of the bystanders. It was time to change from showman into salesman.

Once he felt the prickle of several eyes, he lifted his head and stopped his obsessive pacing. Cold-blooded men and women whipped their tongues in his direction. The furists clicked their claws together in the silence, and the humans rubbed at their chins and wondered what would happen next.

Zero twirled the cane in his fingers and pointed it at a pile of suits he had been circling.

"I am giving away my prized collection in exchange for tokens. Who wants one?"

A murmur, merged into a hiss before finally succumbing to the lower tones of the cold-blooded. One furists stepped free of the crowd. She fluffed out her charcoal fur and waved her paws at the pile.

"What about that oil slick jacket?"

Zero nodded. "Any, and all."

He scooped the hanger up with his cane and displayed it to all the eager eyes.

"Three tokens for this set."

The charcoal furist clapped her paws together. "Yes, that would be prefect to decorate my scratching post."

Zero controlled his shudder and nodded frantically. "You'll have the most stylist scratching post that ever was."

"I'll give you four tokens for the black silk one."

Zero bowed his head at the nervous cold-blooded that had distanced himself from his friends. They hissed at him to return, but Zero waved him forward in encouragement.

"May it give you all the alluring looks in the world."

The crowd trickled forward, but it wasn't enough. Zero needed them to compete to claim his wardrobe.

He twirled the cane hypnotically fast then scooped up a jade suit that sparkled with movement.

"Now this, this is the same shade as your eyes," Zero said, leaning towards a furist.

He spun away and lifted the garment up high. "But it would complement your divine scales…"

The cold-blooded grew brighter with Zero's compliment.

Zero pouted and stepped slowly away. He turned to the group of humans and snapped his eyes to one in particular. The emerald-haired man he had seen at the theatre. The one he hoped to seduce with his invention and invite back to the palace.

He shook the suit, and the colour sparkled to life, making the audience gasp. "Or maybe it'll suit your hair."

Zero moved back to the pile of clothes and lay the jade suit on top.

"Anyone interested?" he said, tapping his cane to the ground.

The crowd stormed forward, and voices fought to be heard. Zero danced around the square, twirling his cane and flipping his hat. He turned the trade of his beloved suits into a performance and the crowd responded. They argued and offered more tokens to outdo each other. Zero goaded them, complimented them, and thanked them wholeheartedly.

By morning his suits were gone, destined to be made into scratch posts or used as stylist blankets for the cold-blooded in winter. Zero even heard one human say he would turn his checked blazer into slippers. He shuddered at the image of the man's feet pressing his treasure clothes into the floor.

The jingle in his pocket, was the only comfort. He had enough tokens to trade for three weeks of food, and housing in the tower.

"What about the hat on your head?"

Zero froze at the voice. Without turning, he knew the slow drawl belonged to Apollo.

"It's not for sale," Zero muttered.

Apollo tutted and marched around Zero in a circle. "I'll give you one hundred tokens for it."

Zero gasped and swayed on his feet. One hundred tokens, he'd never seen that many at once. He lifted the hat from his head and swallowed to relieve his tight throat. He turned it in his hands and stared with his mouth hanging open. It was not the most glamorous hat. The edges had worn, the colour had faded, and it didn't have the structure it once had.

"Your dad's hat," Apollo snorted, "have you sunk that low to not only give up his fortune, but his hat too."

Zero swallowed awkwardly and gazed at the hat in his hands. He breathed deep and exhaled with his eyes closed. His dad and he were never close, no one in the century spoke about their parents as passionately as

Logan had. It was the principle that made him reluctant, and Zero pushed his ego aside and held the hat out for Apollo to take.

Apollo snatched it from his hands and aggressively dusted the top. The humiliation was worth it if it allowed Logan to get back to his dad.

"He would be embarrassed if he could see you."

Zero turned his head. "Just give me my tokens and leave."

Apollo reached in his jacket and tugged a jangling bag from his pocket.

"I would've given you this earlier, and you could've left the palace with your dignity still intact." Apollo smirked. "You're playing hard to get but eventually you will come to me."

Zero snatched the bag from his hand. "No, I'd rather die."

He swirled on the spot and marched away to the car stop. The whole time he felt Apollo's eyes following him.

Warm golden light bathed the flat again, and Zero breathed heavily, dropping on to the sofa.

His arms ached after heaving his suits and accessories into the car, and the sting of seeing Apollo had sapped his last remaining energy. He raised his hand to grab his hat, but it passed through air and he stilled. He dropped his hand into the tangles of messy hair and clutched them tight. No hat, no sparkling clothes, or mirror shined shoes. Zero felt naked, and the empty chasm of his wardrobe made him shudder. He only kept three suits, and they were bland and unworthy of envious glances.

He was about to request sleep, but the flat spoke first.

"Sir, Honey is on the way."

Zero nodded and unbuttoned the top of his shirt. The button pinged off and rolled across the floor. The day before he would've verged on a panic attack, but he glared at the gleaming circle and turned to the window.

The car appeared, and the docking door opened. Zero leaned forward, balanced his elbows on his knees, and waited for Logan and Honey to stroll into the room.

Logan entered first, and his attention snapped to the pile of sparkling tokens on the table. His skin blanched, and his head bowed forward. Zero's chest ached to see him that way, to see the effect the tokens had on Logan. Honey's expression was the opposite of Logan's. She gasped in amazement and bobbed up and down.

"Well done!" she said.

Logan snorted and turned his head. "Yeah...well done."

Zero shuddered at Logan's bitter tone. The urge to soothe Logan with the truth rose, and he stood with his hands up in surrender.

"I have a better chance of getting you home."

Logan raised his head, and whatever else Zero planned on saying died in his throat. Fury blazed in Logan's chestnut eyes, and he curled his top lip.

"Can't wait."

He turned and stomped his way towards the bedroom.

"Logan."

He tried to follow but Honey side-stepped in front. "You might want to leave him."

She smiled, but it did nothing to calm the raging unease in Zero's chest. His brain fought against the ache of his insides, and he forced himself back to the sofa and sat down.

"I think you should leave him until he accepts you made the right decision." She turned and gestured to the pile of tokens. "All this for a few hours of sex."

Zero shook his head. "I didn't have sex with Apollo. I couldn't do it."

Honey's eyes sharpened, and she lowered her brow suspiciously. "Then where did you get all these?"

Zero reached for his hat, and when the silk didn't brush his fingertips, he curled his hand into a fist.

Honey pointed, deepening her frown. "And where's your hat?"

Zero exhaled deeply through his nose. "I traded it. I traded my hat. I traded my suits and my accessories for tokens."

Honey covered her mouth with her paw, and she blinked in quick succession. She spoke, but Zero couldn't hear her through the muffle of her fur.

"Repeat that?" he said.

She removed her paw and her claws flicked out. "Are you crazy, Zero?"

He snorted with a shrug. "Maybe."

"You traded all your suits? They meant everything to you, maybe not as much as success, but they were a close second. You said you'd sell them as a last resort, to get accepted on another island."

"And you said not to be selfish when it comes to Logan, and I'm sticking by that."

Honey shook her head and clutched her face with her paw. "I didn't tell you to be stupid. Apollo would've paid you... You could've kept your suits and still bought more time."

"Not enough. I don't need a few days to fix it, I need weeks, months maybe."

"You could've made a deal with Apollo, had it a regular thing. That kind of job isn't unknown of on other islands. In fact, it's a job I think you'd enjoy."

Zero stood and stepped closer as he shook his head. "I couldn't do it. I—I didn't want to. Selling the suits, it was a price I was willing to pay to get Logan home."

"But what about applying to join another island? You're still doing that right?"

Zero grimaced.

"Zero! What happens when the food runs out, and they evict you? You have nothing to bargain. You'll-you'll be sent off planet."

Her eyes swelled with tears, and Zero rubbed her shoulder. "It won't come to that. I'll think of something. I'll sell the theatre, bribe my way onto an island."

"The theatre is worthless," Honey hissed.

He stretched his lips into what he hoped was a reassuring smile. "Please don't worry, you know I always have something up my sleeve. It's Logan we've got to worry about."

Honey dropped her gaze. "Logan. You care for him?"

"Do I care, or am I just not being selfish?"

She rolled her eyes with a hiss. Then she stilled and edged closer.

"He cares for you. He cares for you a lot."

"Then I take back all the times I called him amazing and talented."

Honey punched his thigh, and he rocked back with a wince.

"I mean it, Zero. I tried to cheer him up, but I couldn't. I tried to tell him it was only sex, but he didn't want to listen. He was devastated, and that turned to anger, and then sadness again. Twenty-first century humans can be quite unpredictable with their emotions."

"So can forty-first ones, apparently."

Honey studied him intently. "I know you care about him, too, not just because you promised not to be selfish. You didn't go with Apollo because you want someone else…"

"Don't be ridiculous. I want success not Logan."

"You've sold your possessions. You didn't like Felix rubbing on him. You're envious over his magic, but not in a bad way, in a proud, impressed way. You care for him."

Zero breathed deep and readied himself to argue, but no fight came. He smacked his palms to his thighs.

"Yes."

Honey gasped, clapping her paws together. "After Apollo, I never thought you'd care for someone else again."

"I care for you."

"Not in the same way though. You care for him, how I do for Rae…. What's that word, the one that Logan used to describe it?"

"Don't you dare use it, it's ridiculous."

Honey scratched her face, and tightened her brow, but to the relief of Zero she didn't remember the word.

"This is great," she said with her teeth-showing smile.

Zero bowed his head. "Is it?"

"Yes, 'course it is."

Zero waved his hand at the tokens on the table, and widened his eyes, but Honey stared back blankly.

"I'll lose him in the end, it's the way it has to be. He will be going home, and I'll be... I don't know where I'll be."

Honey sagged her shoulders and flattened her ears. "Oh. Maybe if you tell him, he might stay."

"He can't stay. You know he can't, and I don't want to make it harder on him when the time comes."

Honey squinted, then shook her head. "You like him, he likes you. In the end, he will leave, but you still have time to enjoy each other."

Zero laughed and raised his eyebrow.

"Not like that," Honey said, "Well, maybe like that, but other ways too."

Zero didn't answer. He breathed deeply then turned away.

"Just think about it," Honey said.

She leaned forward and licked his face. He turned to her slowly and squeezed her paw.

"Thanks, Honey." He grinned, flicking his head towards the dock. "You better go before the car does."

She sighed slowly through her nose and turned to leave.

"Tell him you care for him," she said over her shoulder.

He smiled to her then moved his attention to the bedroom door with a sigh.

He cared for Logan, the man who was destined to leave. Apollo didn't break his heart, but there was every chance Logan would. Once Logan returned home, all that awaited Zero was the recycle planet, and getting his heart split in two was a certainty there.

Chapter Sixteen

Logan wasn't breathing softly like when he was in the midst of sleep. He was near silent, and when Zero approached the bed, he could see the tense muscles of his back.

"Logan…"

He didn't reply, and Zero sighed then perched on the edge of the bed.

"I know you're awake."

"Well done, you."

Logan tugged the duvet higher and covered part of his face.

"I didn't do it."

The rustling duvet paused, but Logan didn't speak, or remove it. Zero bit his lip, then released it with a wet pop.

"I didn't do it," he said again, louder, he waited with bated breath for a reaction.

Logan slid the duvet down and rolled over to face him.

"What—what do you mean?"

Zero shook his head. "I didn't do it. I couldn't do it."

"The tokens?"

Zero sighed and stood from the bed. He opened the wardrobe, and without looking he gestured inside.

"I traded them for tokens."

He closed the wardrobe once he was sure Logan had seen the empty chasm and pressed his back against the door. He sagged and eyed his shoes.

"Your hat?"

Zero resisted the urge to reach for it and nodded. "That too. Everything, but two plain black suits, and a navy one with missing buttons."

"But you loved your suits."

Zero narrowed his eyes at the stupid word. "I enjoyed owning them, yes. I valued wearing them, but we needed tokens. They were priority over my possessions."

Logan slipped to the edge of the bed and swung his legs out. "You didn't go to Apollo."

"I couldn't."

"So, you tried, and he turned you down?" Logan said bitterly. He shuffled back on the bed, reaching for the duvet, but Zero lurched forward, stopping him.

"No, I got there, and I couldn't do it. I didn't want to have sex with Apollo, and I didn't want to upset you. I didn't want to destroy...us."

"Us," Logan whispered.

He stared into Logan's eyes and offered a small smile. It wasn't returned, and he swallowed awkwardly. He released the duvet they were both holding and slipped his fingers over Logan's. Logan pulled away, and Zero's breath caught in his throat. He had misread the situation, had misread the "us".

"Logan, I—"

He didn't get to finish his words, Logan moved both his hands up to Zero's face, held him still and kissed him. It wasn't a rushed tangle of lips and tongue, their mouths lingered, and Zero allowed himself to be pliant as Logan did as he wished. The gentle kiss almost felt like Logan sought permission, or reassurance. Zero cupped the back of his head and encouraged him down to the bed. Their lips didn't separate, and they shuffled up the mattress into a more comfortable position.

Zero pulled away with a pant. "You sure about this?"

"Yeah, let's take it slow, though, yeah, like real slow."

Zero nodded, then grimaced. "What does that mean?"

Logan's cheeks glowed, and he shifted his gaze. "Not all the way."

Zero still didn't understand and swallowed uncomfortably. "But kissing is all right?"

Logan licked his lips and nodded.

"Touching?" Zero asked as he brushed his thumb against the back of Logan's neck.

"Yeah, that's good too," Logan breathed.

"And...and can I suck you?"

"Jesus."

Zero narrowed his eyes and poked Logan in the ribs. "Less of that. Is that a yes or a no?"

"It's a definite yes. If you wanna—"

"'Course I want to."

They resumed their slow kiss, breaking only to remove Zero's shirt. Every soft groan Logan made, Zero matched with his own enthused sound, louder and surer. The taste of Logan filled him, and he groaned at the addicting flavour, just like his scent, Zero couldn't put a word to it. It was uniquely Logan, and he tasted good, more than good.

Zero rolled Logan onto his back and kissed down the paler flesh of his throat. A gentle bite of collar bone earned Zero a stuttered moan, and a swirl of his tongue around Logan's neat nipple had him almost bucked from the bed.

"Sensitive," Zero chuckled.

He skimmed lower to the hair that travelled beneath Logan's boxers, and smoothed his hand over the strands, following the path they made to his straining erection. There was something erotic about unpeeling Logan from his own silver boxers, and he licked his lips at the sight of Logan's excitement. One touch, and Logan spasmed wildly with a gasp of the irritating name.

"My names Zero, not Jesus."

Logan laughed, but Zero didn't share his amusement. He turned Logan's laugh into a choke when he opened his mouth and slid his lips slowly over Logan's erection.

Logan had requested taking things slow, and Zero took it literally. There was no rush to his worshipping, and the room filled with the heady scent of sex and sweat. Logan's eyes were screwed shut. He withered each time Zero took him close and gasped and shuddered each time Zero denied him.

He learned Logan's body, knew that when he stiffened, and held his breath he edged orgasm. A proud smile stretched Zero lips as he waited for Logan to gather his composure after nearly orgasming. As soon as Logan stopped clutching at the sheet below and stiffening his thighs, Zero took him to the edge again, savouring the experience.

"Please, no more like this," Logan gasped.

Zero pulled back and peeked a look at him. "You told me to go slow."

Logan tossed his head on the pillow with a pitiful whine. "No—Fast, I want it fast."

"Fast, I can do fast," Zero said, before plunging his mouth back down.

Logan slid his hands into Zero's hair and scored his nails to his scalp when he reached orgasm.

His body twitched, and his breathing came in rushes. Zero couldn't help the happy smile that tugged at his lips. He wriggled up the bed, to grin in Logan's wrecked face. Sweat had glued Logan's usually springy hair to his forehead, and his flesh had a shiny complexion. Zero ran his thumb above Logan's top lip, marvelling at the glimmer of perspiration on his cupids bow.

Logan cracked open an eye. "You're evil."

Zero drew back. "How am I evil? I did it exactly as you said, and by the state of you, I think you enjoyed it. I enjoyed it too."

"Almost killed me."

Zero cocked his head. "Your heart may've skipped a beat or two, but I wouldn't have let it stop for good."

Logan opened his eyes and fixed them to Zero's. The black consumed him, and he found himself leaning in for another kiss. He didn't object when Logan picked open the button of his trousers. In fact, he leaned on his hip to allow him more access. Logan wiggled his hand into his pants, and Zero sighed in pleasure at the first moment of contact.

"Smooth," Logan said.

A wave of insecurity hit Zero's cheeks, and he shuffled his face to the pillow to relieve the heat. An uncomfortable feeling settled in his stomach. He hadn't considered Logan might not find him sexually appealing as a forty-first century man.

"I like it," Logan said huskily. "I like it a lot."

They kissed with heated tongues and nipping teeth. Logan had the advantage with his hand working Zero into a sweat.

Zero pulled away and stared down at Logan's hypnotic hands. They moved firmly, and with purpose over his skin. No lazy movements, but a strategy. Logan trailed techniques to gauge his reaction. His nimble fingers changed pace and firmness, and his wrist changed angle and length of strokes.

The sensation overwhelmed Zero, and he grew dizzy with Logan's control over him. The sight of his skilful hands made him pant, and they worked him as easily as they worked the cards. Logan learned an effective routine to perform on him to give him pleasure. One that he couldn't get bored of, or less amazed by.

Zero couldn't hold back. He pressed himself into the mattress and panted through the orgasm gifted to him by Logan's hand.

He dirtied his trousers, one of his three remaining pairs, but he didn't care, he didn't curse and hurry to shove them into the wardrobe for it to clean. He lay still on the bed with a smile on his face.

"Your hand is something else."

"Hands," Logan said with his eyes crinkling. "They're both as good as each other. Sometimes they're even better together…"

Zero snorted and rolled to his side. He tapped the headboard, and a panel opened to reveal a warmed washcloth.

"What the hell?" Logan asked. "How long has that been there?"

"It sensed the movement in the bed and prepared one. It's for when I…find myself frustrated and I'm too lazy to go to the shower."

Logan grabbed the cloth and handed it to Zero. "Maybe not everything in the forty-first century is pointless."

"I'm glad you agree with the sex rag."

Logan grimaced and shook his head. "Maybe not the name."

Zero cleaned himself up as best he could and removed his trousers. He quickly hung his suit in the wardrobe and slammed the door shut for it to clean.

As soon as he slipped back under the duvet, Logan shuffled up and pressed himself close. Logan kissed his shoulder, his neck, his chin, his jaw and cheek. Zero accepted all with a curious frown. It wasn't unusual to have more than one sexual encounter at a time, but the kisses didn't seem heated, and Logan's hand moving at his back wasn't a passionate clutch, but a gentle caress.

"What is this?" he asked.

Logan gazed at him with half-lidded eyes. "What?"

"The small kisses? What do they mean?"

"Means—they're affectionate, like the hand holding. Do you not—not like it?"

Zero hummed for a moment in thought before deciding he did like it; he liked it a lot.

"Yes, just not used to it. Will it not lead back to sex?"

"It doesn't have to. Not every intimate touch has to be sexual."

Logan pulled back and cocked his head. Zero watched in confusion as Logan rolled onto his back.

"Why not do it to me and see how it feels?"

"I'll get turned on again for sure."

Logan chuckled and shook his head. "Just try."

Zero shuffled unsure, these post sex touches were not meant for his time, but he couldn't resist a challenge from Logan and reached for him.

He ran his hand through the thick hair on Logan's head and let the strands tickle between his fingers, and then he trailed his fingers down the softer skin of Logan's throat.

He touched Logan's shoulders carefully, before pressing harder and rubbing down his bicep and along his forearm. The hair on his arm was finer, softer too compared to the trail leading down from his belly button. He shot a glance at Logan and froze when their eyes met.

Zero's heart beat with a different rhythm, not the sex-crazed thump, but a skip, and a stutter at touching Logan this way. He swallowed, hoping to ease the odd sensations that swelled inside him, but it didn't. Stroking Logan's soft skin made his body react unusually. His diaphragm spasmed for breath, and his insides fluttered. The sensations were almost like fear.

"It's okay," Logan said, "there's no need to be scar—"

"I'm not scared," Zero mumbled. "It feels like it but it's not it. It's different."

It was intimidation, and nervousness, and he didn't know why those emotions surfaced after orgasm, they were usually saved for before, and hadn't featured in Zero's body since he was a teenager. Logan made insecurity bubble from his pores. Half of him wanted to flee and the other half of him wanted to crush Logan to his chest.

Zero lifted Logan's arm by the wrist and settled it on the pillow so he could see Logan's hands. The sight of them calmed his internal peril, and he sighed, leaning close to kiss each finger. He held Logan's hand between both of his and studied it with his mouth and fingers. He traced the lines of his palm, slotted his fingers in and out of Logan's and pressed his thumb on a small mark.

"What's this?" he asked.

Logan eyelashes fluttered, and he gasped a shaky breath before whispering, "What?"

"The small chestnut dot," Zero said, pressing it again.

"Oh that, it's a mole, like a brown pigment in the skin. I've got them in other places too."

Zero lowered his hand back to the pillow and rose on his knees to look down at Logan.

"I know. I just never had the right moment to ask what they are. I—I like them."

His heart still beat erratically, but he pushed the odd reactions of his body to one side, and enjoyed Logan displayed for his eyes and hands to feast on.

He moved his hand to Logan's ribs and ran his thumb over another mole. "They are...odd cute."

"Thanks, I guess," Logan breathed.

"No human has marks to their skin here. I haven't seen them before."

He skimmed down Logan's body and found another brown dot on his hip. The tops of Logan's thighs drew his attention and he slid his hands lower.

"This is odd cute too..."

"What is?"

"The hair. No human has hair other than on their head. It's odd cute, and it's made cuter by your bare knees." He shuffled down the bed, trailing his fingers along Logan's calf muscles. "And bare ankles."

"So, you still think I'm odd?" Logan asked.

Zero clambered back up the bed, just about pulling his gaze from Logan's filled crotch.

"'Course I do, odd cute. Literally one of a kind. There will never be another one like you."

Zero frowned and rubbed at his tight throat. Those words had been a challenge to speak, not just his heart and lungs were struggling, but his throat too.

He settled his head on the pillow beside Logan and offered him a small smile. Logan leaned forward and rubbed his nose to Zero's who laughed at the touch.

"See, odd but cute."

Logan tucked his head under Zero's chin and threw his arm over Zero's side. "I think you're odd cute too."

Rather than be offended, Zero grinned, and wrapped his arm around Logan in return. His body settled back to normal, and the fear dissolved to comfort. He nestled his nose to Logan's hair and took a deep breath.

"Did you sniff me?" Logan asked.

"Yes, yes, I did, and you smell good."

Logan didn't say whether sniffing was normal in the twenty-first century, but he didn't object either.

Zero's chest brimmed with a warmth he couldn't explain, and the smile on his face didn't leave even after he drifted, unaided, to sleep.

Chapter Seventeen

Zero woke with his fingers absent of Logan's. He rolled to his side and blinked blearily at the fluffed-up pillow. A voice came from the other room, muffled by the door, Zero could hear the pitch and tone of a man speaking. He groaned and smacked the heel of his hand to his head when he realised the erratic voice belonged to him.

He rolled out of bed, slid a pair of boxers on and strolled into the living room. Logan sat on the sofa, suited, but not efficiently so. His shirt hung loose, and half his collar stuck up. It should've annoyed Zero, but the news floating in the centre of the room irritated him more.

"Turn this off," he muttered to the ceiling.

The hologram faded, and he sagged back into the door relieved.

"I was enjoying that," Logan said.

Zero shook his head. "Now who's being evil..."

Logan shuffled to the edge of the sofa. "I mean it."

"What about me hitting rock bottom and selling all my stuff is enjoyable? Were they commending my sacrifice?"

"Well, no."

"Exactly. No doubt they were calling me a failure and mocking my desperation."

Logan lowered his gaze, but the rose pigment in his cheeks confirmed Zero had guessed correctly.

"I like watching you move. The hat, the cane, the tricks."

Zero snorted. "Not tricks, just routines to add suspense. Pointless really."

"They're amazing. You're like a showman. Playing to the crowd, drawing them in with your charm and skill. My dad would've loved it if I could do all that."

Zero furrowed his brow. "There's still time. It takes practise."

Logan shook his head. "I'm not good in front of groups of people."

"You were fine at Swoshies with the cards."

"They had no expectations."

Zero huffed and strode forward. He dropped down on the sofa, and Logan shuffled till the gap between them had gone.

"They were all blown-away, and I, having watched your tricks over and over, am still just as blown away. It does not matter if you're not a 'showman'. You are still amazing."

Logan didn't seem relieved by Zero's words. He slid the pack of cards from his pocket and began his hypnotic shuffle.

"My dad never put pressure on me to take after him. He wanted me to be my own man, but that doesn't stop people expecting me to be a certain way. Even my mum and my sister look at me as if hoping to see my dad."

Zero opened his mouth to reply, but paused and blinked. "Your dad... Is he dead?"

Logan smacked the pack together loudly. "Yes, about two years ago."

Zero closed his eyes and rubbed at his head. He should've known, should have focussed on the way Logan spoke about his dad, and not ignored the past tense.

"I don't know what to say. I doubt the usual forty-first condolence would help."

"Why what would you say?"

Zero huffed and reached for his hat only to swipe air. "I would say I'm sorry for your loss."

Logan snorted, and his eyes crinkled with amusement. "It's okay. These things happen."

"I thought I was getting you back to him."

"You're getting me back to my mum and sister, my few friends, and my job, but not my dad, he's already gone."

Zero bowed his head. "I can't say I know what it's like. Family dynamics are different in this time."

Logan turned away and hunched forward. "You understand in terms of success and failure though, and I failed him."

"You've done no such thing."

Logan dropped his head into his hands, and a whine escaped him. Zero's heart leapt in his chest, and his fingers itched to do something. He threw his arm over Logan's shoulder and tugged him close. He didn't know if his attempt helped, but Logan didn't shove him away or shout. He sniffed and turned his head into Zero's chest.

"I said to you you're not the only one who's ever failed. I failed."

Zero rubbed Logan's arm and rested his chin on his head. "Tell me, tell me how you have failed."

"I told you my dad was an amazing magician. Loved by all. He ran a magic club, a place where he performed, and people came to watch him. It was always popular; the tickets were always booked weeks in advanced."

Zero squeezed Logan to him and thought of something comforting to say. "Sounds like he was a successful man."

He inwardly cursed himself at the weak sentiment, but Logan didn't seem to mind. He nodded against Zero's bare chest.

"When he died, the club was left to my mum. She didn't want to sell the place, she wanted it to stay running in tribute to him. She needed a showman, and the most obvious person to take over from my dad was me. I knew the tricks, big and small, I knew the venue, and the people. It was the most obvious solution, and I wanted to do my family proud."

"What happened?"

Logan shuddered. "As soon as I saw the audience, I was a shaking mess. I performed routine after routine wrong. They laughed at first, thinking it was part of the performance, but by the end they were silent. They didn't applaud, they gave my mum apologetic looks, and left halfway through my final act."

Zero grimaced. "That's—that's rough... At least you didn't faint on the stage for all to see."

Logan snorted, and the rush of soft air tickled Zero's chest.

"I made an idiot out of myself, failed in my dream."

Zero shook his head and held Logan tighter. "Was it *your* dream, or were you doing what you thought people wanted you to?"

Logan peeled his face off Zero's chest and glanced up. Zero cupped his face and brushed his thumb against his puffy cheek.

"I don't understand..."

"From the age of ten, I've wanted to be remembered. I've wanted to invent something to amaze and astound. To please society and be cemented in history. I failed. That is failure. Did you always want to be a showman?"

Logan shook his head. "No, I did the card tricks for fun—"

"And did your dad ever push you into taking over, or ask you to do more magic?"

Logan flashed a smile and turned away. "No. He was glad he could talk magic with someone, but never thought I'd take over for him."

Zero pinched his cheek lightly. "You have not failed him. You haven't failed anyone. Being a showman isn't for you, and that's okay. You never wanted to be one in the first place."

"People expect me to be like my dad."

"And you can be, but not in the way of performing magic. Be like him and do what you enjoy. Be a success in the job you want to do, not try to fill his shadow."

Logan leaned back and drew his eyebrows together. "I just don't want to disappoint anyone."

"They have no right to be disappointed. It's your life not theirs." He poked Logan in the chest gently. "Do what feels right inside here."

"Do what I love?"

Zero rolled his eyes. "Yeah, if you wanna use that word."

Logan laughed lightly, and Zero thought he had made progress, but then his expression turned serious.

"What about you?"

Zero frowned and shrugged. "Me?"

"You still have time to be an inventor. You're making a time machine right now to send me home, you can be successful, be remembered."

Logan smiled, and his eyes brightened. Zero swallowed uncomfortably and turned away.

"Yeah, maybe. Speaking of the machine, I better get dressed. There's work to be done."

The damp patch of Logan's tears itched his chest, and he rubbed at the skin. He ignored Logan's confused expression and pulled away.

"Zero?"

Logan's gaze followed him to the bedroom, and once he was safely inside, he banged his head to the door and exhaled slowly.

*

Zero secured the last laser to the frame and stood back to appreciate his work. It didn't have the polished gleam or the glamour of the first time, but it didn't need it when he was the only one destined to see it.

"Is it done?" Logan asked.

"We're at the second stage."

"Which means?"

"Testing. It's time to test and adapt till it works."

Logan nodded, then stilled and stared wide eyed. "What do you test it on?"

"Apples, bananas, grapes."

"Like a fruit salad then."

Zero scoffed. He shook his head and strode forward. "Fruit and salad, two completely different things."

"Where do we get them?"

Zero gestured with his hand for Logan to follow. He led him to the back of the stage and stamped his foot. He put on a pair of latex gloves and threw a pair at Logan.

"You'll need these."

Logan rushed to yank them on his hands and rocked on his heels nervously.

"Relax, this is perfectly safe, as long as the gloves stay on."

Logan glared and expanded his nostrils. "I haven't forgotten Hummer you know..."

"That was a necessary lie."

Logan didn't appear happy with the explanation. He stared unblinking until Zero sighed.

He pressed his hand to his heart. "I promise."

Zero dropped to his knees and ran his fingertips along the stage to find the overlap.

"Here we go."

He eased the floorboard up and slid it to the side. Light escaped the hole, and he smiled smugly at Logan beside him before climbing down. A huge rectangle pulsed with light in the corner, it was covered to conceal it, but each throb of light burned Zero's eyes.

"What's the light?"

"Fuel cell," Zero said, "but we're not down here for that yet." He pointed away from the vibrant light.

Logan gasped and smiled. "You're growing your own food."

"No, growing test subjects, everyone knows you shouldn't eat unprocessed food, and it's a secret, not even Honey knows about this."

"Why not?"

"It's illegal. This is a one-way ticket to the recycle planet for sure."

Logan gripped his arm and Zero turned to him confused.

"Recycle planet? I don't understand."

Zero's breath caught in his chest, and he laughed awkwardly. "Was—was a joke, forty-first century humour."

"I don't get it."

Zero grimaced and pointed at the hanging vines. "Apples, grapes, bananas. Just like I said, the fuel cell makes them grow faster."

The distraction worked, and Logan turned to the hanging fruits.

Zero watched intently as Logan breathed deep through his nose to draw in the scent. He hummed in pleasure, licked his lips, then reached for a shiny apple.

Zero nodded in approval. "Yes, that one will be a good start."

Logan's face sagged in disappointment. "I was thinking maybe I could eat it."

"You'll get ill."

"I won't. I promise, please let me have it."

Zero turned away from Logan's pleading face, but he could still feel the intensity of his gaze. It made his insides jittery, and he sighed.

"Fine, eat it."

Logan cupped the apple in both his hands like a precious gift, and Zero shook his head at his awe. He picked a different apple and climbed out the hole in the stage. Logan followed, admiring his apple. He sunk his teeth in with a crunch and Zero shuddered.

"That's weird."

"It tastes good."

Zero shook his head and moved over to the arch. He rubbed his thumb over the apple in his grip and then placed it gently on the floor beneath the arch.

"You see that button on the wall?"

Logan turned, and pointed. "That huge red one?"

"It's scarlet, but never mind. The big button, push it."

Logan took another bite of his apple before moving to the wall. "This one here."

"Yeah—"

"'Coz I don't want to get it wrong and have you hate me again."

"Just push the button!"

Logan chuckled, then slammed his hand down. The lights in the theatre dimmed, and Zero rubbed at his face while watching the distributor. Zero cracked his knuckles while he waited, and after a few seconds it flashed gold signalling full capacity.

"Let's see how this goes."

He flipped the switch, and the lasers hummed with the building energy before beams of light shot from them and struck the apple.

It exploded and chunks of apple flew across the stage. Zero rubbed his chin in thought. It wasn't unexpected. He needed to adjust the angles to get the lasers to distribute energy equally.

He turned to Logan who stood on the other side of the stage with his eyes wide and his mouth hanging open. He didn't move, even after Zero strode towards him. He stayed in the same position. The half-bitten apple lay on the stage, and Zero bent down to get it.

He waved the apple in front of Logan's eyes. "Told you this would make you ill."

Logan snapped his jaw shut and shook his head. "You're expecting me to get in that?"

"Not yet, obviously. We'll work our way up to you."

"I think we need to work our way down first."

Zero snorted and flicked his chin to the button on the wall. "Can you turn it off?"

"Yes, I think that's for the best."

"That was only a test," Zero said, frowning at the teeth marks in the apple. "I'm not gonna let that happen to you."

"You can't be certain though, can you?"

Zero breathed heavily through his nose. "No. I can't."

"At least...at least it will be quick."

Zero wagged his finger. "Yes, that it would be. Now, do you want this back?"

He held the apple for Logan to take, but he grimaced and shook his head. "No thanks."

"Good, you're learning," Zero said with a smile.

Chapter Eighteen

"Sir, Honey has arrived."

Zero dusted his hands together, then held the door open for her. "And why am I being subjected to this visit?"

She hissed and swiped at him. "Subjected? I wanted to check you were still alive and hadn't been vaporised."

"Not yet, but plenty of apples have gone that way."

Honey screwed up her face and stuck her tongue out. "Can't believe you touch them raw."

Zero raised his hands and twinkled his fingers. "I wear gloves."

"I hope so, and I hope you don't let Logan handle them like that."

He gripped the back of his neck and gave what he hoped was a reassuring smile. "Of course not."

Honey narrowed her eyes, then brushed past him farther into the flat.

She scanned the room, peeked a look around the sofa, and under the table. She crept as if the shadow she stalked would leap out at her.

Zero narrowed his eyes. "He's asleep."

Honey straightened and flattened her fur. "Asleep?"

"Yeah, twenty-first century humans sleep more than we do."

Honey cocked her head and wiggled her nose. "I can smell him."

Zero sniffed the air then shook his head. "Your nose is better than mine, but it's not unexpected, he's been here for weeks."

She shook her head. "No, I can smell him in here...on you."

Zero shuffled away with an unconvincing laugh. Honey grabbed his arm and spun him round. She widened her eyes and sniffed harder.

"You told him how you feel. You've had sex—"

"No no no," Zero said waving his hands. "No sex, we...we take things slow."

Honey drew back smacking her lips together. "What's that mean?"

"No idea, but we do everything but...the last thing."

"And-and how is...everything?"

Zero sucked in his cheeks to stop his smile but failed and as soon as Honey pointed a claw at him. He let his lips expand and ducked his head. Heat expanded in his cheeks, and an odd hiccup escaped his throat.

"What was that?" Honey asked.

"Nothing, I coughed."

She narrowed her eyes and Zero waved her attention away.

"Logan and I, it's great. Different, but great."

"How's it different?"

Zero drummed his fingers to his chin and hummed. He didn't know himself, and when he tried to think about why, his head hurt.

"I—it's more intense. It feels like my whole body is involved not just...you know, and then afterwards. Lying beside him, and kissing, and touching. It's—it's enjoyable. Really enjoyable."

Honey moved closer purring and bristling her whiskers. She smiled, showing off her sharp teeth.

"What?" Zero huffed.

"You feel what I do with Rae. It's nice to know I'm not odd."

Zero rolled his eyes. "It is odd, but it's not a bad thing. If it feels right, I don't see the problem, but—others might."

"Why?"

"It's not normal, and you know how society reacts to the unknown."

Honey bowed her head and flattened her ears. "I know, I just wish it wasn't so."

He shrugged and moved away. Honey followed. She puffed up her amber fur, and her soft purr rang in Zero's ear.

He lifted an eyebrow. "What is it?"

"What did he call it, what was the word Logan used?"

"I can't remember."

"Yeah, you can."

"So much emphasis on that twenty-first century *word*, there's no room for it here."

Honey's purr stopped abruptly, and she stared at him. "Why don't you like it?"

"It's stupid. It's all stupid."

"You said it feels right."

Zero threw his hands up. "Yeah, but it's still stupid. It doesn't belong here for a reason, and when Logan goes, he'll take it back with him. It's better I don't use it, in case we're overheard."

Honey flattened her ears. "Oh."

"Oh, indeed."

"When he does go, all you will have is your memories of him."

Zero snorted and glared out the window. "Memories of making the machine, the machine that took him from me."

Honey edged closer and pressed her paw to his forearm. "Make memories away from the machine."

Zero pointed at the bedroom. "What do you think we do in there?"

Honey's claws clicked out in threat and she hissed angrily. "I don't mean that. Outside the theatre, and outside of the bedroom. Make memories, for both of your sakes."

"Like what?"

"You could take him dancing?"

Zero huffed and pulled his arm from her paw. "I'm banned remember."

"The cinema."

"Also banned."

"Is there somewhere you haven't irritated someone?"

Zero hummed and shook his head. "Nope, I'd say pretty much everyone hates me here."

Honey narrowed her eyes and wriggled her nose. "Think of somewhere. Don't let all his memories of you be about that machine and sex. You've always wanted to be remembered, Zero, and you can be. Logan will remember you in a way the forty-first century can't."

Zero rubbed at his temples. "It's not the same."

"It's better," Honey said puffing her chest out.

Zero recognised the look in her eyes, the determination to get her point across. He didn't want it to end in a scrap, mainly because she would win. He sighed and waved his hand in the direction of the bedroom door.

"Fine. I'll show him...something."

Honey relaxed her stance and smiled.

"Good," she said, "but not the recycle yard."

"Why do you think I'd take him there?"

She narrowed her eyes. "That place excites you, but it's dirty, dusty, and Hummer is gagging to sink his fangs in you. Logan's scared enough of me and Rae, if he see's Hummer he'll probably faint."

Zero grinned and squeezed her paw. "I'm not that stupid, give me some credit."

"I give you none, and it's a generous none."

She left the flat, and Zero watched her car dropped down towards the surface. He rubbed his chin and thought of somewhere special to take Logan.

*

In the morning Zero strolled into the bedroom and clapped his hands. "Enough, time to get up."

Logan groaned, fidgeted and then went still with a soft breath. Zero rolled his eyes and gripped the corner of the duvet.

"Must I always resort to these measures?"

He yanked the duvet away, and Logan whined as if wounded. He rolled into a tight ball and muttered words Zero didn't recognise.

"I don't know what you're saying, but I know it isn't nice."

Logan moved his arms from caging his head and glared. "Did you have to do that?"

"Yes," he said, clapping his hands. "Now, come on. We don't have much time."

Logan shuffled up on his elbows, paused to yawned, and sat up in the bed. Zero flared his nostrils at his slow display.

"Time for what?"

Zero didn't answer. He turned and shoved open the wardrobe. The empty space tightened his gut, but one glance over his shoulder at Logan loosened the coils. He selected the navy suit and held it out for Logan to hurry up and take.

Logan staggered from the bed, waved his hand for the suit three times before finally grasping the material.

"Can I have a shower?"

Zero tapped his foot to the floor. "No time. When we get back."

Logan clumsily walked into the washroom with the suit dragging along the floor. Zero grimaced but didn't comment. He moved into the living room and watched nervously out the window. He had requested a car, and it flashed impatiently in the dock.

Logan appeared a few minutes later and yawned into his hand.

"So, where we going?"

Zero pointed up, and Logan blinked blearily at the ceiling. Zero rolled his eyes and took his hand.

"Come on, we're running out of time."

He led Logan to the car, tugged him inside, and slid the door shut. His heart thumped beneath his ribs, and he realised he was nervous, nervous of taking Logan to one of his favourite places on the island.

"So where now?" Logan asked.

Zero tapped the car's dashboard. "The roof."

Logan leaned forward. "The roof? Why?"

"I'm taking you to one of my favourite places."

"So it's all scrap metal and wires."

Zero chuckled. "No, quite the opposite."

He reached back into the car and pulled out the emergency kit. Logan tapped his finger on the painted skull on the front of the box.

"Now I'm nervous."

Zero shook his head. "Don't be. I told you the cars used to be unreliable, they crashed into each other, turned on their sides, and drifted off into space. The kits were in case of emergency."

"So, what's the emergency right now?"

"There isn't one, but I needed these."

He retrieved two heat collars and two respirators from the kit and slammed the lid shut.

"The cars would float off, the temperature would drop, and the passengers would freeze. These will stop that from happening."

"And the respirators?"

Zero tapped the window. "Have you tried breathing outside at this height?"

"Point taken."

"They concentrate the thin air. You have to take it slow, no—no screaming."

Logan gripped Zero's arm. "Why would I scream? What the hell is on the roof?"

"Nothing bad. I said it as a precaution."

Logan quickly snapped his collar on and shivered as the immediate heat covering his skin.

"Wow, how does it work?"

"It's a heat force field. They use it in the walls of the flat, and any other building."

Logan sighed and relaxed in his seat. "This, we need this in the twenty-first century."

Zero clapped his hands by Logan's ear. "Don't you dare go back to sleep. We're almost there."

The car pulled into the dock, and Zero quickly snapped the collar around his neck. He shifted the respirator on his face and turned to Logan to ensure he had put his on correctly. Logan glared at him, so Zero pinched his cheek gently.

"Odd cute."

Logan brushed his hand away. "You showing me or what?"

Zero nodded and slid the door open. The wind rustled his hair out of position, but he didn't try to fix it with the respirator strap around his head. He would tolerate looking ruffled for Logan's sake.

He took Logan's hand and led him out of the dock door onto the roof.

Glittering snow covered the top of the tower. Wind had made ripples in the white blanket, and it looked almost like a white beach.

"Wait for it."

He positioned Logan so he was facing the east, and their fingers tangled as they waited for the sun. The first beams hit the tower block, and the snow transformed into a rainbow of colour. It shimmered in the light, and Zero heard Logan gasp beside him. He enjoyed tinkering with wires, and fusing metal, but the other side of him marvelled at colour and texture.

They stood holding hands and watched how the snow changed colour the higher the sun climbed. It didn't lessen in beauty, the shades changed, and the sparkle intensified. He had bought suit after suit hoping to recreate the roof of snow, but every time he stood surrounded by the glistening colours, he knew it was impossible.

"Amazing," Logan whispered.

Zero hummed in agreement. They stood for another twenty minutes admiring the natural light display. There was no need for words, and surprisingly the silence wasn't uncomfortable.

Logan detached his fingers from Zero's and stepped away. Zero cocked his head in confusion when Logan bent down.

"What you doing—"

A compact handful of snow struck him in the face and he rocked back. He heard Logan's laugh through the respirator and glared at him.

"What are you doing!"

Logan crouched down and gathered another handful of snow. Zero skipped a few steps back to avoid being hit by the fast-moving lump.

"Snowball fight."

Zero stepped out of the way of another snow clump. "A what?"

"You make balls out of the snow and throw it at each other."

"This a twenty-first century thing?"

Logan patted another snowball together. "Yes, it's fun."

"Fun?"

Zero stared at the snow trails Logan had made. No longer smooth and unruffled, but clumped, and messy.

"How is this fun—"

A snowball hit him in the chest, and he growled.

"Come on Zero, you scared of having fun?"

Zero narrowed his eyes and leaned down and glared at the snow. The patch he crouched in front of was even, it twinkled, and sparkled, and a part of his mind yelled at him not to disturb it.

He delved his hands into the snow and raked it together to form a ball.

"Come on, see if you can hit me," Logan said, dancing.

Zero threw a snowball in his direction, and Logan dodged out the way and laughed.

"Right, you're in for it now."

He hurtled after Logan, making more snowballs to pummel him with. He laughed when he landed one and laughed harder when Logan chased him in return. The soft snow compressed under their feet, and their hastily made snowballs exploded on impact and littered the even surface. Zero didn't care that the smooth layer of the roof became messy, and uneven. He didn't care that the colours and the sparkles he had marvelled at were forgotten under laughter and joy at chasing Logan down.

He wrestled Logan to the snow and pinned him down. He couldn't see Logan's lips beneath the respirator, but the crinkle around his eyes and the brightness in his face expressed an infectious happiness. He grinned back, with an unknown warmth throbbing in his chest.

Logan struggled free and pelted ball after ball at Zero as he tried to stand.

"You better run," Zero growled.

His heart pounded, and his throat grew hoarse from laughter. The heat collar could only do so much, and soon a bitter bite of ice affected the tips of his fingers. Logan didn't seem to be affected by the cold, he continued gathering snow and rushing around the roof top.

"What do you call his again?" Zero asked.

"A snowball fight. I can't believe you've never had one. Have you at least made a snow man?"

"A what man?"

Logan dropped the snow in his hand and frowned. "Snowman...come here."

He beckoned Zero closer, and he went tentatively, ready to skip away if needed. Logan kneeled in the snow and pushed a lump of snow along the white surface. The ball gathered more snow, and grew bigger, wider, more like a snowball than their handfuls.

"Snowball," Zero said. "So I can throw that one at you? Make you into a snow man?"

"If you wanna kill me."

Zero sat on the roof and observed Logan roll the ball around the top. He stopped once it was up to his hip and started on another one. The second ball was smaller, halfway up Logan's thigh. He gestured for Zero to come over.

"Help me put it on top."

The snowball was surprisingly heavy, and they heaved it onto the bigger ball with a pant.

"Are you finished now?"

Logan panted and moved away. "Not quite."

Zero frowned at Logan's staggering form and rubbed his hand on his back. "Take it easy."

"I'm almost done."

The ventilator whistled, and Zero eased Logan to the snow. "Just sit, breathe."

Logan wheezed his breaths, and his head flopped unsteadily on his shoulders.

"Come on, let's go back to the car."

Logan shook his head. "Not yet, I'll rest up."

"You need more concentrated oxygen."

"Please, I'm having fun." He gripped Zero's hand and squeezed. "At least let me finish the snowman."

Zero huffed and flexed his stiffening fingers. "Fine. But I'll do it."

Logan pointed at the snow. "You need to make a smaller one."

Zero nodded and dropped to his knees. He raked the snow into a pile with his hands, and tried to force it into a ball, but it crumbled.

"Small snowball, and then roll it," Logan said.

Zero did as Logan told him and grinned at the rolling ball. It gathered momentum and grew. Every few rolls he paused at Logan's direction and patted the snow tight.

"Enough," Logan said, "otherwise it'll be too big. You've got to put it on top."

Zero bent his knees and heaved the snowball into his arms. His ungraceful walk got a chuckle from Logan, but he ignored it and carried on walking like something unfortunate had happened in his boxers.

He lifted the ball on top and stood back hoping to see some resemblance to a man, but there was none.

"A snowman," Logan breathed.

Zero turned to him with a fierce frown. "It looks nothing like a man?"

"It has a head, and a body."

Zero spun around to glare at the balls of snow. "Does it?"

"It just needs some coal for his eyes and mouth, and a carrot for his nose."

"Now I know you're mocking me."

Logan laughed and shook his head. "I'm not, I swear it."

"Well, I don't have coal or a carrot."

Logan heaved himself to his feet and stumbled over. "Doesn't matter. It's a unique snow man, probably the first one to be built in your time."

"Yes, I imagine it probably is, and no wonder. I get the snow part, but the man?"

Logan pressed his head to Zero's shoulder with a small laugh. Zero wrapped his arm around his shoulders and held him close. He wanted to kiss him, but the best he could do was press the respirator to the top of his head. Logan leaned back and grinned, and they brushed respirators like they did noses in the night.

"Come on. Let's get back in the car. I can't feel my fingers."

Logan nodded, and they strolled back to the car, with Zero's arm around Logan's shoulders, and Logan's arm around his waist.

Zero didn't know whether it was a memory worthy of being kept by Logan, but it was one he would treasure, even if the idea of a snow man was stupid.

Chapter Nineteen

The apple vanished. It dispersed into millions of microscopic particles that floated in the arch. Zero punched the air as he rushed to flick the switch on the transformer again for another burst of energy. Electricity swelled and pulsed before fading back to nothingness.

On the floor, beneath the vibrating arch, sat the apple. Intact, shiny, and in the exact same position it had been placed. Zero clapped his hands together and strolled forward. He grabbed the apple and spun around to face Logan.

"It worked," Logan said. He paused, the smile stretching his lips. "Didn't it?"

Zero studied the apple with a frown. He placed it on the scales beside the stage. It registered as the same weight as before, was the same size in his hand and had the same colouration, but something was different. He brought the apple up to his nose and gave it a sniff.

Logan rolled his eyes. "You thought it smelled gross before you put it in."

Zero ignored him and gripped the apple with all his fingers. He twisted his hands in the opposite directions. The apple split with ease, and Zero grimaced at the black insides.

Logan took a step back and wrinkled his nose. "So I'll look like I'm okay on the outside, but inside I'll be rotten."

Zero shrugged. "People say that about me all the time."

Logan flicked his arm, and he chuckled. Logan didn't share his amusement, he glared with a troubled look in his eye.

"It might not look like it, but its progress. We're getting closer."

"I guess it's not exploding anymore, that's got to be a good thing, right?"

Zero nodded, but Logan didn't look reassured.

"Relax, we're doing fine."

He held the ruined apple at a distance as he moved over to the recycle chute. He dropped it inside, smacked his lips together in distaste then added his gloves to the chute too.

"How much time did it take before?" Logan asked.

"A long time, but I know what I'm doing now."

"Do you?"

Zero rubbed at his chin and hummed. "Well kind of."

Logan sunk his teeth into his lip and rocked back on his heels. "You're going to kill me."

Zero waved the comment away but didn't promise he wouldn't. He flapped his hand towards the machine.

"I will test it, just like last time."

"But you thought it teleported, not time travelled. How can you test that?"

Zero squeezed his temples. "Perhaps—perhaps there were signs I chose to ignore."

"Like what?"

"I could take the atoms of apples, grapes, bananas and other fruits apart. But they didn't always reappear the same."

"What do you mean?"

Zero sighed and sat cross-legged on the stage in front of the arch. Logan stared at him intently before joining him.

"It was rare, really rare, so rare I didn't think it was significant—"

"What was?"

"The apple would come back different, or not come back at all."

Logan flicked his chin out for him to continue and he put his hands on his head then sighed.

"Sometimes they vanished, and I thought the atoms might have floated into the atmosphere."

"Now you think you were sending them somewhere?"

Zero grimaced. "Sometimes maybe, but other odd things happened. I built the other arch to receive the atoms and reform what went inside. A small percentage of my tests had unexplainable results. One apple changed colour, another changed size. I ignored it, thought the machine had arranged the atoms slightly differently, or mutated them. Other apples would be duller in colour or have a longer stalk. I ignored it because the other ninety-nine times it had been a success. The apple had been identical, not just identical but the same apple. But maybe I was wrong all along."

Logan dropped his head into his hands. "I'm never gonna get home."

"I know the amount of energy I used that night, and I will use the same again, all controllable variables will be the same and it should work, but I can't be certain."

"I could end up vaporised."

"I'll test it on the fruit till I'm satisfied, then try it on a life form. If it successfully rebuilds the atoms, then the chances of you being vaporised drop dramatically."

Logan nodded. "That sounds good right."

"Right, I won't vaporise you, but I could end up sending you somewhere else."

Logan clacked his tongue and laughed lightly. "Oh, you mean like the apples."

"Yes, like the apples, bananas, and grapes that have vanished unexpectedly."

"I wonder where or when you've sent all that fruit?"

Zero shrugged. "No idea."

"Let's hope you weren't responsible for the apple dropping into Eve's hand, hey?"

Logan laughed, and knocked his shoulder into Zero's, but he only glared back in confusion.

"What? Did something bad happen to this Eve?"

Logan clacked his tongue and squinted. "You could say that."

"Well, I hope Eve learned quickly and only chose processed food from then on."

Zero jolted to attention when Logan laughed. He hadn't tried to be funny, but Logan laughed with his hand on his chest and his eyes crinkling.

Zero flicked his hand at the machine. "Better get back to it."

Logan nodded, and drew his knees to his chest to watch as Zero dashed around the arch, measuring angles, and analysing the lasers under a magnifying glass.

By the end of the day on the fifth trial, the apple reappeared perfectly, and after that Zero tried a bunch of grapes, and a banana. All reformed with no flaws or differences. He smiled to himself and twirled the banana in his hand. It was a poor substitute for a cane, but he was too thrilled with himself to care.

"Think I've got it," Zero said over his shoulder.

There was no reply, and he turned to Logan, then snorted softly at the sight of him curled on his side, with his suit jacket under his head. Zero shrugged off his own jacket, stepped softly across the stage and laid it gently on top of Logan's sleeping form. He shuffled, snuffled, and tucked his chin under Zero's jacket.

Zero spun around and strolled up to the machine. He buzzed with adrenaline, and rushed to place the banana underneath the arch for another test.

*

The next night Zero invited Honey to the theatre to help with further testing. He didn't expect Rae to stroll in behind her, scenting the air with a grimace.

"What's she doing here?"

Rae narrowed her eyes and darkened her scales. Honey stood in front of her with her chin high and arms folded.

"I invited her."

Zero pointed at the machine. "This is all top secret. You know I don't like people watching me work."

"Logan's here," Rae hissed.

"He's different, he doesn't understand any of this. He won't steal any of my ideas."

"Well, thanks for making me feel like an idiot," Logan muttered.

Rae moved past Honey and up to the edge of the stage. "I'm not interested in your ideas."

"Yeah, you would say that," Zero snapped.

Honey clicked her claws out, and the sound rang around the theatre. "Enough. I invited her along. If you want my help, you'll have to put up with Rae being here."

Zero flashed a look at Logan, then bowed his head. "Fine…just…no touching."

Rae's scales changed back to turquoise, and she climbed up on stage and held her hand out for Honey to take. They grinned at each other, a smile that lasted longer than necessary.

Zero shook his head and huffed. The noise broke the lingering smile, and Honey narrowed her eyes at him.

"You said you needed me?" she said.

Zero clapped his hands. "Yes, I do. I need you to flick the switch on the distributor. Like the time before."

The irritation vanished from her face. She flattened her ears and widened her eyes in worry. "You sure?"

"I'm sure. I think I've cracked it."

"Think?" Honey gasped. "Only think?"

"I don't know anything for certain, I just need you to remember to flip the switch. One flick and it breaks down atoms, another flick to restore them."

Logan strolled forward and pointed to the distributor. "I've been here the whole time, why not ask me to flick the switch, I'm not as stupid as you think I am."

Zero shrugged. "Thought you might protest."

Logan stepped closer with his hand on his heart. "I want to help. Please."

He flicked his chin out and pleaded with his eyes and twitching eyebrows. Zero sighed and squeezed his brow.

"Seems I've wasted your night, Honey."

She waved her paw. "We're here now, we might as well see how it goes."

Zero turned to the machine with a long-drawn sigh. He slid his jacket off his arms and threw it in Rae's direction. She caught it, but narrowed her eyes, and rattled her tongue in annoyance.

Zero smirked and rolled the sleeves up to his elbows. Logan stepped forward frowning and shaking his head.

"What you doing?" he asked.

Zero rolled his shoulders and cracked his neck. "Making myself comfortable."

"But why?"

"It's time to test the machine, that's why."

Logan continued to frown, and Zero tapped him on the head. "Stop doing that."

Honey moved to Logan's side and gripped his arm in her paws. "Don't worry, I felt exactly the same the first time he tested it."

Logan backed away and brushed off her paws. "What? I don't understand."

Zero rolled his eyes. "The fruit was a success, now we need a living test subject."

"Living," Logan whispered. He whipped his attention back and forth between Zero and the machine. "No way!"

"Perhaps it's a good job you're here, Rae. I might need you to stop him doing something stupid," Zero said over his shoulder.

"With pleasure."

She strode forward and reached for Logan's arm. He darted out of the way of her striking hand and rushed towards Zero.

"Wait just a minute, you can't do this. You only got it working yesterday."

Zero nodded. "Yes, it's been working well for twelve hours, and there's no time like the present to test it again."

"This is madness." Logan yelled. He ran to Honey. "Tell him, tell him this is stupid."

Honey shrugged. "It needs to be tested, and if he says it ready, then I trust him."

Logan spun back to Rae. "You, surely, you can see this is stupid. He could vaporise himself."

"I wouldn't have come otherwise."

Logan turned back to Zero and pressed his hands together. Zero had no idea what the gesture meant and glanced at Honey who seemed just as confused.

"Please, Zero. Don't."

The tone of his voice hit Zero hard in the chest, and his heart skipped a beat. Logan's eyes were huge, and his flesh had blanched to a shade Zero hadn't seen before.

"I couldn't bare it if something happened to you. I can't see you come apart like the fruit, I just can't."

Honey stepped forward and held her forearm up for Logan to see. "I'll cover your eyes."

Logan drew his eyebrows together and shook his head. "No. Just don't do it."

Zero rubbed at his tightening throat and shuffled in his shoes. "It needs to be tested on a living thing."

Rae crept silently towards Logan. His back was to her, and there was no hint in his features he was aware of her presence.

"Not you, please, find something else."

"I trust in my machine, and all inventors experiment on themselves."

"Please—"

Rae struck and wrestled Logan's arms behind his back. He struggled, and snarled, but Rae held on tight to the bucking human.

Zero turned to Honey and nodded. She bounded to the side of the stage to hit the button. Logan fought to be free of Rae's grip, but her fingers curled like vices, and she clung to him.

"Zero, this isn't worth risking your life. I'll stay here, I'll stay with you."

Zero gasped at another skip of his heart, an unknown emotion sparked in his body, but he quickly shook his head and drowned it with doubt and self-loathing.

"You'll stay to spare me from possible harm, not because you want to be with me. That is why I must test the machine. I must get you home."

The lights on the distributor flashed gold, and he flicked the switch to prep the machine. He raised his hand in the air to bow with his hat, remembered it wasn't there and tried to make his hair stroke look casual.

He stepped towards the pulsing light. "See you soon."

Logan shouted behind him, panicked, and pleading, but Zero's ears dispersed and there was no sound, or sight, or sensation, only nothing.

Zero gasped and blinked. He fell forward and managed at the last minute to move his hands to catch himself before colliding with the floor. A high-pitched ring rattled his brain, and his eyes burned with fire. He had forgotten the pain of being reformed, forgotten the ache in his chest, and the parched sensation in his throat.

Honey helped him to his feet and patted along his arms and legs. She helped him to the scales, and he stood unaided, albeit bowing forward and jittery.

"Everything seems intact," Honey said.

Zero nodded, then gripped the back of his neck to knead the muscles. "Yeah, I feel okay."

He grimaced and turned his attention to Logan.

His eyes were wide, his mouth had slackened, and behind him Rae stood with an identical expression on her cold-blooded features. She loosened her hold on Logan's arms, and he stumbled forward, rocked back on his heels, before launching himself across the stage.

The air left Zero in a whoosh, and he took a few steps back to compensate for Logan's weight. Arms tightened around his back, and Logan's hair brushed against his face. The scent of Logan invaded him, and he sighed at the odd comfort it gave him.

"I'm fine—"

"You're not fine, you're stupid, an idiot. You're a stupid idiot."

Logan didn't loosen his hold, and Zero felt compelled to embrace him back. He wrapped his arms tight around Logan and muttered words of reassurance into his ear. Logan didn't reply, he held on tighter and buried his face into Zero's neck.

"I'm all right, and even better than that. The machine works."

Logan didn't reply, and Zero moved his hand up to the back of his head to card his fingers through Logan's soft hair. Logan shivered at the contact, and Zero grinned and pressed his upturned mouth to Logan's cheek.

"No need to be scared," he teased.

"Of course, I was scared, you great idiot."

Zero pursed his lips and rubbed his chin against Logan's face. "I like the great part…"

Logan chuckled lightly, and the sound loosened the tension in Zero's chest.

He glanced up to see Rae and Honey both staring at him, stunned, and he stopped his roaming fingers and dropped his hand. He distanced himself from Logan, gave him a comforting pat on the shoulder and strode to the side of the stage to shut down the electricity.

The gobsmacked expressions didn't leave Rae and Honey, but they did turn to follow him around the room with their jaws hanging loose.

"What?" he snapped.

Rae's tongue stilled in the air, and her eyes were wide enough Zero feared them falling out.

"Yeah, the machine. I admit it must be shocking to see for the first time, but I don't know why you're shocked, Honey."

Honey snapped her jaw shut and shook her head. "Not the machine. That with Logan."

Zero scratched the back of his head. "What, I don't know what you're talking about."

"The hug."

Zero blew a breath threw his teeth. "Wasn't a hug, was just—just keeping him upright. Anyway, it's time I focus on the final part of the machine. I need to find the right coordinates of dead space, then load the machine with enough power to send the atoms there."

"And how long will that take?"

Zero shrugged. "Impossible to say, maybe a week, maybe two."

Honey turned to Logan with a huge grin. "Hear that, you could be home in as little as a week."

Logan dropped his gaze to the stage and toed the boards with his feet. "A week."

Zero spun away and yanked the collar of his shirt. "So, I'm tired. Time, we go back and get some sleep."

Rae and Honey left the theatre with beaming smiles, but Logan walked beside Zero in complete silence. They waited in the designated spot for a car, and one travelled down from the sky. Zero rocked on his heels as he watched their descent, but Logan eyed the ground with a troubled expression wrinkling his features.

He opened his mouth, but no words flowed, and he stood looking as stunned as Honey and Rae had moments ago.

"Well, this is a surprise."

The voice yanked him away from any thought of Logan, and he turned sharply to face Apollo.

He smirked, wearing his familiar gold suit, with the added addition of a top hat. Zero swallowed uncomfortably and shuffled back a step. The air around his head felt cooler without his hat covering him.

"What do you want?" Logan snapped.

Apollo fixed his gaze on Logan and looked him up and down. "Such rudeness, and especially from a man from Far Away...it might get you in trouble."

Zero stepped in front of Logan and flicked his chin out at Honey. She understood and moved forward to grip Logan's arm.

"What do you want, Apollo?"

"I was wandering the square, basking in the amazed looks, and I saw you and your...fellow life forms. Thought I would say hi and allow you to gasp in wonder and longing at my medallion."

Zero shook his head. "Not interested."

Apollo pulled out the medallion and held it high enough for them all to see. Rae gasped, but one hiss from Honey and she fell silent, and dropped her gaze to her feet.

"And I wanted to see if you'd thought anymore about coming to see me at the tower?"

Logan knocked into Zero's back, and Honey hissed and gripped him harder.

"He's not interested in you!"

Apollo turned his attention back to Logan and frowned. "This one, this one needs to be careful."

"No, you do," Logan snapped.

Zero stiffened, as did both Rae and Honey. Apollo's mouth popped open, and he blinked slowly.

"Was that a threat?"

"No, it wasn't," Zero said raising his hands in surrender. "He's had a bit too much to drink."

"Does he not know what happens if you threaten one of the elite?"

"Of course, he does."

Zero flashed a look back at Logan. He struggled in Rae's grip, and Honey's paw muffled any shouts from his mouth. Zero gave him a pleading look, and Logan's features softened, and his taunt body relaxed.

The car beeped behind them, and never in his whole life had he been more relieved to see Apollo's stupid signature floating beside him.

"It's failure after failure with you Zero, and now you're entertaining that freak from Far Away."

Rae widened her eyes and gasped, Honey stumbled back with her ears flat to her head, and Zero's mouth hung open. Apollo sniggered and brushed his hand up the hat on his head.

Zero's heart thundered in his chest, and after a few mute seconds he found his voice. "Don't you ever call him that word."

"I just did, because that is what he is, and that is what you are fast becoming. You are a disaster Zero, and nobody in their right mind will accept you on their island. You and the Far Away freak, are destined to be shipped off planet. It's already been decided, you have two weeks left here. I offered you a chance to stay, and you turned it down. You know all that awaits you now is death."

Zero stepped forward, till his nose almost rested against Apollo's. "I welcome it if it means I get away from you."

He turned, took Logan by the hand and pulled him into the awaiting car. Rae and Honey bundled in after, and Zero slammed the door shut as hard as he could. Apollo grinned smugly, took the hat off his head and wiped it against his sweaty brow.

The anger that rose in Zero's body rattled his bones. He pressed his teeth together till his gums ached and clenched his hands till the skin almost split.

"I'll kill him!" he snarled.

Honey dug her claws into his shoulders, Rae tightened her fingers around his arms, and between them they managed to pin Zero to his seat.

The car rose, but even two hundred meters off the ground, Zero still wanted to hurl himself out, in the hope his body would land on Apollo and pummel him into the ground.

Chapter Twenty

Honey only retracted her claws once they were inside the flat. The wounds stung, and oozed, but after a few seconds the blood stopped escaping, and clots formed on top. Zero brushed his fingers over the itchy scabs with a grimace.

"Sorry about that," Honey said.

Zero didn't reply, he stomped through the flat and collapsed on the sofa. Rae's scales darkened to near black, and Zero glared at her.

"What?"

She looked down at herself and whipped her tongue out. "I'm not angry at you. I'm angry for you."

Zero bit the side of his cheek and bowed his head in apology. "Oh, thanks, I guess."

Honey joined Zero on the sofa and rested her paw on his thigh. "What you gonna do?"

Zero flapped his hand towards Logan who stood across the room. "I'm going to get him home, just like I said I would."

"But what about after?"

"I don't need to think about that right now."

Honey hung her head, and her whiskers twitched with sadness. Rae strolled forward and hooked her arm over her shoulders.

"Don't worry, Zero will think of something."

Logan edged forward hesitantly. He tracked the floor as he moved and drew his eyebrows together. "What does being sent off planet mean?"

Rae opened her mouth to speak, but Zero raised his hand fast and waved it.

"It's nothing for you to worry about."

Logan shook his head. "I am worried, and I want to know."

Honey's cheek's twitched erratically, and her eyes filled with tears. Rae shushed her and hugged her close.

"It must be bad," Logan whispered.

Rae darted a look at Honey, then Zero, then Logan. She rattled her tongue between her lips with a sigh.

"It means he'll be sent to the recycle planet."

Zero balled his hands into fists. "What the hell did you say that for?"

"He needs to know."

"He doesn't need to know. He won't be here for that!"

Honey wailed, and Rae rocked her forward then back. She hissed in rushes, the same way the cold-blooded comforted their young. A few months ago, Zero would've recoiled in shock, but Logan had numbed him to oddness.

"The recycle planet. The place where all your waste goes? Why do they send you there? To organise it, to work there?" Logan asked.

Zero clutched at the escape Logan had given him. He smiled and bobbed his head in encouragement. Logan seemed to relax, and the confusion left his eyes, all until Honey peeled her face away from Rae's chest.

"They send life-forms there to die."

Zero cursed and glared at her, but he doubted she could see him through her water-clogged eyes. He turned to Logan in the hope he could laugh off her comment, but that hope vanished in an instant.

Logan's jaw dropped in horror, and his bottom lip trembled.

"They what?"

Zero gripped the back of his neck with a growl. "I'll be okay."

"How?" Honey whined. "If that's what society has decided there's no going back. They'll ship you off there, no food, no water. I've heard rumours life-forms resort to cannibalism, just to last a few days before succumbing to poisonous fumes."

Zero lifted his head and gripped Honey's face in his hands. "Stop, stop thinking about it."

"What if I can't?"

"You have to, just as I do. For the sake of me, for the sake of Logan, don't think about it. It's not important right now."

The damp fur beneath his hands tickled his fingers, and he rubbed his thumb against her broad cheekbone. He nodded, and she sniffed, flicking her whiskers and nodded back.

"I'm not being selfish, just like I promised, and I will get Logan home. What happens afterwards...I don't know."

"There has to be a way," Logan shouted.

Zero turned to him, and his breath hitched when he saw Logan's puffy wet cheeks. "There is no need for tears."

"There is if you're going to die."

Zero stood abruptly and gestured to himself. "I am not dead yet, and there is still work to be done to get you home. I will not sit in the flat and mope about my life."

Logan shook his head. "There has to be a way."

"A way for what?"

"You can stay here."

Zero turned to the window. "There isn't. I've disgraced myself enough, and no other island would want me."

"What if—what if you redeem yourself?"

"It would have to be a pretty huge redemption."

Logan moved across the room and gripped Zero's arm hard. He blinked back his tears and bit his lip.

"What?" Zero asked.

He released his lip, but it continued to wobble, distorting his voice. "What if you do what you claimed you could?"

Zero narrowed his eyes and flashed a look back at Rae and Honey who were equally clueless.

"Teleport."

Logan grinned and clutched his fingers tighter around Zero's forearm. Zero closed his hand over Logan's and peeled his fingers away. Irritation displaced pity, and he stepped away from Logan with a sneer.

"I've spent all my time fixing the machine to get you home. You think in a week I can create a teleportation device?"

Logan shook his head. "You don't have to. Do it my way, a twentieth century magic trick."

"Cards, cups, and fur balls. They're one thing Logan, this would have to be huge, it's not possible."

Logan nodded eagerly. "It is, I've seen it done."

"Maybe in your time, not here."

"Please Zero. I need a few bits, and it'll work."

Zero turned to walk away, but Logan gripped his hand and slotted their fingers together. "Put your trust in me, like I'm putting mine in you. We can do it."

"Teleportation, I've tried, for years. I've tried, it just isn't possible, perhaps it will never be."

"But tricking people into thinking it is can be done. What will happen if they think you appear on the opposite side of the stage? What will happen if we trick them all, and they truly believe you can do what you claimed?"

Zero closed his eyes and bowed his head. "If we convinced all of them, if they thought I had moved by self through space, I would be worthy of being remembered. I would move into the tower and be basked in wealth till the end of my time."

Logan nodded. "Just like you've always wanted. I can give you that, you've got to trust me."

"But it's a trick. Once you've gone, I won't know how to do it."

Logan pulsed his fingers around Zero's. "Make something up, say it needs more charge, or more lasers, just make something up. They only need to see it once to believe it. Please, let me try."

"It's a risk, if we're caught trying to deceive, they will ship both of us off planet with no warning."

Logan flicked his chin out in determination. "If you do exactly as I say, it won't go wrong. It will be amazing."

There was gentle pressure to Zero's other hand. Softer, and a press rather than a clutch.

"It's worth a try," Honey whispered.

Zero smiled weakly and held her paw. "I guess so."

She grinned, and leaned forward to lick his face, but Logan beat her to it and kissed him on the lips. Honey widened her eyes and laughed lightly at the display.

"So, what do you need?" Rae said, brushing her hands together.

Logan dropped Zero's hand and rubbed his chin. "The first thing on my list...I think I'm gonna need your help."

Rae frowned and lashed her tongue at the air. "Mine?"

"Yep."

*

Zero paced back and forth along the fence. "This is such a bad idea."

Rae nodded. "I don't often agree with him, but this time I do."

Logan strode forward and blocked Zero's path. "Trust me."

"This isn't about trust, this is life or death," Zero shouted, pointing at the fence.

"Exactly, and I'm going to save yours," Logan said, smacking a fist to Zero's chest.

"So, who's going to do it?" Rae asked.

Logan flicked his chin out at her. "Well, I thought since you're a cold-blooded, too, it's best it comes from you."

Rae widened her eyes and flushed her scales with black pigment. "You brought me along as bait."

"Not bait, I brought you along to speak to your fellow life-from, to come to an agreement."

Rae sighed. "Fine. If all goes wrong, I can outrun you."

Zero punched the air. "That's the spirit, unless I trip you, of course."

Rae hissed and stalked forward, but Logan quickly intercepted.

"Please, Rae."

She stared at him, ran her forked tongue along her top lip before nodding. "Okay, let's get it over with."

Rae jumped up onto the platform outside the recycle yard and allowed herself to be scanned.

"I wish to speak to Hummer."

A rattle began, distant at first but it came closer, and through the beams of the fence Zero spotted the colossal life-form. He stomped his feet. His crest seemed to hiss like the sound of spitting raining, and his lava coloured eyes pulsed from his face.

"Jesus," Logan muttered.

Despite the thump in his chest, and the skip in his diaphragm, Zero still managed to roll his eyes.

"Sorry, but your ex can't help you."

Logan shook his head, but his eyes stayed fixed on Hummer. "Not my boyfriend, it's just an expression."

"An expression for what?"

Hummer stopped at the fence, and the rattled ceased. Zero didn't think he would miss the sound of him, but the silence ringing between them all was so much worse.

"Shit," Logan gasped.

"It's an expression for shit, good to know."

Hummer opened his mouth in what looked like a yawn, but Zero knew he wanted to show off his impressive fangs. One had a split, and poison dribbled down. A shake of Hummer's head dispersed droplets everywhere, and the ground fizzled where they landed.

"What?" Hummer growled.

He didn't address his question to Zero, or Logan, but Rae stood on the platform.

"We've come to purpose a trade."

Hummer shook his head again and more poison flew out of his mouth landing on the ground. Zero gripped Logan's arm and tugged him back a few steps. Hummer's attention snapped to them, and the buzzing in his crest reared up till they were forced to cover their ears.

"Enough!" Rae snapped. "We've come here to trade tokens for scraps of rubbish. I did not come to be deafened."

Hummer stopped his threatening display and glared at her. "Tokens? For what, there's nothing of use here."

"We will give you ten tokens, for two broken down meat containers, and full-length mirrors, four of them."

Hummer scratched at his crest. "You want broken machinery, and mirrors?"

"Yes, yes, we do, and we want help getting the containers to Zero's theatre in the square."

Hummer bristled and shot Zero a disgusted look. "This sounds like it's illegal."

"Yes, it probably is, but I can double the tokens to twenty if that's more of an incentive."

Hummer ran his tongue along his broken fang, then nodded. "I could get this fixed."

Zero clicked his fingers. "You certainly could."

"Then my bite will be hard enough to sever."

"Whatever makes you happy, I guess," Zero said.

Hummer nodded. "Okay, tonight. I'll box them, and if anyone asks, I'll say they're replacement chairs."

"And what should I say happened to the old ones," Zero said, lifting an eyebrow. "Just in case someone asks."

Hummer leaned forward until the scales surrounded his nostrils grazed the deadly laser. "You can tell them you irritated me, and I threw you at them... repeatedly."

Zero swallowed uncomfortably and stepped away. "Well, now that's sorted, we better get going, Rae, Logan."

Rae jumped down from the platform, and Logan rushed to his side. They moved swiftly in the direction of the tower blocks with the eyes of Hummer still on them.

"That went better than predicted," Zero muttered. "We're still alive."

He didn't expect Rae to laugh, but she tipped her head back and hissed with her tongue dancing in the air. She recovered and flashed her turquoise scales.

"I wonder how Honey got on."

Zero brushed his hands together. "It's time to find out."

Honey launched herself at Rae as soon as they entered the theatre. They performed their routine of kissing, hugging and the dopily gazing into each other's eyes.

"Now that's over, do you have any news for me?" Zero asked.

Honey released Rae and clapped her paws together. "Yes. A week from today, the theatre will be filled out."

Zero frowned and scanned the hundreds of seats. "Filled out?"

"Yes, and the performance will be broadcast on the news and played in every living room on the island."

"How the hell did you manage that?" Zero asked. "After my disaster months ago, I assumed no one would ever take me seriously again."

Honey shook her head. "Oh, they don't take you seriously at all."

Zero narrowed his eyes. "So why are they coming?"

"I said if you failed, you would voluntarily leave for the recycle planet."

Rae dropped her head back and laughed at the ceiling.

Zero pinched the bridge of his nose. "So, what you're telling me is instead of two weeks left on this island, I have one."

Honey bobbed her head and twitched her whiskers. "Yes, if it goes wrong."

"Which is more than likely."

Logan stepped forward and gripped Zero's forearms, he turned him, so he no longer faced Rae and Honey.

"Trust me. It will work."

"A week," Zero mumbled, slumping. "How am I meant to fix the time machine and make a teleporter—"

Logan rested his forefinger against Zero's lips to quieten him. "You concentrate on the time machine. Let me prepare the magic trick."

"My life is resting on a magic trick," Zero said bitterly.

"Yes, but it's one the forty-first century couldn't make a reality. Trust the twenty-first to save you."

Zero flashed a look back at Honey who flicked her chin in encouragement, and Rae who nodded with certainty.

"I literally have nothing left to lose," Zero said.

Chapter Twenty-One

Hummer delivered the goods, alongside a few of his cold-blooded associates. He snatched the tokens from Zero's hand and left the theatre with a stomp and a droning rattle. Logan hid the containers behind the curtain and began work "setting up" the trick.

The days passed, and Zero found himself hating the curtain with a burning passion. If he only had a week, he wanted to see Logan for as much of it as he could. Even when they got back to the flat, Zero couldn't save the minute details of Logan's eyes or smile for his last living seconds. Logan was asleep before his head hit the pillow, sometimes he succumbed to unconsciousness during the car ride.

Zero watched him sleep with the odd warmness pulsating in his chest. He smiled when Logan's lips twitched, and his eyelashes fluttered. Their hands stayed locked together, and even after waking, Zero didn't release Logan's fingers. He focused on the sensation of holding Logan and having him hold him back even in the mists of sleep. This, he didn't know what it was or how to describe it, but it was one thing from the twenty-first century he wished he could keep, but only with Logan.

Two days before he was scheduled to reveal his brand-new teleportation machine to the world, the meat containers still looked the same.

Zero turned to them and grimaced. "It's not going well, is it?"

Logan patted the side of one and a metallic ping echoed around the theatre. "It is. Almost ready for show time."

"All the clunking and the banging and I expected to see some difference."

"I've made all the difference in the world. It's perfect."

Zero rolled his eyes and turned away. The containers were far from perfect, covered in dents, discoloured from rain, and etched with deep scratches. The sight of them irritated Zero's eyes, and he didn't dare touch them.

"I guess they do look perfect in some lights," Zero muttered.

Logan clapped his hands. "Exactly, knew you'd come around."

"They look a good size for a coffin. I only expected mine to be sparkly, and carved with intricate patterns, but I guess it doesn't matter when they're fired off into space."

"Stop being dramatic," Logan said, then he paused. "You don't really fire coffins into space?"

"Space is a bit of an exaggeration. They launch them to the very top of our atmosphere. They fall back to earth, burn up, vaporise, and linger in the air for all us on earth to breathe in."

"You're joking, right?"

Zero shook his head. "No. No I'm not."

Logan flapped his hand. "That's not important right now. Getting these ready is."

"Ready? Ready for what? What could two broken down meat containers possibly do?"

Logan grinned and tapped his finger to his nose.

Zero frowned and mimicked the odd tap to his nose. "I have no idea what that means or the one-sided blink for that matter."

Logan closed his eyes and laughed lightly. "Just trust me okay."

The lights of the theatre buzzed, and then its voice sounded, crackly and distorted.

"Sir, Honey is at the door."

Zero rubbed at his chin. "Let her in."

She bounded down the aisles, breathing fast with her tongue hanging out. "I got what you asked for."

Logan rushed to the edge of the stage and held his hand out for her. He heaved her up and smiled brightly. "Brilliant."

"What did you need?" Zero asked.

Honey bounded towards him and revealed what she cradled in her arm. Fur, silver fur from one of the furists.

"And he needs that because…"

Honey glanced down at the fur. "No idea."

"It needs to look like your hair," Logan shouted.

Zero screwed up his face in outrage. "This? This does not look like my hair, how dare you!"

Logan sighed. "From a distance it will."

He rushed forward and took the fur from Honey's arm. He ruffled the clumps in his fingers and pouted his lips.

"Thank you," he said, bounding off behind the curtain force field.

Zero folded his arms. "My hair is nothing like that."

"No, the fur's softer," Logan shouted.

Zero flared his nostrils and stamped his foot to the floor. A chuckle crept round the curtain, and he growled and spun to face the arch.

He stilled at the tentative touch to his hair and gritted his teeth. "Honey, what are you doing?"

"Seeing if Logan is right."

Zero ducked away from her paw and narrowed his eyes. He edged forward and whispered by her ear. "Well?"

"The fur is softer."

Zero growled and turned away. "Thanks for the support."

She brushed her face against his cheek, vibrating the flesh with her loud purr. It tickled, and Zero couldn't stop the smile on his lips from forming.

"Off with you, you'll be late for work."

She nodded, then fled the stage with her ears flat on her head.

"So, what you doing behind there?" Zero yelled.

Logan poked his head through, and the fur Honey had given him covered his hair.

"What do you think?"

Zero rubbed at his chin. "I think you look ridiculous."

"I'm not offended. I'm trying to look like you after all."

Zero narrowed his eyes, and Logan mimicked him.

"Are you done messing about?"

Logan ruffled the fur on his head. "This is part of the trick. We have to look similar—same hair, same suit."

"Absolutely not, I am an individual."

"For the basis of this trick, you're not. I need to be near identical."

"I'm hating this idea more and more."

Logan chuckled and beckoned him behind the curtain. "Come on."

"Is it ready?"

"Almost, I'll give you a demonstration."

The meat container looked the same, inside and out despite all the noise.

"Go around the container, study it, make sure it's all solid."

"Do I have to touch it?" Zero asked.

"Yes, yes you do. Go on."

Logan flicked his chin out and Zero sighed, then moved around the meat container with his hand brushing the side.

"Yes, it feels solid."

"Test the inside too."

Zero rolled his eyes and banged his fist to each side of the container. "Yes, it feels like a normal broken meat container."

Logan picked at his smile, nodding enthusiastically.

"I'm going to get inside. I need you to shut the door and count to five, then open. No touching the inside, and to get me back, close the door, count to five, then reopen."

"What do you mean to 'get you back'?"

Logan chuckled and strode into the container. "Shut the door."

Zero exhaled forcefully reaching for the door to slam it shut. He tapped his foot on the stage five times, then swung the door open.

He narrowed his eyes, ready to glare at Logan, but he had gone. Zero blinked, and when that didn't work, he rubbed his eyes.

"Where—where."

His words failed him, and he circled the container with his jaw hanging open. He touched the back, and the sides, but didn't venture into the container.

"Logan?" he gasped.

He had vanished, and not seeing him, when he had expected to, made Zero's heart thump and his breathing skip.

"Come back."

His hoarse voice shocked him, and he rubbed at his throat and swallowed dryly. He remembered what Logan had told him and slammed the door shut. His foot tapped the floor faster than before, and he swung the door open on a count of three.

Logan stood, grinning ear to ear. "That was a bit close, I said five seconds—"

Zero gripped him and pulled him from the container. He positioned Logan behind him and backed them both away.

"I don't know what that is, but it's not a meat container!"

Logan grabbed his hips, and chanted his name, but Zero continued to move backwards until they neared the edge of the stage.

"Zero, its fine."

"It's not fine, that thing took you."

"It didn't. I adapted it. It was a trick, only a trick. I didn't go anywhere."

Zero glanced over his shoulder. "You were there, and then you weren't. There was no way of getting out."

"I didn't get out. I was there the whole time. I swear."

Zero stopped shuffling and glared angrily at the meat container. Logan moved around him to stand in front and grabbed his face.

"I didn't really vanish. It's a magic trick, you saw what I wanted you to see."

"I wasn't ready for you to go. I don't think I'll ever be ready."

Logan released his face and rocked back on his heels. "Zero—"

Zero raised his hands. "It's okay, you don't have to say anything."

Logan breathed heavily, and Zero opened his mouth, poised to apologise again.

"It's not like I haven't thought about staying," Logan whispered. "This place is terrifying, and if it weren't for you, I wouldn't even consider."

"Then why not stay?" Zero asking, daring to hope.

Logan lowered his gaze. "I disappeared. I vanished for real, and that panic you just felt, that fear and uncertainty, that is how my mum, my sister, my friends, that is how they feel and how they've felt since I've been here. I can't put them through that. I can't stay here, knowing I could be ruining their lives."

Zero pressed his lips together and nodded. Family were not fondly spoke about in the forty-first century, but he could see how much Logan's own meant to him, by the way his eyes filled, and his face creased with worry.

"I need to let them know I'm okay, I need to take away that fear. You understand, right?"

Zero exhaled slowly and fixed his eyes to Logan's. "I understand."

Zero rushed to the other side of the curtain and took a relieved breath when Logan didn't follow. He needed a moment to gather himself, reign in his panic, and apply his logic and cleverness to complete his machine.

*

The arch whirled. It spat out sparks and then levelled itself. Zero waited patiently holding a breath, and it responded by glowing gold. The floor shook, the twirling white light appeared in the centre and reached for him. It beckoned him towards the white light, but he resisted, and turned away. Zero switched off the machine, then kneeled in front of it panting.

He had done it. The machine had found the right point in space, the place where time didn't exist, and atoms could be exchanged. He had completed the machine that would take Logan from him, the machine that would freeze the warmth in his chest forever.

He thought it would take hours, and push his brain power to the limit, but the arch had synced with the dead space with ease.

Logan stepped out from behind the curtain. "What was that about?"

Zero swallowed awkwardly and blinked away the burning in his eyes.

"I've done it," Zero whispered.

"What do you mean?"

"It's ready. I found the coordinates in space, or at least the arch did."

Logan sat by Zero's side and squeezed his thigh. "Coordinates?"

Zero nodded. "The place in space where time has stopped."

Logan shook his head, and darted a look at the machine, then back to Zero. "I don't understand."

"Existence is a balancing act. Every force has an equal negative force. With all the orbiting, the expansion, the gravity, there had to be an opposite, a point where the forces balanced perfectly."

"Like the eye of a storm?"

Zero tilted his hand left to right. "Kind of. It's a dead space where time, gravity, expansion doesn't apply, and I found it. That is where the machine transmits the dispersed atoms. The other arch is designed as a responder and pulls them back from that dead place, and they reform. That was my theory of teleportation."

Logan pointed at the pulsation fuel cell Zero had heaved out from under the stage. "That give it the energy?"

"Yeah, without that it wouldn't work. It's from one of the space-liners that crashed in the ocean. It has the power to transmit the particles as a signal, then pull them back. Or so I thought…"

Zero dropped his head forward and rubbed at his temple. "I didn't count on it going wrong, and pulling you through dead space into my time, but that is what happened. My arch, adapted, beauty, and well crafted, linked with your plain one of the past, and they formed a gateway."

"Hey," Logan snapped, knocking his shoulder to Zero's, "Don't call my dad's plain."

Zero snorted softly. "Sorry."

"This gateway…will it always be there?"

Zero shrugged. "I don't know for certain."

"Take an educated guess," Logan mumbled.

"The universe has changed from a few months ago, we are not in the same place and never will be again. I thought it would be a struggle to find dead space again, but it did effortlessly, like it was drawn to that point. Like it needed to restore itself, to fix the link I made in time. If there is enough electricity, if the arch is functioning, it will be able to link to its opposite."

"So, what you're saying is…I could come back? It would be like a real transporting door?"

Zero closed his eyes and puffed air out his nose. "In theory, yes, in practise, no."

"Why not?"

"The first time it exploded. I had to rebuild the arch. There is every chance when you go through, it will overload and explode again. I have one fuel cell left to get you home."

Logan drew his eyebrows together and squeezed Zero's thigh hard. "But you could get more, right?"

"They're not easy to come by. I was lucky finding the two in the ocean. A ship crashed years ago, it rarely happens, but I saw the wreckage and scavenged what I could."

"But you could find more, right? One day?"

Zero shuffled and turned away, Logan cupped his face and tried to draw him back, but he refused.

"What, in years? What would be the point, Logan? Once you go through. I won't want to reform the gateway."

Logan's hand dropped, and his breathing hitched. "Why not, would you not want to see me?"

Zero gasped and looked up to the ceiling. "More than anything, but it wouldn't be good for either of us. You talk of love, of finding someone and settling down, having children out of choice, putting each other first. That is what awaits you, love and happiness, not from me but someone else. It would be torture for me to wait years to see you, knowing you got what you desired, and I didn't."

"But you're gonna be in the palace, the trick will work, trust me."

Zero squeezed his eyes shut and shook his head. "That's not what I want anymore."

"Then what? Tell me."

Zero struggled to his feet, but Logan gripped his ankle and stopped his run.

"Why would it be torture?"

Zero grimaced and shook his head. "It would be uncomfortable to see you like that with someone else, that's why it would be torture."

"But why?"

Zero rubbed at his aching chest, he focused on the uncomfortable squirm in his gut, and the chill to the blood flowing around his body.

"I don't know. I can't describe it. Just thinking about it hurts. When you go through the arch, that has to be it. It will hurt, more than I can imagine, but the small glimmer of light will be knowing you'll be happy, you'll find this love you seek, and find your own path to success. You go back to your life, and I go back to mine, whether on the recycle planet or in the floating palace. When that machine breaks, I will not make another, even if I was able."

"Zero—"

He lifted his leg sharply to dislodge Logan's hand, then rushed to the front of the stage. His eyes stung, and he blinked the pain away before clapping his hands together.

"Right, I'm done. Do you need any more help setting up your trick?"

Logan didn't answer, and Zero clapped his hands again. "I'll take that as a no, I'll leave you to it. See you at the flat."

He jumped down, and walked briskly to the door, doing his best to stay calm. If this was "love", he didn't want it in his life. It was infectious, disrupted his bodily functions, and ached his chest. Zero couldn't picture the twenty-first century, but when he tried, he imagined a lot of life-forms crying, and staggering around as if intoxicated, all for the idea of love.

Chapter Twenty-Two

Zero pursed his lips and exhaled through them slowly. The air didn't pass out smoothly, it stuttered, and he tried again. With no cane to spin or hat to fiddle with, he resorted to clenching his fists and releasing them over and over while getting his breathing under control. It didn't work, his body vibrated with nerves, and he shifted his weight from foot to foot to disguise it.

The curtain flickered, and the noise of the crowd crept through the force field. Not the voices of frustration, but doubt, and ridicule. The rushes of air left Zero louder and wavering. They drowned out the chatter on the other side, and he concentrated on the static hiss he created.

"Zero?"

He started at Honey's voice and pressed his hand to his thumping heart.

"You scared me..."

He offered a weak smile, but it felt uncomfortable and he quickly dropped it.

"Look at the state of you."

Zero glanced down at his all-black suit. It wasn't glamourous by anyone's standards, but it didn't deserve her horrified expression. He wanted to wear the navy suit, but Logan had been adamant they both wear black.

"Not the suit, you."

She wiped her forearm across his sweaty brow, then flicked out her claws and gently tousled his hair. He leaned into the touch and shut his eyes.

"I'm nervous," he said, flexing his fingers.

"Logan's plan will work."

"What if it doesn't? It's bad enough I'm destined for the recycle planet, but I don't want to be shamed before I go there. The one failure was enough, I don't want another one over my head—"

Honey withdrew her claws and pressed her soft pad to his lips. He opened his eyes and peered into her dark pupils. All he saw was his own panicked reflection.

"It will work. Trust this magic, this trick or whatever it is. I'm a bit upset you didn't show me it first."

"I can't implicate you in any of this. If we're caught deceiving, I don't want your name involved. If it does go wrong, you know how to run the machine to send Logan home, it's all ready."

Honey dropped her paw and twitched her brow. "Have you told him?"

"Told him what?"

Her pupils narrowed to slits and she hissed. "That you want him to stay?"

Zero bowed his head and didn't answer.

"I know you do. You like him, Zero, you're happier around him, and the fact you haven't snapped at me proves it."

Zero snorted softly. "You told me not to be selfish, and I'm sticking to it. I won't spend my last days making him feel guilty for wanting something more than me. He has more to go back for, than he has to stay."

"You're really going to let him go?"

"There's nothing to keep him in the forty-first century, and there's plenty to go home for. It's best for him."

Honey bobbed her head and dropped her angry stance. Her ears perked up and she looked around the stage. "Where is he?"

Zero tapped his nose, and Honey frowned before poking his nostril with a claw.

"Ouch, what was that for?"

"Thought you had an itch," she said, scanning the darkened area of the stage.

"Logan is fine," Zero said. "He's in position."

"In position?"

Zero nodded and pointed to the flickering curtain. "Think you better get in yours, it's almost time."

"What about making the audience wait?"

A bead of sweat trickled from Zero forehead and itched his skin. He pointed to the trail of moisture.

"If I wait any longer, I'll bolt from the theatre."

Honey narrowed her eyes. "I'd pounce on you, and Rae would squeeze you till you passed out."

"That's nice to know."

Honey grinned in reply, leaned up on her tiptoes to lick him, thought better of it, and wiped her arm along his brow again.

"See you after," she said before vanishing through the curtain.

Zero's heart quickened after she'd gone, and he bowed his head and stared at his shiny shoes. A droplet of sweat landed on his polished toes, and he blinked in quick succession. He cursed, straightened, then wiped his brow along his forehead. The sweat tickled his head, itched behind his ears, but the worst area was his armpits. He wanted to remove his jacket, but he remembered Logan's words. They had to look identical, and they had to get their timing perfect.

Zero closed his eyes, released a lingering sigh, and pressed the button of the remote in his pocket. The curtain disintegrated, and the voices faded with it.

The stage echoed with Zero's reluctant steps, and air whistled through his nose as he tried to calm himself.

Apollo sat in the centre of the theatre, with his feet on the seat in front. Decimal sat with his arms crossed, and beside him King narrowed his eyes and flicked out his tongue. Felix took up two chairs and Hummer took up three. Zero shook his head and focussed on Honey. She didn't sit, she stood and clapped her paws together. The soft pads made no sound, but it didn't matter. She was there, and she cheered him on.

"I am here today to show you something that will change our world forever."

He pointed at the broken meat container, and the audience stirred with laughter. Zero ignored them and pushed on.

"Imagine one of these in every home."

"A meat container? I wish."

The voice travelled fast, and a rapturous laughter came as an after wave. Zero shook his head.

"It's not about the container, it's about what I can make it do."

"Keep meat?"

A different voice, feminine. A furist Zero didn't recognise. Her claws slid out slowly, and her ears were flat on her head. Those around her chuckled, but Honey stood from her seat and hissed louder than Zero had ever heard. The unknown cat settled back in her seat with her eyes wide, and Rae grabbed Honey to calm her. She rubbed

Honey's arm and spoke low and fast to her. Honey's fur flattened, and her ears pricked up. Their display caught the scrutiny of those sitting close. They narrowed their eyes and pointed with repulsed expressions.

Zero stamped his foot to the stage to pull everyone's attention back. The same repulsed faces settled on him, and he glared back.

"I-I have altered this meat container, and now it can do the most remarkable thing. I will walk into it and appear in—"

"The one up there on the clear force field," Apollo shouted, "Yes we've heard it. Last time you at least dressed it up. A meat container, really?"

The audience erupted into fits of laughter, and Apollo stood and held his hand high to acknowledge the noise. His gold suit caught the lights of the theatre, and near blinded Zero. He dropped his gaze to the stage and blinked to relieve the burn.

Zero opened his mouth to explain more, but no words followed. He snorted, pressed his hand to the meat container, and looked up to the other one floating a hundred meters above them.

"Wait and see."

The audience's laughter followed him inside, and he shut the door, thankful that it muffled some of the cackles. He positioned himself at the back corner and slid the mirrors to conceal him just like Logan had shown him. He crouched down and held his breath.

The meat containers had been programmed to open their doors after five seconds and Zero crouched to wait out the longest five seconds of his life. He could tell the countdown finished, not by the creak of the door, but the silence that fell over the theatre.

He closed his eyes and waited. The muteness was interrupted by a clunk, the other meat container swinging open on cue, and then a gasp in unison from the audience. Zero swallowed awkwardly, and bit into his clenched fist. He didn't know whether it was a gasp of bewilderment, or one of horror. Did they know it was Logan on the platform, silver fur, and a matching suit couldn't possibly convince the audience. He was two inches taller than Logan, and an inch wider.

The door of his container clunked shut a few seconds after Logan's, and Zero pushed the mirrors back into position. He huffed, braced his hands on the door then pushed through with a forced smile tilting his lips.

Every life-form in the theatre had the same expression. Their eyes were wide, their mouths were hanging, and they sat statue still.

Honey reclaimed her hanging jaw and stood in her seat. She clapped her paws together hypnotically quick. In a room of silence, Zero could hear her soft pads touching, and he grinned towards her.

Her near silent clap cued the rest of the audience, and they stood, applauded, whistled and cheered. No mocking on their faces, only amazement, and as he paced the length of the stage to bow at each end, the sound increased. Faces no longer hung in shock but smiled and Zero was faced with hundreds of sets of teeth. Even Hummer smiled, and his dripping fang soaked into his shirt.

Apollo didn't recover from the shock. He didn't reclaim his jaw, and he didn't revive his stinging eyes. He stared unblinking, and his image was blocked out by the standing ovation.

Zero's heart slowed beneath his ribs, his breathing returned to normal, and he spread his arms wide and absorbed the sound wave of astonishment. He longed to hear the appreciation, the amazement, and it warmed his heart, but not with the same power Logan could.

He snapped his eyes up and looked to the container hovering above. He hadn't concluded the trick, and he rushed to the edge of the stage to lower the floating force field. The meat container lowered slowly and stopped on the stage. Zero hoped Logan was in position and rushed over to open the door. Empty space stared back at Zero and the audience, and he smiled.

"Imagine this, every flat, every venue, every workplace. No more floating cars, no more undergrown tram, or fast-ferry across the sea. Instantaneous transportation."

The audience bobbed their heads, and their happy hum of approval spurred Zero on.

"Time for work, then step through this and you'll be there. If you forget your ID card, or you're hungry, go back to your flat in the blink of an eye."

King climbed up on his seat and cocked his head. "May we come up on the stage and see it?"

"Yes, you can walk around the containers, but no touching, the containers are surrounded by an invisible force field. Dangerous if you don't know what you're doing."

They accepted his words and widened their eyes. The first row of the audience stood and made their way onto the stage.

The next hour was filled with every audience member circling the meat containers, muttering their amazement before shaking Zero's hand eagerly.

Honey bounded over with Rae close behind. She leaned up and licked his cheek, and he grinned and patted her head.

"That was incredible, how did you do it?"

Zero shushed her and flicked his head for her to follow. They moved to the edge of the stage, close enough that Zero could still see the containers, but far enough away that no one could hear them.

"It worked perfectly, and, no, I didn't really transport myself."

"But I saw you up there," Honey said, "On the platform."

"You saw what you wanted to see."

Rae straightened and peered above the crowd on stage. "Where's Logan, I thought he'd want to see his trick work, or at the very least congratulate you."

"He's resting."

Zero grimaced at his poor excuse and turned away. The unknown furist who interrupted him crept over and bowed her head.

"I'm sorry for doubting you."

"That's okay, I'd doubt me too."

She frowned, then smiled, and bowed to Honey by his side.

Even though it was fake, success still inflated Zero, and he grinned, and puffed his chest out proudly, but in the centre of his chest, there was a hole, an unknown shape that no amount of clapping or cheering could fill.

Decimal walked up to him with a grunt, all three eyes wide in amazement. King joined him and flicked out his chin in appreciation.

"Well done. I'm sorry we ever doubted you."

Zero pressed his hand to his heart. "You had every reason to doubt me. My first attempt was a disaster."

Both Decimal and King barked with laughter. Zero joined them but forced the sound in his throat. They moved aside and revealed the emerald-haired human. No lust rose in Zero's body, only an intense ache for Logan.

"Hi, I'm Pointer. What you just did was amazing."

Zero tilted his head forward. "Thank you."

"I was wondering if maybe you'd wanna meet up? After this?"

Zero shook his head. "Thanks for the offer, but I'm busy tonight."

"Sometime next week? I'll request to see you at the tower."

Next week, when Logan had gone home, and Zero was left to dwell on him for the rest of his life. He didn't want anyone else, knew he couldn't have what he had with Logan with anyone else, but he was leaving. Logan would go back to his town and find a man more suited, and Zero would be stuck in the palace, no longer wanting to bask in the riches of remembrance.

His throat tightened, and he cleared it before forcing a smile. "Maybe."

Pointer grinned and pursed his lips. "Maybe? Does that mean I'll have to join a queue to see you? If so, that doesn't worry me. I'll be happy with one night of pleasure with you."

A coil in Zero's gut tightened fast, and he sagged forward with a forced laugh. "I'll let you know."

Pointer grinned brightly, turned, and strutted down the stage.

Zero closed his eyes and exhaled slowly. One night of pleasure, he got more than just pleasure with Logan. His hand twitched, and he glanced down as he spread his fingers wide, ready to accept Logan's.

At first, he thought the hole in his chest was the knowledge his victory was hollow, but his eyes were drawn to the container that had been floating on the force field. The hole in his chest expanded until it robbed him of breath. He wanted Logan, he wanted him there, he wanted him in his arms and in his bed.

"Are we all done?" Zero said clapping his hands. "I need to pack the machine up."

The audience grumbled and reluctantly left the stage. Honey stayed by his side, smiling brightly.

"That means you too," he said.

Her cheeks rounded, and she stuck out her bottom lip. "I wanna stay."

Zero flicked his wrist towards the containers. "I'm just going to pack these away, and I'm really tired. Think I'm gonna go straight to bed."

"You sure?"

Zero nodded and pressed his hand to his mouth as he yawned. Rae slid her arm around Honey's and pulled her close.

"Come on, we can go back to mine."

Honey's sad face perked up, and she laughed and gazed at Rae adoringly. No disgusted looks were thrown their way. The remaining crowd only had eyes for Zero.

"Come on," he shouted, "time that everyone's out."

He moved to the centre of the stage and waved his hand to move the audience along. They climbed down, shot amazed glances back before pushing through the theatre doors. Honey and Rae were the last to go, with

Rae's arm secured around Honey's waist, and Honey's thrown over her shoulder.

The door closed behind them, and Zero raised his head to the ceiling. "Seal it."

He rushed towards the second meat container, empty to everyone else but him. He knew the trick, knew two mirrors joined at a right angle concealed a small area behind. The container appeared empty, but it never had been.

He folded the mirrors back with his heart thumping and sat squished on the floor was a sweaty Logan. He glanced up, smiled and in an instant the hole in Zero's chest filled and he gasped, reaching for him.

He tugged Logan up by his lapels and pushed him to the side of the container. He held Logan's face in his hands, thumb on each cheek, and fingers covering both ears. He wanted to speak, but no words came. Instead he pressed his lips to Logan's in a bruising kiss, then released him and stepped back.

"Sorry," he mumbled.

Logan smiled and touched his lips. "It worked then?"

Zero nodded, before throwing himself forward and kissing Logan again. They were small kisses, firm, but brief, and Logan grinned at the attention, until his grin morphed into a soft chuckle. Zero kept kissing him, not lusting kisses but a way of expressing how much Logan meant to him.

"Sorry, I just wanna kiss you," Zero said, before feeling stupid at his admission.

Logan gripped Zero's hips and pulled him forward till their midriffs pressed together.

"I like it, but maybe we should—"

"Take it slow, I know…"

Logan shook his head and licked his lips. "I don't wanna take it slow anymore."

Zero leaned to press their mouths together, but Logan stopped him and pushed his hand to his chest.

"Not here. At the flat, in the bed. I want my first time to be somewhere comfortable."

Zero nodded. "Of course," he paused, and pulled a pained expression. "Are you sure about this?"

"Yes. I'm sure, surer than sure. I want you, Zero."

Logan smiled and moved to connect them. The kiss was sloppy, and eager, and Zero grinned instead of kissing back.

"Wait, wait. At the flat." He laughed. "Can't kiss me like that here, we'll never get out of this container."

Logan bit his lip, glancing away.

"Logan?"

He laced his fingers through Zero's and tugged. "Let's go."

Chapter Twenty-Three

Most of the audience had already left the square, but a few stood waiting for cars. Honey and Rae were among them, and they turned towards Logan with matching frowns.

"Where were you?"

Logan opened his mouth to reply, but Zero got there first.

"Resting, I told you they sleep more where he comes from. He was curled up at the back of the stage."

Rae stopped frowning and nodded, but Honey's frown intensified.

"I looked in the dark and didn't see him."

Zero waved his hand dismissively. "He was asleep under the stage."

Honey shuddered. "With the fruit and veg."

Zero shushed her and darted a look behind himself. "I don't wanna get arrested."

"What are you talking about? You're destined to live in the floating palace, you can do whatever you want," Rae said, spreading her arms wide.

Zero flexed his fingers around Logan's and grinned when they pulsed back. "Right now, whatever I want, is Logan, and Logan alone."

Honey held her paw out towards her car. "Take ours."

"Thank you."

Zero moved forward, but he jolted back when Logan didn't move. "What is it?"

Logan's fingers detached from his, and he strode away. Zero gawped as Logan walked right up to Apollo and snatched the hat from his head. There were shouts of outrage, and Zero hurried forward only to stop in surprise. Both King and Decimal were arguing with Apollo over the hat, and more joined the gaggle surrounding the golden suited human.

Apollo huffed and walked away, and when the crowd dispersed Logan stood with Zero's hat in his hands. He walked up and lowered it over Zero's hair.

"Thank you," Zero whispered.

Logan smiled, took his hand and led him into the awaiting car. Honey waved them off, and Rae lifted an eyebrow and sniggered to herself. The car rose in the air and flew to Zero's flat on the eight hundredth floor for what Zero hoped was the last time.

His and Logan's fingers stayed tangled, and with Zero's other he stroked the hat on his head. It needed a wash, to be disinfected and dusted, but it was his and under his possession again.

"You can't wear that when we're having sex," Logan mumbled.

Zero stuck his bottom lip out. "You don't think it suits me?"

Logan shoved him with his elbow. "You know it does, but not when we're doing the deed."

Zero raised an eyebrow. "Doing the deed? Is there no end to your odd-cuteness?"

The car docked, and Zero slid open the door and helped Logan out. There was no pretence of where they were heading, they walked briskly into the bedroom, and Logan shut the door behind them.

The easy smile faded from his lips and he pressed his back against the door. The heated promise dimmed in Logan's eyes, and Zero edged forward and cupped his face.

"It's okay, we don't have to do anything... I'm happy just lying in bed, holding hands."

Logan bit his lip and turned his face into Zero's hand. He closed his eyes, and his soft breath tickled Zero's palm. "I just want it to be good."

Zero rubbed his thumb against Logan's cheekbone. "It will be."

"Do you remember what I said about sex...about how I feel about it."

Zero dropped his hand and took a step back. "I remember. It's okay if you don't feel that way about me. We don't have to—"

Logan pushed off from the door and launched at Zero. Their mouths connected, and Logan wrapped his arm around Zero's neck as he backed him towards the bed.

The back of Zero's knees hit the frame, and he fell to the mattress.

"Sometimes you're so stupid," Logan said breathlessly.

"Me? My IQ is 350, what about you?"

Logan leaned down and pushed their mouths together again silencing Zero's outrage. Logan's movements were uncoordinated, sloppy, and their teeth knocked together. Zero laughed into the lock of mouths, and tried to slow Logan's onslaught, but there was no controlling the kiss. Logan straddled his lap and rocked forward till Zero lay on his back.

Logan leaned back, gasped at the air then grabbed the hat on Zero's head and threw it across the other side of the room.

"Slow down." Zero laughed, but Logan made no indication he had heard.

His fingers picked at Zero's buttons but made little progress with the tremor in his hands. A blush grew on his cheeks, and Zero could feel Logan's nerves rattling his body. He stopped smiling and frowned at Logan's desperate display. On anyone else it would look normal, rushing to undress, but Logan panted, and his eyes shimmered, not in lust but some other emotion.

Zero gripped his wrists to slow him. "Easy, there's no rush. Calm down."

Logan leaned back, and his throat bobbed awkwardly. "I'm trying to be sexy."

"Stop trying. You are already." Zero leaned up on his elbows. "You're sexy, you're cute, you're like no one I've ever met."

Logan averted his gaze. "Sex is about pleasure here. How am I meant to be good if I've never done it before? How am I supposed to make sure you remember me?"

Zero's stomach twisted into knots, he snapped his jaw shut and swallowed before answering. "I'm never going to forget you Logan, how could you even think it."

"I heard everyone talking about the palace, how they would request to visit you, how they wanted to be with you. I have this one chance to make an impression, to make sure you remember me."

"If that's why you're doing this, then it's wrong."

Logan shook his head. "It's not the only reason. There's the most obvious one. The one I think you feel, too, but I want you to think back on this moment...and be...be amazed. I want you to think this is worthy of remembering."

Zero closed his eyes and breathed out slowly. "Logan, you don't have to worry about me forgetting you, that's impossible. You constantly amaze me, your card tricks, your magic, your odd-cuteness. You. Sex with you will be amazing too, far more amazing than simple pleasure."

"I want it to be good for you."

"How about yourself?" Zero said. "You rush like this, do you really think you'll enjoy it?"

Logan retreated farther and stood from the bed. "I've made an idiot out of myself."

"No, you haven't. You're worried about not being remembered. I of all people understand that, but I promise you right now, I will not forget you."

"Why?"

Zero grit his teeth and growled. He softened his expression and looked up to Logan with pleading eyes. "Don't make me say it okay. You know why..."

Logan stared at him long and hard, then nodded. "Can we try this again?"

"Yes, and we'll do it our way, not the forty-first century one."

Logan nodded, and joined him on the bed. There was an awkward shuffle, a soft laugh from both of them and then Zero brushed his thumb against Logan's cheek and he relaxed into the caress.

"We'll take this slow," Zero whispered, and Logan nodded in agreement.

Zero's heart pounded, not just from arousal, but the excitement of getting to map out Logan's body with his mouth and hands. He had done so before, but never while chasing his and Logan's release. The body beneath his roaming fingers shuddered, and the skin dotted with sensitive dots. Zero kissed along Logan's collar bone, rubbed his face against the soft fuzz on his pecks, and brushed his hands along Logan's legs all the way to his hairless ankles. They were worshipping touches, designed to burn every detail of Logan into his memory, and relax him to a state where nerves couldn't fester.

Logan eyes were closed, but his face wasn't tightened in worry or pain. Zero straddled him, then nose nudged Logan's cheek to make sure he hadn't dozed off.

Logan's eyelashes fluttered, and he smiled dopily. Zero chuckled lightly and leaned back. He looked down at Logan, and their crotches that were both bare and engorged, desperate to get acquainted, but before Zero indulged in that need, he grabbed Logan's wrist and lead his hand to his heart.

Logan splayed his fingers out on Zero's chest, and Zero mapped them with his own. The clever hands of magic, that could move cards with ease. He lusted for all Logan's body, but had a soft spot for his hands. Zero stared down at Logan with a soft smile on his lips but jolted forward with a gasp of laughter when Logan tweaked his nipple.

"Brave," Zero muttered.

Logan licked his lips and flicked his chin out. "I'm ready now."

Zero nodded and reached for the headboard. He slid a panel away to reveal a nozzle. It squirted an adequate amount of lubricant into his palm, but he held his hand under for more. He knew it would be uncomfortable for Logan and wanted to limit the rawness as much as he could.

Logan tensed at the first attempt at stretching him, and Zero stopped immediately.

"We can stop—"

"No, I just thought it would be cold."

Zero frowned and shook his head. "It's body temperature, like always."

He tried again and told Logan to relax. Words were not enough, and he leaned down and pushed their mouths together. He twirled his tongue around Logan's hesitant one, and after a few seconds of kissing, his arms came up and hooked around Zero's shoulders. The bolder Zero got with his fingers, the more forcefully Logan kissed him. It was a game of give and take, each time Zero slid a finger inside, and then out, Logan copied the motion with his tongue in Zero's mouth.

He moved his fingers away and drew back from the kiss. He didn't ask, he just nodded, and Logan nodded back.

Logan tensed at the first penetration, and he looked down to where their bodies joined. The sight didn't relax him, and he tensed harder until Zero feared moving forward or back.

"Relax."

Zero was thrown at his own strained voice, and decided words were not the answer, but gentle reassurance was. He wrestled his head against Logan's until he stopped staring down at them and looked up at the ceiling, and they slotted their mouths together. Gentle coaxing from his tongue got a response, and Logan relaxed into the lock of mouths with a soft sigh.

The slow pace, and the tenderness of their touches, unsettled Zero, and the odd warmth grew in his chest. He pulled away from Logan's mouth and pressed his head by the side of his throat as he continued to move his hips. Logan didn't tense, he clung on to Zero's back as if it could save him from a fall. Zero blinked the burning away from his eyes. If Logan were to recall his first time, he didn't want him to remember Zero becoming overwhelmed and sobbing into his neck.

Zero braced his forearm on the bed to take his weight and reached down with his other hand. He inwardly sighed in relief when he gripped Logan's erection. He was still aroused, despite the intense situation they found themselves in.

Zero's hand movements lacked rhythm. He rocked his hips out of time, but it didn't matter. He could feel Logan's skin tighten, and the wetness coating his hand made it easier to slide. Logan neared the edge, but before he succumbed to pleasure, he scratched his nails down Zero back to get his attention.

"Will it hurt?"

Zero couldn't speak. He shook his head instead, and Logan relaxed with a stuttering sigh.

Logan's orgasm hit, and Zero stilled his hips while Logan tightened around him. He grunted and strained every muscle in his body to resist rocking back into Logan's body. Despite his desire to find his own release, he made a silent promise not to hurt Logan, and refused his body's urges.

Only when Logan had melted into the mattress below, with his release trickling between them, did Zero proceed. He watched Logan intently for any sign of pain, and instead he got a smile of encouragement.

He finished with a groan and dropped his body down on Logan's sweaty one.

After a few minutes of contented silence, Zero shifted and rolled to his side. Logan retrieved the sex-rag, or washcloth, as Logan liked to call it.

He cleaned his chest and between his legs and then shoved it back in the compartment for it to be cleaned.

Zero found his hand and squeezed his fingers. "So?"

"It was perfect."

Zero propped his head up on his hand. "Yeah? It didn't hurt."

"A bit sore, but better than I was expecting."

"Well, that's a back-handed compliment."

Logan snorted and rolled on to his side. He ran his hand along Zero's side with a soft smile stretching his lips.

"Lie on your back."

Zero frowned but did as Logan said. "Why?"

Logan reached for the lubrication nozzle, and Zero frowned. "I think once is enough for today, I don't want it to hurt you."

Logan rolled his eyes. "It's not for that."

"Then what are you going to do with it?"

Logan rubbed his hands together till they shone with stickiness. "A massage."

"Massage? What's that?"

"I'm gonna rub your body."

He straddled Zero, then leaned forward and pressed his hands to Zero's chest.

"I think I'd like it if you rubbed me lower...just a suggestion."

Logan chuckled and began moving his hands. Zero glared, hoping if he didn't react to the strange caresses Logan would shimmy down his body and "massage" something else.

His eyes fluttered, and despite him wanting to continue his glare, he couldn't. He closed his eyes and concentrated on the sensation of Logan's hands rubbing his skin. It felt good, not as intense as an orgasm, but a pleasant tingle rushed across his body and he shivered.

Logan pressed hard, moved the hard muscles till they lost their resistance. Zero bit back a moan and breathed heavily to catch his breath.

Logan kept his fingers together and moved them over Zero's flesh in a circular motion. The flesh seemed to soften with the attention, and when Logan moved to Zero's shoulders and neck, he released a groan through paralysed lips.

"You like that?" Logan asked, stilling his hands.

"Yes," Zero breathed, and Logan continued.

Not the burst of an orgasm, or the comfort of their post-orgasm touches. It was different, a different kind of pleasure, and Zero buzzed with it.

When Logan separated his fingers and probed Zero scalp, he couldn't help the breathless moans of appreciation. His throat grew hoarse with vocalisation, but he didn't flush in embarrassment, or turn away. He accepted what Logan gave him and surrendered to him.

"Your hands," he mumbled.

Logan chuckled. "I think you like them more than me."

Zero frowned, but Logan rubbed his fingers against his brow and he immediately relaxed. "They're part of you, don't ever lose them."

"I'll do my best not to."

The massage continued, each arm, each leg, Logan touched with the hypnotic movements, and Zero melted into the mattress below. Sleep tugged at his eyes, and he fought it, until Logan started running his fingertips over the features and angles of his face.

"Sleep," Logan said, and Zero couldn't fight it off any longer.

Chapter Twenty-Four

Zero woke with the gaps between his fingers colder than ever. He rubbed the heel of his hand into his eye sockets and rolled on his side. Logan had gone, and by the cool sheets, he had been out of bed for a while. It was the day he was going home, and part of Zero wanted to curl up in bed and never get out, but the other part, the more dominant one, pushed the last remainders of sleep away. Zero yawned and stretched out his limbs before forcing himself to stand. His body still felt jellified from Logan's hands, and he smiled to himself when he thought back to their night of pleasure.

He stumbled into the bathroom, had a quick wash, and shave and moved into the living room with a forced enthusiasm for the day.

Logan sat on the sofa with a food pouch in his hand, he squeezed the contents into his mouth while staring out the window. He didn't even notice Zero's dramatic stroll into the room.

Zero's smile faltered, and he watched Logan for a few minutes until it looked like he was about to turn his head, then he clapped his hands.

"Today's the day."

Logan looked up at him. The small dent appeared at the top of his nose, and he dropped his gaze. "Yeah...about that."

Zero frowned. "What about it?"

Logan didn't answer, and Zero joined him on the sofa, placing his hand on his knee. "It's okay to be nervous."

"I'm not nervous."

"And it's okay to... To be sad to say goodbye."

Logan shook his head. "It's not that."

Zero retracted his hand and leaned forward to stand. The words hurt, but it wasn't Logan's fault he was handling the situation better than him. Logan gripped his arm and stopped him from moving away.

"I was wondering...if the machine could send other stuff back."

"Like what?"

Logan's eyes burned into his, but he didn't understand the meaning of the look.

"A letter?"

Zero rubbed his chin considering, then gave up the pretence. "What is a letter?"

"Ya' know, a written message, with pen and paper?"

Zero pursed his lips before trying the words slowly. "Pen, and paper...nope. No idea."

Logan huffed and shuffled his shoulders. "You don't write letters here, how can you not write letters?"

Zero waved his hand. "We don't, but theoretically what would your written message say?"

Logan bit his lip, then glanced up and connected their gazes. It was another meaningful expression, but Zero floundered and shrugged his shoulders.

"It would say I was happy. It would tell my family they didn't need to worry about me, and that I'd chose to leave."

Zero bowed forward and circled his fingers into his brow. "I don't understand."

"I've found something in this century I want to stay for."

Zero moved his circling fingers to his chest and rubbed over the rampant muscle. "What is it?"

"It's not a something, but a someone."

There didn't seem to be enough air in the room, and Zero flapped his hand by his face to draw more in. Logan didn't seem affected by the drop of air pressure. Zero could feel the heat in his cheeks, but there was no blush on Logan's face. He panted at the air, before gripping the collar of his shirt to shake.

"It's hot in here, isn't it?" he said.

Logan smiled, then reached for his wrist and stopped his crazed tugging of the shirt. He grabbed both of Zero's hands and turned him till they were facing each other.

"I want to stay with you, if you'll have me."

The words pushed the remaining air from Zero's lungs, and he struggled to pull more in. He stayed, with his eyes wide, and his body unresponsive until Logan tapped his face.

"You hear me?"

He nodded, gulped at the air then panted franticly. "Sorry, I just didn't expect it."

Logan licked his lips, then leaned forward and kissed him. Zero didn't react, it was hard enough to breathe let alone start an onslaught of mouth and tongue. Logan pulled back and pressed their foreheads together.

"So, you want me to stay?"

Zero opened his mouth but no words flowed. He wanted Logan to stay, more than anything, but couldn't bear him being unhappy, or living with regret.

"What about your family? Your friends?"

Logan closed his eyes in an extended blink. "It will hurt not seeing them, but it will hurt more to let you go. That's why I thought about a letter, sending a message back to my time so they know I'm all right."

"A message," Zero said, "you can do these messages?"

"Yes, I can write. I just need something to write with and something to write on."

Zero stared back blankly and Logan rolled his eyes.

"If not pens or pencils, do you at least have something that can cut? Something sharp?"

"I'm sure we can improvise. Are you sure about this?"

Logan nodded, and a smile twitched his lips. "I laid in bed thinking about it all last night, and it is selfish of me wanting to stay, but sometimes in life you have to be selfish or the amazing things will pass you by. If I can send my family and friends a message, something they will know is from me. They might understand."

"What will you tell them?"

Logan snorted softly. "I'll say I've gone off exploring, off on an adventure, and that I'm happy."

"You think they will accept that?"

"I hope so."

Zero nodded slowly, then shook his head. "Are you sure about this?"

"I'm sure about how I feel about you," Logan said, then he climbed off the sofa and held out his hand. "I want to stay here, but I must send a message home first."

Zero took his hand. "You want to do it now?"

"Yes, but we need one more thing."

Zero stared at him expectantly, and Logan lifted an eyebrow.

"You need your hat."

The whole drive to the surface, Zero expected Logan to change his mind. He readied his facial expression for the moment, understanding and sympathetic, while on the inside he would die. Every time Logan opened his mouth to speak, Zero's heart leapt into his throat and almost choked him, and he shuffled in his seat to hide his unease. His hair underneath the hat tickled with sweat, and he feared taking it off in case a tidal wave dripped down his face.

"Can't believe you don't have paper," Logan muttered, but Zero barely heard him above his pounding pulse.

His heart and his lungs continued to falter with hope, but Zero refused to let his mind be swamped by the emotion. He couldn't lose his mind; he couldn't let it be seduced by Logan's promise. It would be all he had left if Logan changed his mind and chose to leave.

When they got to the surface, Logan unlinked their fingers, and wiped his hand on his trousers with a grimace. It was enough for Zero to pant for breath again and stir up the sick feeling in his stomach. Logan turned to him with a frown and focused on Zero's twitching hand.

"You're sticky."

His mouth bobbed open and closed, and then he found his voice. "I'm sorry, I'll work on it if you stay."

"I am staying. I told you I am."

Zero laughed lightly, but it came out shrill and odd. He cursed himself and pushed open the door. The tremor didn't just affect his hands, but his legs, and he felt his body jittering as he walked across the square to the theatre.

Once inside, Logan blocked his path, and grabbed his face. "What's wrong? Are you sick? Do I need to call someone? What number is it here?"

"Number?"

"Yeah, for an ambulance."

Zero pointed to the ceiling. "You ask, and it'll call one, but I don't need one."

"Then what's wrong with you?"

"No idea. I keep thinking you'll change your mind about staying."

Logan sighed, and a grin lifted his lips. He continued to squeeze Zero's cheeks between his hands. "Stop worrying. I want to stay, and I am staying."

Zero shut his eyes and forced his vibrating body to relax. He breathed in deep, and exhaled slow, and after a few minutes, he calmed enough to grin, and nod.

"I'm sorry. You have the ability to make my body react in strange ways."

Logan stoked his hands against his cheeks, and down his throat before performing a rub of his shoulders.

"I don't know if I've told you, but I really like your hands."

Logan chuckled. "Yes, you've told me a lot. Now, come on, we need to work out how to send a message back to my time."

Zero had no idea what paper was, and when Logan explained it was made from trees, he stared back blankly before a memory sparked.

"The same thing you said you can climb in your century?"

"You can do a lot with trees," Logan said.

Zero couldn't shake the image of the spindly food vines from his head.

"I just need something to write on?"

"A meat container?"

Logan shook his head. "Something smaller."

Zero rubbed at his chin. "I might still have some bananas under the stage."

"Nope, not a banana, they'll think I've gone mad."

Logan strolled to the end of the stage then back again. He stilled and tapped his foot on the metal slat below. "This?"

"A section of the stage?"

"Just a slat of it, I'd need something to etch a message in though."

Zero wagged his finger in the air. "A steel manipulator."

"A what?"

"Small laser, perfect for scoring metal. Would that work?"

Logan nodded. "If it'll make a mark, it will work."

Zero clapped his hands. "It's with my tools."

Logan removed one of the loose slats that covered the growing fruit and veg, and Zero passed him the laser.

The theatre flickered, and sparked, and then its voice filled the room. "Honey is at the door sir."

"Let her in."

She moved down the aisle with a deliberately slow pace. Her cheeks hung with sadness and her eyes drooped. Zero rolled his eyes, but Logan looked up and gasped.

"You look beautiful, are you going somewhere nice?"

Honey looked down at her outfit in despair. "What are you talking about?"

Logan gestured to her. "The white dress, it's nice."

He turned to Zero for help, but he sniggered into the back of his hand.

"It's a mourning dress," Honey said.

Zero stopped laughing and flicked his chin out towards her. "No one has died."

"But he's going home, and once he's home he'll have died in our time."

Zero shook his head. "He's not going home."

He wanted the words to sound confident but heard the dip in his own voice. Logan looked to him and gripped his hand.

"I'm staying here. In the forty-first century."

Honey's jaw dropped open comically wide, and her pupils expanded and engulfed her lime irises. "Really?"

Logan nodded, and she leapt up on the stage and bounded towards him. She licked Logan's face, and he turned away with a grimace.

"Really?" she said again. "Did Zero tell you how he felt, did he use that word?"

Zero gripped the back of his head and growled. "Honey, enough of that please."

Logan turned to him and raised his eyebrows. "I'm sure he'll tell me how he feels later, and I think I'll get him to use that word."

Zero snorted. "Don't hope for too much."

Honey patted her paws together. "This is brilliant. Where will he stay if you're in the palace?"

"I'll tell everyone the transportation machine was both of ours, it's true, after all."

"And if they ask you to run it again?"

Zero shrugged and lifted his lips in a coy smile. "I'm sure me and Logan will be able to do it a few more times, and new inventions are prone to break anyway. I'll be remembered as the first to do it, and someone else will take on the baton and do it their own way. Maybe the trick will even inspire them to do it for real."

Honey jumped up and down on the stage. "Wait till I tell Rae. She'll be so happy."

"Will she? Is that even possible?"

Honey swatted him with her paw. "I can't believe it, there's so much Zero hasn't shown you. He hasn't taken you dancing, or to the movies, or to the beach island, or to the moon on a day trip."

Zero rolled his eyes. "That's because I've been banned from all those places."

"Not anymore, not now you're destined to be remembered."

Zero shook his head and dropped his gaze to the stage. He laughed lightly through his smile and finally voiced his realisation. "I don't care about that anymore. All I care about is Logan."

Honey purred so loud Zero could feel it in his chest, and she darted forward to lick his face, and then Logan's again. She leaned back, frowning.

"So, what you doing here then?" she asked.

"Logan's writing a letter home," Zero said, gesturing to the plank of metal, and the laser held in a peculiar way in Logan's hand.

Honey hummed to herself, then paused and frowned again. "What's a letter?"

Zero waved his hand with a sigh, and she bounded giddily towards him.

"The letter will mean he'll stay?" she asked.

Zero couldn't stop his smile from forming. "Yes."

"Then he better get on with it," she said, then narrowed her eyes at Logan.

"I'm doing it," he said.

Zero and Honey watched in interest as Logan made marks on the metal. They cocked their head, and frowned, then both retrieved their ID cards from their pockets. Logan used the same language, both Zero and Honey could read the symbols, but they had never tried scrawling them.

"He could get a job as a card maker," Honey whispered.

Zero pursed his lips. "I think you're right."

The lights fluttered, the walls vibrated, and then the theatre spoke again.

"Sir, Apollo is at the door."

Zero sighed and pinched the top of his nose. "Tell him to go away."

"Sir, he has your medallion from the palace."

Zero raised his eyebrows and shot a smug look to Honey, who returned it.

"Better let him in then," he said loudly.

Logan stopped lasering marks and moved to Zero's side. He squinted his eyes when Apollo came into view, and Zero laughed and ruffled his hair.

"I think you hate him almost as much as me," Zero mumbled.

"More," Logan grunted.

Apollo climbed on stage, and Zero didn't know if he was imagining it or not, but the gold of his suit appeared duller than the day before. Honey hissed, and puffed her fur up, and Logan's stared unblinking with his nostrils flaring.

Apollo raked his fingers through his long hair, then reached into his jacket. He pulled out a shimmering medallion and held it for Zero to take.

"Here, seems you'll be joining me in the palace."

Zero gazed at the medallion and didn't feel the sense of accomplishment he expected. When he looked at Logan, he felt it, that and so much more. He tapped the gold circle on the back of the hand. "Me and Logan will be joining you in the palace."

Apollo sneered and shot a disgusted look towards Logan. "No, just you. He did nothing—"

"The teleportation machine was a team effort, you can tell them. Not just me, but Logan, Honey, and Rae helped create it. We should all receive a medallion, and a flat in the palace."

Honey gasped and pressed her paw to her mouth. Her eyes fogged with moisture, and she blinked the tears away.

"The palace will not allow this," Apollo snapped.

"Yeah, they will. Otherwise I'll refuse to demonstrate teleportation again."

Apollo staggered back with his mouth hanging open. "You can't do that."

"I can, and I will, if they refuse. Now if you'd kindly leave, that would be most appreciated."

Apollo dropped his attention to the stage and sighed slowly. "I get why you hate me, Zero, but we're both destined for remembrance, it's time to let the past go."

"Let the past go?"

Apollo raised his head and nodded. "Yes, you and me, both great inventors. You are not meant to hang around with the likes of these two. Don't lower the standard of the elite by asking for them to be remembered too. We all know you made the machine, not them."

Zero shook his head then turned his attention to Logan and gave him a brief smile.

"You're wrong, it was not me that made this machine, but Logan, and he, alongside Honey, will not lower the elite. They will elevate it. They aren't just worthy of being remembered, but they're the right kind of people to be remembered. Kind, and generous, not selfish."

Logan smiled and leaned up on his tiptoes to get to Zero's lips.

"Freaks!" Apollo roared.

He darted forward and snatched the laser from Logan's hand. He snarled, lunged, and Zero didn't have time to get his hands up to take the brunt of the lasers burn. Time slowed, and he awaited pain, but tilted, and landed heavily on his side. Instead of searing pain, he heard the agonised scream of Logan, and he glanced up from his horizontal position with horror paralysing his features.

Honey pounced with her claws out and sunk them into Apollo's face. She hissed, slashed, not stopping her assault, until Apollo had left the stage with blood pouring from many wounds.

Zero scrambled across the stage to get to Logan. He pulled him into his lap and checked him over. The black shirt he wore hid the injury, and at first Zero didn't think it was that bad. Then he split the material, and saw blood leaking from Logan's body, not clotting or slowing. Logan groaned, and his eyes fluttered open.

"You're gonna be okay," Zero said, stroking his thumb to Logan's cheek.

He held his hand to the wound and called for Honey. She rushed over and dropped to her knees.

"Why isn't it stopping?" Honey sniffed, the air and her eyes grew round. "It doesn't smell the same, it doesn't look the same, and it's not acting the same. Zero, what do we do?"

Zero gulped for air, not knowing how to help Logan. The wound wasn't healing, and the blood loss paled his flesh. He needed help, but not from Zero's century.

Logan's flesh cooled against Zero's hand, and he swallowed uncomfortably. "Honey, put the machine on."

"What?"

"Just do it," he shouted, rearranging Logan in his arms. She rushed to the arch at the back of the stage and smacked her paw on the button on the wall. The sick feeling in Zero's gut returned, but worse than ever before. His eyes stung, but he didn't attempt to blink back the tears, he let them run.

"Logan?" he gasped.

His brow tightened with pain, but he didn't reply.

Zero stood, with Logan close to his body. He shook him gently, and his eyes twitched open.

"Why did you do that?" Zero asked.

Logan's blanched lips moved into a small smile. "You know why."

He closed his eyes, and Zero shook him again, but they didn't reopen. Logan's face relaxed of all pained lines, and he hung limp in Zero's arms. The warmth in Zero's chest froze, and his lip wobbled with the onslaught of fear.

The machine whirled and spat out sparks of white. Zero breathed deep and stepped across the stage towards light. Just before he walked into the arch way, he paused, turned to Honey and gazed into her tearful eyes.

"I love you," he said, then stepped inside.

Chapter Twenty-Five

Zero spluttered in the darkness and held Logan close to his body. His knees ached from them pressing into the floor, and his chest heaved with the need for oxygen. The smell of burned metal, and melted plastic assaulted his nose, and he shook his head before coughing into his shoulder. The air wasn't just filled with the fumes of burning, but it had an itchy quality and scratched Zero's throat, and he cleared it forcefully.

"Lights." He shouted, rocking forward on his knees. He shook Logan but there was no response, and he couldn't see his face in the dark.

"Please Logan, hang in there," he whispered close to Logan's ear. He lifted his head to the ceiling. "Lights!"

The building didn't respond, and Zero growled getting to his feet. He peered into the dark and blinked in quick succession to adjust his sight. Light steamed through a rectangular gap, and Zero rushed over in the hope it was a door. The door didn't slide but burst opened when he shoved his shoulder to it. He stumbled outside and dropped to his knees again at what confronted him.

The buildings were different, not as tall, and not symmetrical or coloured the same. Huge leaved growths were dotted about the path, reaching up for the sky. The air felt different to breath, cloggier, and filled with a bitter scent. There was human's moving along the pathway, some on contraptions with wheels and others being tugged up the path by four-legged life-forms.

Odd containers moved in the distance, and one turned and came closer. Light's beamed from the front of it, blinding Zero and he winced curling his body over Logan's. Nothing happened, but he was too scared to move.

"Are you all right?"

Zero shook his head and glanced towards the voice. The woman rushed towards him and kneeled. Her long black hair hung in curls, and her navy shirt hung loose on her body. She leaned forward, and a loose length of white fabric dangled from her neck.

"I'm a nurse, can you tell me what happened?"

She reached for Logan, but Zero curled his arm protectively around him and shuffled away.

"I can help him," she said, nodding in encouragement.

Zero loosened his arms and let the woman see Logan's wound. She grimaced and removed the long stretch of fabric from her neck. She bunched the material and pressed it to Logan's stomach.

"Hold it here. I'm going to call an ambulance."

Zero nodded frantically and did as the woman told him. She spoke fast into a small box, and Zero could hear a voice talking back to her.

"Can you tell me what happened?"

Zero dropped his gaze down to Logan's ashen face. "He got stabbed."

The woman nodded with the box still to her ear. "The ambulance is on the way."

The white fabric turned scarlet, and warm blood seeped through to Zero's fingers. The scarlet contrasted with Logan's pale face. Even his chestnut hair seemed darker in comparison to his bleached flesh.

"Hang in there, Logan, you hear me. I've got you home."

The ambulance didn't descend from the sky, nor was it rounded like all the vehicles in the forty-first century. It travelled along the ground with lights and noise blaring. Zero winced at the sound, then it abruptly stopped, and rumbling ceased with it.

Humans climbed out and rushed towards them. The black-haired woman spoke to them, and a man wearing a lime green jacket, with silver stripe detail took Logan from Zero's arms.

"I need to check him over."

Zero nodded and watched wide eyed as the man laid Logan onto a plastic board.

Another man wearing the same uniform, gripped Zero's elbow gently. There was no hair on the man's head like the cold-blooded, but he had skin not scales, and his eyes were human.

"I'm Matt, a paramedic from the ambulance service, what's your name?"

Zero hummed, then blinked slowly and turned to him. "My names Zero."

"Zero? That's an odd name."

"So is Matt."

Matt frowned and reached into his pocket. He retrieved a small light and shone it in Zero's eyes. "Impressive contacts, but you might be more comfortable without them in."

"Without them in?"

Matt gestured with his middle and forefinger to Zero's eyes. "Take them out."

Zero pushed away from him and struggled to his feet. "You want me to take my eyes out! What kind of madness is this?"

Matt held up his hands and shushed him. "You need to calm down, I think you're in shock."

Zero bobbed his head. "I think you're right, but I don't see how removing my eyes would help. If this is the kind of treatment you suggest, I don't want you around Logan."

"We're going to stabilise your friend and get him to hospital."

Zero glanced over to Logan. Blankets had been laid over him, and a plastic contraption was being held to his face.

"I couldn't bare it if something happened to him."

Matt reached for his arm, and Zero allowed it. Fingers tightened around his wrist, and he sagged forward, raising his eyebrow at Matt's odd display.

"Your pulse is fast. You need to calm down."

"That's a little hard."

Matt flicked his head back to Logan laid out on the floor with two paramedics over him.

"Your friend's in the best hands. My colleagues will take good care of him."

Matt slid his hand up to Zero's shoulder and gently coaxed him towards the ambulance.

"Let's get you inside."

Zero leaned heavily on Matt and climbed into the vibrating box. His heart jumped to his throat, and he covered his mouth to stop a sob when he saw Logan's chest exposed and covered it what looked like wires.

"It's to measure his heart rate, blood pressure, oxygen levels," Matt said.

Zero nodded, then mimed the plastic contraption over his lips. Matt studied him, before realisation stuck.

"It's an oxygen mask. Can you see some of his colour has returned to his face?"

Zero shook his head. "He's practically white."

Matt gripped his forearm and encouraged him farther inside. "Take a seat."

Zero slumped down with his eyes fixed on Logan.

"What's his name?" Matt asked.

"Logan."

He nodded. "Logan what?"

Zero opened his mouth then snapped it shut. He shrugged, and Matt turned to one of his colleagues.

"Did he have anything on him?"

"ID, his next of kin are being notified as we speak."

Matt nodded, then flicked his chin out at Zero.

"What's your relationship to Logan?"

Zero bit his lip before replying, "We're both human."

Matt leaned closer and stared intently in Zero's eyes. "Have you taken anything tonight?"

"No, didn't even have time for breakfast."

"Then I'll ask you again, how do you know Logan?"

Zero swallowed and dropped his gaze to his shaking hands. "I met him a few months ago, I care for him greatly."

"He's your boyfriend."

Logan wasn't a boy, he was a man, but the friend part was more-or-less right.

"Yes." He breathed, then turned his attention back to Logan limp on the small bed.

"Were you two off to a party tonight?"

Zero glanced down at his plain suit. "No, I'm completely under-dressed for a party."

Matt laughed and scratched his head. "It's eccentric, I'll give you that, but the hair and the hat work for you. Not sure about the purple eyes though."

Zero tugged the skin beneath his eyes so Matt took notice. "They're mauve."

Matt laughed again and turned back to his colleagues. He studied Logan, and the beeping machine, then turned back to Zero.

"Your boyfriends stable."

"Is that good?" Zero asked.

"Yeah, that's good. We'll know more about the extent of the injury once we're at the hospital. His next of kin should arrive soon after us."

"Next of kin?"

Matt nodded. "Most likely his close family."

"His mum and his sister," Zero whispered.

The ambulance rocked and swayed. The seats vibrated, and the street blurred as they travelled. It didn't take long for them to arrive at the hospital, and Logan was wheeled inside.

Zero tried to follow, but Matt stopped him. "You can't go in there. I'll take you somewhere for you to sit and wait."

"Wait? I don't want to wait. I want to know he's going to be okay."

"You've got to let the doctors and nurses do their job, come on."

Matt led him down a corridor and patted a plastic chair for him to sit on. Zero sank down reluctantly and held his head in his hand.

"There's a coffee machine there, and a vending machine if you're hungry."

Zero flashed a look where Matt pointed, pouches of different shapes and colours were behind a sheet of plastic.

"I'm not hungry," he mumbled.

"Eating or drinking might calm your nerves," Matt said, glancing over his shoulder. "I'll buy you a coffee, but then I've got to get back to my shift."

None of it made sense, but Matt grinned, and Zero forced a grin in return. "Thank you."

"Just stay here, and when Logan's family get here, we'll tell them where you are. They will contact you."

"Contact me? The ceiling will tell me?"

Matt frowned and pressed the back of his hand to Zero's forehead. "I'm gonna get someone to come check on you too."

"I'm fine, it's Logan who's hurt, not me."

Matt hummed and bobbed his head. He moved to the narrower machine and feed it tokens. When he returned, he held a white container full of a copper liquid. He held it out for Zero and he took it with a forced smile. The container was softer than he expected, and he frowned at the odd material.

"I've got to go. Someone will come talk to you when there's news on Logan."

Zero nodded sombrely. "I have to wait."

Matt squeezed his shoulder, then took off in a sprint down the corridor.

Zero bowed forward in his chair and tapped his foot to the floor. He jogged his arm, and the unknown liquid escaped the container, and ran down the side of the white material to his fingers.

He cursed, swapped hands, then shook the stinging one. A scalding hot liquid was supposed to calm him down. The century's rituals made no sense. He glanced up the corridor and saw another human with a container of liquid. They raised it to their lips, blew gently, and then slurped it into their mouth.

Zero breathed deep and copied the woman at the other end of the corridor. He grimaced at the bitterness and spluttered. The coffee did nothing to calm him. He stood and placed it in a metal cylinder full of empty coffee holders, then he slumped back in the chair and held his head in his hands.

The hospital bustled around him. Some people rushed the corridors, others hobbled, and some were pushed in chairs on wheels. A child of the species walked by with an apple in his hand, he took a big bite and crunched the piece loudly. Zero saw another human biting into a banana, and an elderly man popping grapes into his mouth. Zero shivered at their eating habits, and their odd clothes. The coffee was a popular choice for the people passing-by the corridor, and the bitter fumes filled the space. Zero smacked his lips in distaste and glanced away.

He took the hat off his head and ruffled his hair, then shoved it back on top firmly. He picked at his fingernail, huffed, and shuffled, and did everything he could to distract himself from reliving the past few hours, and the unknown ones to come.

Zero tapped his foot to the floor, and when he got tired of that he drummed his fingers on his knee. He stood, paced the corridor before returning to the safety of the chair.

No one came for him, and he stared at the map on the wall with no idea of how to find Logan. Matt had told him someone would come along and get him, that Logan's family would contact him. He rolled his hat in his hand, flicked it, and flipped it, then shoved it down on his head with a growl.

Zero sagged back in his seat and stared blankly out the opposite window. The memories began to flow, and his chest grew tighter till he clutched at his shirt. He thought of Logan, pained, and pale. He thought of Honey, and how he would never see her again. The two most important life-forms in his life, and he had already lost one that day. She wasn't to be born for centuries, and Logan lay somewhere in the hospital on the tipping point of life and death. Zero's eyes stung, his lip trembled, and a strangled sound escaped his throat.

The night's darkness changed to the early morning light before his eyes, and they stung from his barely blinking gaze.

"Here…"

He glanced up at the elderly women. She smiled, creasing the skin around her lips and eyes. Her shaking hand held another coffee container, but the scent was sweeter.

"The coffees run out," she said.

Zero took the container with a weak smile. "Thank you."

The woman sat down on the chair beside him. "You're waiting for news?"

Zero swallowed uncomfortably. "My boyfriend's been hurt. I just want to know he's okay."

The woman patted his shoulder. "Have faith."

"Whoever this faith is, I don't want them, I want Logan."

Her laugh sounded strained, and she coughed into her hand. "Trust that the doctors and nurses will do their best by him. Now, drink up, it'll make you feel better."

Their silence only broke when Zero slurped the drink. It wasn't bitter like the coffee, but sweet and comforting. He lifted the drink and turned to the woman.

"What is this?"

"Hot chocolate."

He nodded. "Much better than coffee."

"I agree with you," she said with a light laugh.

Zero finished the hot chocolate, and the woman rubbed her hand on his shoulder gently.

The woman got to her feet with a groan. "I hope your friend is all right."

"Me too," he said, lifting the container. "Thank you for this."

She smiled and moved slowly down the corridor. Zero went back to crushing his head between his hands in an effort not to think of the worst-case scenario.

"Zero?"

He blinked to awareness and turned to the voice.

Matt stood, no longer wearing his lime green jacket, but a short-sleeved T-shirt.

"What the hell are you doing here?"

Zero stood, but his legs fuzzed with numbness and he stumbled. Matt steadied him and stared intently into his eyes.

Zero waved the stare away. "I sat here just like you told me."

"Did no one come to get you?"

Zero shook his head. "No, no one's come. I don't know what it means, but it's not good is it…"

Matt's lips popped open, but no words followed. He took Zero by the elbow and led him down the corridor.

"I'll help you find out what's going on."

"Thank you," Zero mumbled.

Matt didn't let go of his elbow and took him through the winding corridors. He spoke in a hushed voice to a woman dressed in navy, then he turned with a grin on his face.

"Logan's going to be all right."

Zero gripped Matt's arm. "Can I see him?"

"Come on. He's in the recovery ward."

After another seemingly endless march through the hospital, Matt stilled outside a full-length curtain, and flicked his head for Zero to go inside.

The first thing he saw was Logan still covered in wires, with the mask over his face, but his eyes were open, and they brightened when they caught sight of Zero.

"Who are you?"

Zero turned to the woman next to the bed. Her eyes tracked Zero's frame, and her face tightened in disgust.

"I'm Zero, Logan's boyfriend."

The woman jumped up and pointed her finger at his chest. "I said this to the nurses before, Logan doesn't have a boyfriend."

"I've known him for a few months."

"Liar, I saw him yesterday, he didn't mention you, he's never mentioned you, I would've remembered."

Zero pinched the top of his nose. "Yesterday?"

"Yeah, we had lunch, so don't go telling me you've been in a relationship with him, he would've told me."

Zero frowned. "Who is he to you?"

"He's my brother, and our mum will be back soon."

Zero scanned the woman's appearance. Her hair was the same shade as Logan's but that was the only similarity.

"Why did you tell the paramedics you were his boyfriend, he doesn't even know you, and why the hell are you dressed like that?"

Zero glanced down at his clothing. "Like what."

"Like a freak" the woman yelled.

Zero staggered back and dropped his eyes to the floor.

"Don't call him that," Logan croaked.

He had removed the plastic from his face and shuffled up on the bed.

The woman turned and shushed Logan. "Rest, don't worry about him."

"What he said is true. He's my boyfriend, Faye, please, please let me speak to him."

She rocked back on her heels and crossed her arms. "Speak—"

"Alone."

Faye bunched her lips, then turned her head. "Fine, you've got five minutes, and then five minutes to convince me and mum this isn't the morphine."

She knocked her shoulder into Zero as she left, and the curtain swayed behind her.

Logan twitched his fingers, and Zero rushed to slot his between them. He collapsed in the chair by the bed and exhaled in a rush.

"I thought I'd lost you."

"They stopped the bleed, gave me a transfusion."

Zero nodded and pulsed his fingers around Logan's. "I'm just glad you're all right."

Logan's eyes filled with tears, and one dripped down his cheek. Zero cupped his face and wiped the tear away.

"The arch...did it break?" Logan asked.

"I think so. I could smell burning when I got here, and there was no light flowing."

More tears ran Logan's face, each time Zero rubbed one away, another dropped from his bottom lashes.

"I'm sorry."

Zero frowned and shook his head. "You have nothing to be sorry for."

"You're stuck here because of me."

Zero snorted. "It's a small sacrifice for your life. I'm not going to lie, though, this place is terrifying. I didn't appreciate the coffee, and people are biting into raw fruit like it's completely normal."

Logan chuckled. "It is normal here."

"There's some good, too, though. Matt the paramedic and a woman in the corridor. They helped me. This century will take some getting used to."

The smile faded from Logan's face, and he stared at their joined hands. "Why? Why bring me here? Why do that?"

"I wasn't going to let you die, was I?"

"But why?" Logan asked.

Zero leaned closer and whispered in his ear. "You know why."

Logan closed his eyes and a soft laugh escaped his lips. "I wanna hear you say it."

Zero wetted his lips and nodded. "I, Zero of the forty-first century, love you, Logan of the twenty-first."

Logan beamed at him despite his sore looking eyes, and paler than usual skin.

"What the hell was that?"

They stopped gazing adoringly at each other and turned towards the open curtain. Faye stood with her arms folded, and by her side was a similar looking woman with more wrinkles, and silver streaks in her hair. Matt was there too, with a rectangle board hugged to his body.

"Mum, Faye. This is Zero."

Faye waved her hand. "Yeah, we heard. What was that about the thirty-first century?"

Zero spluttered on air "I'm not from the thirty-first century, how insulting."

Logan squeezed his fingers, and he snapped his mouth shut.

"He role plays a lot. Pretends he from the future."

Matt tapped his finger to his chin. "Explains a lot, but is he always in character?"

"I'm not in character," Zero snapped.

Matt smirked and retreated through the curtain. Faye narrowed her eyes and flicked her chin out.

"The future, flying cars, and robots?"

"Yes, did Logan tell you?"

Faye rolled her eyes. "It was an educated guess."

The older woman strolled forward with a frown creasing her forehead. "What happened to my son?"

Zero swallowed awkwardly. "He was stabbed. He was stabbed protecting me."

"Why, why would someone want to hurt you?"

Zero glanced down at himself. "Because I am who I am. I dress like this. I act like this."

"That's why they stabbed you?" Faye asked.

"Yes. It was my fault for being me. For being a freak as you put it."

Faye dropped her head and took a step back.

The older woman shook her head. "It's not your fault. It's the fault of whoever did this. What happened to the attacker?"

"He ran away," Zero whispered.

The woman exhaled heavily through her nostrils. "I hope he gets what's coming to him."

"You're Logan's boyfriend. Logan's secret boyfriend he didn't tell us about," Faye said slowly.

"Yes, and I love your brother more than anything and everything, and if me being in the twenty-first century doesn't prove it, I don't know what will. I want to be with him, but only if he wants me too."

He turned back to Logan and brushed his fingers through his hair. Logan's eyes dropped, and his smile wasn't as intense as moments ago.

"'Course I want you, Zero," he slurred. "I love you, loved you when we made snowmen on the roof, loved you when we kissed in the meat container, and when we performed the vanishing trick in front of all the snake and cat people."

Faye stepped forward and peered down at her brother. "Jesus, he's delirious."

"Who is this Jesus?" Zero asked with a frown.

Faye groaned, but her mum stood beside her and smiled. "Ya know what, I think your dad would've liked him..."

Logan's eyes were shut, but he nodded with a smile on his face. "I know he would have. I love him, Mum. He makes me happy."

She stepped forward and shushed him. "Get some rest now."

Logan tugged at Zeros fingers. "Promise me you won't leave, you'll stay."

"I'm staying. I promise."

Epilogue

Zero ran his fingers up the wooden frame. Behind him on the stage, lay the door, badly charred.

"It really was a door then," he said.

Logan moved up to him and gripped his hand. "Yeah."

Zero exhaled slowly through his nose and stared at the empty space in the frame. A few times his mind had deceived him into seeing sparks, but he knew it was impossible for the connection to be fixed. He wasn't going to see Honey again, and the knowledge pained him.

"She'll be all right," Logan whispered.

Zero forcefully coughed and dropped his gaze to the stage. "I know she will. She has Rae, and they'll take care of each other."

"Like I'll take care of you."

Zero turned to Logan but couldn't smile. "I don't want to be a burden. I don't want you to feel you have to be with me because I'm stuck here."

Logan shook his head and stared at him with a serious expression. "I want to be with you Zero, here, there, anywhere."

Zero looked at Logan's stomach and pictured the scar underneath his T-shirt. "You almost died because of me."

Logan shook his head. "Apollo is to blame, not you. I'd do it again. It hurt, but I'd do it again in a heartbeat."

"Why?"

Logan chuckled and dropped his head to Zero's shoulder. "You know why."

Zero chuckled, and a comfortable silence settled over them.

"This century is…strange."

Logan laughed lightly.

"Not scared, are you?" he said, lifting his head.

Zero tugged his fingers. "Yes, yes, I am."

The amusement left Logan's features. "We'll be all right here, I'm sure of it."

"How can you be sure?"

"We've got each other, and I love you."

Logan leaned in and pressed his lips to Zero's. He accepted the kiss and wrapped his arms around Logan's back. The leisurely kiss pushed away the doubt in Zero's body, and he pulled back and rubbed his nose against Logan's.

The door to the club creaked open, and Logan tugged away sharply.

"Urgh, less of that," Faye said walking forward with a box in her hand.

Logan jumped off the stage and took the box from her. He flicked his chin towards the door, and she left with a loud sigh.

"What is that?" Zero asked.

Logan walked up the steps to the stage slowly. He grinned to himself, and his cheeks filled with rose pigment.

"I know it'll never be the same as Honey, not by a long shot, but maybe...when you think about Honey, you could talk to her..."

Zero narrowed his eyes. "Who is her?"

Logan looked pointedly into the box, and Zero did too. "A kitten, a baby cat."

The tiny life-form had the same amber fur as Honey, and the same piercing lime eyes. The kitten turned to Zero and opened her mouth.

Zero frowned and flashed a look to Logan. "I don't understand what she said."

Logan chuckled and scooped out the life-form. "She can't speak, Zero, she's a pet. You've got to take care of her."

Zero took the kitten from Logan carefully and stared into its fierce eyes. "Ya' know what, it does have the same traits as the furists."

"I told you so."

"Does that mean we can get a...what did you call them? A spake?"

"Snake? And no...no snake."

Zero pouted, and Logan sighed. "Maybe one day, let's see how it goes with the cat first."

The kitten swung its claws out and caught Zero on the nose. He didn't recoil or drop the kitten. He laughed. "Just like my Honey."

"You've got to give her a name."

Zero bobbed his head. "Easy, Little Honey."

Logan rolled his eyes. "Little Honey it is."

Zero grinned at the small kitten biting at his thumb, then leaned close to kiss Logan on the mouth.

"Thank you," he whispered.

About the Author

Tilly lives in a small village in the UK, surrounded by fields, and meadows.

By day, she's looks after her two lively boys, but by night...she's usually asleep, too exhausted to write, but sometimes she gets lucky, sometimes she settles down with a nice cup of tea and sinks into a story.

She hopes you enjoy them.

Email

tillykeyesauthor@outlook.com

Other NineStar books by this author

Sweet Revenge

Also Available from NineStar Press

Connect with NineStar Press

www.ninestarpress.com

www.facebook.com/ninestarpress

www.facebook.com/groups/NineStarNiche

www.twitter.com/ninestarpress

www.ingramcontent.com/pod-product-compliance
Lightning Source LLC
Chambersburg PA
CBHW051601100726
47898CB00001B/183